"Ellie," he broke in. "You talk a little too much."

"And I won't allow you to silence me!"

"Won't you?"

She gasped. Because he was lifting the fingertips of his left hand to let them trail across her full mouth, brushing away a tiny cold snowflake that had landed there, then letting the pad of his finger travel on down to her deliciously-pointed little chin.

And he leaned in, and kissed her.

Just a touch. That was all Luke ever intended. Just one brief, sweet meeting of lips...but the joining of their mouths, her soft skin against his, sent lightning bolts through him, astonishing him. He saw that her eyes were closed, he realized that her lips were slightly parted, and his heart drummed, his loins pounded. She was wonderfully sensual—and she was an innocent. *Stop there*, Luke ordered himself. God help him, everything about her shouted a warning for someone like him to stay well clear.

But he didn't.

Author Note

You'll see that my book is set in 1815, in the months before Waterloo—and my heroine, Ellie Duchamp, is a French refugee who has been sent by her English relative Lord Franklin to the safety of his mansion in Kent.

But nearby is the run-down estate of the disreputable ex–army captain, Luke Danbury, whose brother has been lost in France and labeled a traitor. As soon as Luke discovers the secret of Ellie's past, he ruthlessly resolves to blackmail her to dig out the truth about his brother—but he hasn't reckoned on the sparks of attraction that fly instantly between the two of them!

The lonely Kent coast is beset by rumors of smugglers, intrigue and French spies. On the same side now, Luke and Ellie battle to uncover the truth—but can they really have a future together when the exposure of Ellie's past might very well ruin them both?

Here is their story, which I really hope you'll enjoy.

Lucy Ashford

The Captain and His Innocent

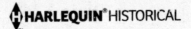

ISBN-13: 978-0-373-30729-6

The Captain and His Innocent

Printed in U.S.A.

HARLEQUIN®
www.Harlequin.com

Lucy Ashford studied English with history at Nottingham University, and the Regency is her favorite period. She lives with her husband in an old stone cottage in the Derbyshire Peak District, close to beautiful Chatsworth House, and she loves to walk in the surrounding hills while letting her imagination go to work on her latest story.

You can contact Lucy via her website: lucyashford.com.

Books by Lucy Ashford

Harlequin Historical

The Major and the Pickpocket
The Return of Lord Conistone
The Captain's Courtesan
Snowbound Wedding Wishes
"Twelfth Night Proposal"
The Outrageous Belle Marchmain
The Rake's Bargain
The Captain and His Innocent

Harlequin Historical e-book

The Problem with Josephine

Visit the Author Profile page at Harlequin.com.

Chapter One

Kent, England—1815

In the grey light of a January afternoon, two dark-clad men stood on a lonely shingle beach gazing out to sea. 'Soon we won't be able to see a thing out there, Captain Luke,' muttered the older one restlessly. 'This wretched mist that's rolling in is as thick as the porridge they used to give us in the army.'

'Be grateful for that mist, Tom.' Luke Danbury's eyes never shifted from the forbidding grey sweep of the sea. 'It means the Customs men won't spot Monsieur Jacques's ship out there.'

'I know, Captain. But—'

'And I wish,' Luke went on, 'that you'd stop calling me *Captain*. It's over a year since you and I left the British army. Remember?'

Tom Bartlett, who had a weatherbeaten face and spiky black hair, glanced up warily at the taller, younger man and clamped his lips together for all of a minute. Then he blurted out, 'Anyway. I still think you should have sent me as well as the Watterson brothers to bring in Monsieur Jacques. It would be just like the pair of them to lose their way out there.'

'Would it?' Luke's face held the glimmer of a smile. 'While you and I were soldiering in the Peninsula, Josh and Pete Watterson were in the navy for years—remember? Those two don't lose their way at sea, whatever the weather. They'll be here soon enough.'

Tom looked about to say something else; but already Luke was walking away from him to the water's very edge, a low sea breeze tugging at his long, patched overcoat and his mane of dark hair.

'Well,' Tom was muttering to himself as he watched him, 'I hope you're right, Captain. I hope those Watterson brothers will row the French *monsieur* to shore a bit faster than their wits work.' He glanced up at the cliffs behind them, as if already picturing hostile faces spying on them, hostile guns pointed at them. 'Because if the Customs men from Folkestone spot us, we'll be clapped in irons fast as we can blink, you and me. And that's a fact.'

The other man stood with his hands thrust in his pockets, studying the mist that rolled ever thicker across the sea. As if his gaze could penetrate it. As if he could actually see the coast of France; could even perhaps picture the far-off place where last year his brother had vanished without trace.

Bitterness filled Luke Danbury's heart anew. He clenched and unclenched his gloved right hand, thinking… *News.* He had to have news, one way or another. He was tired of waiting. He needed to know—for better or worse.

Behind him Tom Bartlett, once his loyal sergeant-at-arms, had started grumbling again softly, but broke off as Luke shot out his hand for silence.

Because Luke's sharp ears had registered something.

And, yes—a moment later, he could see it, a rowing boat slowly emerging from the mist, with two men pulling at the four oars, while another man in a black coat and hat leaned forward eagerly from the bow. Tom was already wading into the shallows, ready to reach out a hand to the black-clad passenger and help him ashore as the boat's keel grated on shingle. 'There we are now, *monsieur*!' Tom was calling in welcome. 'You'll enjoy being back on dry land again, eh?'

'Dry land, yes.' Jacques laughed. 'And with friends.'

Tom preened a little at that praise, then turned to the Watterson brothers, who were making the oars secure; brothers who looked so like each other, with their mops of curling brown hair, that they might have been twins. 'Well, you rogues,' declared Tom. 'I always said the navy's better off without you. You took that much time, I thought you'd lost your way and rowed to France and back.'

The brothers grinned. 'The army's certainly better off without that gloomy face of yours, Tom Bartlett. Though you'll cheer up a little when you see what's weighing down our boat.'

'A gift from Monsieur Jacques?' Tom was nodding towards their passenger, who was already deep in conversation with Luke Danbury a few yards away.

'A gift from Monsieur Jacques.' The brothers, after dragging the boat even further up on to the beach, were reaching into it to push aside some old fishing nets and haul out a heavy wooden crate. 'Brandy,' they pronounced in unison. 'Monsieur Jacques rewards his friends well. Come on, you landlubber, and give us a hand.'

'My men have dropped anchor out there for the night,' Monsieur Jacques was saying to Luke. 'A good thing you caught sight of us before that mist came down, my friend. A good thing that your Customs men *didn't*. How long is it since I was here?'

'It was late October.' Luke's voice was level.

'As long ago as that…' Jacques glanced at the men by the boat and gave Luke a look that meant, *Later, my friend. When we are alone, we'll talk properly.* Then he went striding across the shingle to where Luke's men had placed the crate of brandy, withdrew one bottle with a flourish and uncorked it with his penknife.

'Here's to the health of the valiant fishermen—Josh and Peter Watterson!' He raised the bottle and drank. 'To the health of Tom Bartlett! And most of all to your own very good health, Captain Danbury!'

Jacques passed the bottle across to Luke's right hand—but Luke swiftly reached to take the bottle with his left, which, unlike the other, was ungloved. His eyes were expressionless.

'*Pardon.*' Jacques looked embarrassed for a moment. '*Mon ami*, I forgot.'

'No matter.' Luke's voice was calm, though a shadow had passed across his face. 'To the health of everyone here. To freedom's true friends, in England and in France.'

'To freedom's true friends!' echoed the others.

Luke drank and handed the bottle back to Jacques. 'And may justice be some day served,' he added, 'on the British politicians in London, with their weasely words and broken promises.'

'Justice.'

'Aye, justice, Captain.' One by one, the little group on the shore by the cliffs passed round the brandy bottle, echoing his toast sombrely.

At last Luke turned to Tom. 'I intend to take Jacques up to the house for the night, of course. But before we set off, I want you to check the road for me, Tom.'

'The London road, sir?'

'Exactly. I want you to make sure there are no spies around. No government men.'

Already Tom was on his way, hurrying along the beach to a path that climbed steeply up the cliff. The Wattersons still hovered. 'Josh. Peter,' Luke instructed, 'I'd like you to take that brandy to the house and warn them there that our guest has arrived.'

'Aye, Captain.' They set off immediately.

And so, with the afternoon light fading, and the sea mist curling in and the cries of the gulls their only company, Luke and the Frenchman were alone. *And I'm free*, thought Luke, *to ask him the only question that really matters*. The question he'd asked of so many people, so many times, for the past year and a half.

'Jacques, my friend.' He was surprised that his voice sounded so calm. 'Is there any news of my brother?'

The Frenchman looked unhappy. Uncomfortable. Luke's heart sank.

'*Hélas, mon ami!*' Jacques said at last. 'I have asked up and down the coast, as I sailed about my business. I have asked wherever I have friends, in every harbour from Calais in the north to Royan in the south. And— there is nothing.' The Frenchman shrugged expressively. 'Your brother disappeared with those other men at La Rochelle in the September of 1813. Sadly, many of them are known to have died. As for your brother—we can only hope that no news is good news, as you English say.' His face was taut with sympathy. 'But I do have something for you.'

Reaching into the inside pocket of his coat, he handed Luke a small packet wrapped in oilskin. Luke, cradling it in his gloved right hand, peeled it open with his left—until at last a gleam of colour flashed in his palm. Ribbons. The glitter of brass. War medals, engraved with the names of battles: Badajoz, Salamanca, Talavera. Luke felt fierce emotion wrench his guts.

He looked up at last. 'Where did you get these?'

'From an old French farmer's widow. She found them lying half-buried in one of her maize fields—she has a small farm that adjoins the coast near La Rochelle. Realising they were British, she gave them to me, and asked me to get them home again. They could be your brother's, couldn't they?'

Luke nodded wordlessly. They could. *But even if they were*, he told himself, *this doesn't mean he's dead. He might still be alive over there. A prisoner, perhaps. Needing my help...*

He mentally rebuked himself, because he'd suddenly noticed the dark shadows beneath the Frenchman's eyes and realised how weary he was despite his outward cheerfulness.

'We'll have time enough to talk later,' Luke said. 'I would be honoured, Jacques, if you would come to the house, to dine with us and stay for the night as usual.'

'Gladly—though I must leave before dawn tomorrow. It's not safe for my crew to keep the ship at anchor once daylight comes.' Jacques gripped Luke's shoulder almost fiercely. 'You know that I'll do anything I can to find your brother. I owe you this, *mon ami*, at the very least—'

He broke off, realising at the same moment Luke did

that Tom Bartlett was back, his feet crunching on the shingle. 'There's travellers on the high road, Captain!'

'Revenue men?' Luke's voice was sharp.

'No, Captain, it's a fine carriage. With two grooms as well as the driver, and luggage aplenty strapped on the back.'

Luke felt his lungs tightening. 'Does it look as though the carriage has come from London, Tom?'

'Aye, that would be my guess. Can't make out the coat of arms on the door. But the horses, they're Lord Franklin's all right—I recognised the four fine bays that he keeps stabled at the George Inn close to Woodchurch.'

'And is Lord Franklin in the carriage?'

'I caught sight of a middle-aged woman and a younger one, by her side. But was his lordship in there as well?' Tom shook his head. 'I couldn't see and there's the truth of it.'

Luke made his decision—he needed to know exactly who was in that carriage. 'Tom, see Monsieur Jacques up to the house, will you? I'll join you as soon as I can.' Even as he spoke, he was already setting off along the beach, towards the path Tom had followed.

Tom guessed his intention and was aghast. 'You'll never catch up with those four bays of Lord Franklin's!'

Luke turned calmly to face him. 'They'll have to stop, Tom. Don't you remember that half the road's fallen in a little beyond Thornton, after that heavy rain a week ago? Lord Franklin's coachman will have to take that particular stretch of road very slowly, or he could risk breaking a wheel. There's woodland I can take cover in. I'll be able to observe the carriage and its occupants at leisure.'

'But if Lord Franklin *is* in the carriage, Captain, what are you going to do?'

Luke let the silence linger for a moment. 'Don't worry. I'm not going to kill him. At least—not yet.'

And with that, he turned his back and once more headed swiftly towards the cliff path.

Tom sighed and smiled resignedly at Jacques. 'Well, *monsieur*,' he said, 'let's be off up to the house, shall we? There'll be logs burning on the fire and my good wife will have a pot of stew keeping hot on the stove. And thanks to you, we've brandy to drink…' He hesitated. 'I take it there's no news yet of the captain's younger brother?'

Jacques shook his head. 'No news.'

'Then we can still hope,' said Tom, 'that he'll turn up safe and well!' He set off once more, cheerful at the prospect of hot food. But Monsieur Jacques, following behind, looked sombre.

'Safe and well?' he murmured under his breath. 'Sadly, I doubt it, my friend. I doubt it very much.'

Chapter Two

Ellie Duchamp, nineteen years old, gazed out of the carriage window at the alien English countryside and remembered that she had hoped to travel to Bircham Hall on her own. To have the time, and the silence perhaps, to come to terms with all that had happened to her in the last few months.

But she had had no period of grace in which to contemplate how or why her life had changed so rapidly, ever since Lord Franklin Grayfield, wealthy English aristocrat and collector of art treasures, had found her in a garret room in Brussels. Ever since, he had told her she was his relative and would thenceforth be in his care.

No time or silence—far from it—because beside her in the carriage was the female companion Lord Franklin had provided for her, Miss Pringle, a very *English* spinster, who had arrived at Lord Franklin's Mayfair house a few days ago. Who could not conceal her excitement at being entrusted to escort Ellie to his lordship's country residence, Bircham Hall, in the county of Kent.

Yesterday, as they prepared for their noon departure, Lord Franklin himself—middle-aged, polite as ever—had stood outside his magnificent London mansion in

Clarges Street to watch as Ellie's trunk was strapped to the back of his coach. Miss Pringle, as she took her leave of his lordship, declared ardently that she would take as much care of Ellie as if she were her very own daughter. And Ellie soon realised that to her new companion, *taking care* meant one thing only—talking.

All the way through London, Miss Pringle had talked. She had talked through the city's suburbs and through the green fields beyond Orpington. She had talked all the way through their halts at the various coaching inns where the ostlers raced to change Lord Franklin's horses.

Ellie had told Miss Pringle at their very first meeting that she understood English perfectly well; but Miss Pringle insisted on speaking slowly and enunciating every syllable with the greatest care. And Ellie was being driven to the limits of her patience.

Lord Franklin had announced that although the journey to Kent could be achieved in one day, he felt Ellie would be more comfortable with an overnight stop at the Cross Keys in Aylesford. Ellie had hoped that the evening meal they took in the private dining room there might silence her companion a little, since Miss Pringle keenly enjoyed her food. But somehow, Miss Pringle managed to eat a substantial amount and also produce as many words as ever at exactly the same time.

'Of course,' Miss Pringle pronounced, 'Lord Franklin has always honoured my family with his esteem, Elise.'

Elise was Ellie's French name, the name she'd been christened with. Her French father and English mother had always called her Ellie; but she didn't trouble to correct those who preferred to call her Elise, since they were strangers, who knew nothing of her life or her past.

'My dear father,' Miss Pringle went on through a

mouthful of ham and peas, 'was the vicar of Bircham parish, you know, for many years. And since my papa's sad death, Lord Franklin—well, *no one* could have been kinder, or more considerate! It was a great sadness for me to have to leave the Vicarage on Papa's demise— but Lord Franklin understood perfectly. He said to me, "My dear Cynthia, we cannot have you leaving Bircham, when you have been such a valuable part of its life for so many years." Those were his exact words! And in the end, Lord Franklin found me a cottage—the very best of cottages, I might add!—in a most *superior* part of Bircham village. I have really been more than comfortable there, and of course I have had my many charitable works to keep me busy.'

Miss Pringle leaned closer. 'But when I heard from Lord Franklin that he wanted me to come up to London to accompany you to Bircham Hall itself and to live there as your companion—well, I was so very honoured. To think, Ellie, that he is your long-lost relative! And as you'll know, he is off travelling again very shortly. Taking advantage of the end of this horrid war with France to go and observe the art and classical buildings of Paris. Lord Franklin is *forever* travelling and enlarging his wonderful collection of artistic treasures. Which is, of course, how he met *you*. In Bruges, was it not?'

'In Brussels,' Ellie replied tonelessly, pushing aside her plate. 'If you have no objection, Miss Pringle, I am rather tired and would like to withdraw to my bedchamber now.'

But the next morning, at breakfast, the inquisition started again.

'So...' Miss Pringle began, over her toast and marmalade, 'Lord Franklin came upon you in Brussels. But to think, that he should turn out to be your mother's second cousin—you could not have wished for a luckier stroke of fate!' Suddenly her eyes fixed on Ellie's shabby travelling cloak and dowdy bonnet and she said, a little more hesitantly, 'You know, I was led to understand that Lord Franklin generously furnished you with a quantity of new clothes in London.'

'He did,' Ellie answered. 'But I prefer to travel in more practical clothing.'

'Very wise.' Miss Pringle nodded. 'Very wise, since you will find, I think, at Bircham Hall that *practicality* is of the utmost importance.'

Ellie wanted to ask her what she meant. Was it chilly there? Was it uncomfortable? But it couldn't, surely, be as frugal or cold as some of the dire places she'd taken shelter in during the last year or more. And then it was time to go out to where the carriage stood in the yard of the inn.

There, the ostlers, under the careful eye of the coachman, were harnessing up four beautiful greys, and Miss Pringle saw Ellie gazing at them. 'Lord Franklin keeps only the best, of course,' she declared, 'at each posting house. This is our next-to-last change, I believe, and by this afternoon we shall be at Bircham Hall. How my heart lifts at the thought! And there you will meet Lady Charlotte, who is sure to give you a *wonderful* welcome...'

Was it Ellie's imagination? Or did Miss Pringle's confident tone falter just a little at the mention of Lord Franklin's widowed mother?

'My mother,' Lord Franklin had told Ellie, 'used to come to London occasionally, but never does so now. I have sent word to inform her that you will be arriving at Bircham Hall and have asked her to ensure you will be happy there.'

But how will Lady Charlotte really feel? Ellie was wondering rather wildly as the carriage rolled on through the Kent countryside. *How can she relish the prospect of having a nineteen-year-old French girl—a penniless orphan—suddenly foisted upon her?*

One thing was for sure—Ellie would know soon enough.

They made slow progress, as slow as the previous day. Miss Pringle talked on as the road led them up and down hills, past farms and the occasional village, past fields of sheep, and dark woodland.

And then, soon after the final change of horses, Ellie could see the sea. The afternoon light was fading, and from the far horizon a low mist was rolling in across the expanse of grey waves; but even so, she pressed her face to the carriage window, realising that between the shore and the road lay a bare expanse of heathland. She glimpsed the sturdy tower of a small and ancient church, and nearby stood a lonely old house with sprawling wings and gables, set on a slight rise and shrouded by stunted sycamores.

She craned her head to gaze at it, but the carriage was entering woodland again and the house had already disappeared from view. A house of secrets, she suddenly thought.

Ellie, her father would have fondly said. *You and your imagination.*

A sharp pang of renewed loss forced her to close her eyes. By the time she opened them again, the carriage had rounded the next headland and the sea was visible once more. Down below was a cluster of little houses around a harbour, with an inn and a wharf where fishing boats were tied up and men mended their nets.

Miss Pringle was still talking about Lord Franklin. 'His family—the Grayfields—can, I believe, trace their ancestry back to Tudor times...'

Ellie glanced down at her small black-leather valise on the carriage floor. She wondered what Miss Pringle would do if Ellie were to seize her valise, jump out of the carriage, run down to the harbourside and beg one of those fishermen to take her away from England's cold and hostile shores. *I am homesick*, she thought with sudden anguish. *Homesick for the Paris of my childhood. For the happy times I spent there with my father and mother. I'm even homesick for Brussels, where I endured those last desperate months with my poor, dying papa.*

'Oh, look at that mist.' Miss Pringle was shuddering. Ellie realised her companion was looking out of the window also. 'And soon it will be dark. January. How I hate January. It's this sort of weather, they say, that brings out the smugglers. Lord Franklin does his very best to stop their obnoxious trade, but they are desperate renegades. It's even said they're in league with the French— and after all, on this part of the coast, France is less than twenty miles away.'

The fishing village was no longer in sight. The road was heading inland again to carve its way through thick oak woodland, and Miss Pringle talked on. But suddenly she cried out in alarm.

'What is this? Gracious me. Why have we stopped?'

Ellie noted the fearful expression on her companion's

features. *Highwaymen*, that expression said. *Robbers*. *Murderers*. 'Please,' said Ellie. 'Calm yourself.'

By then one of the grooms, distinctive in Lord Franklin's navy-and-gold livery, had appeared at the window of the carriage. 'Begging your pardon, ladies, but it appears that half the road ahead of us has fallen away, no doubt because of the recent rain.'

Miss Pringle put her hands to her cheeks. 'Oh, my goodness. Oh, my goodness...'

'No reason at all to be alarmed, ma'am,' said the groom hastily. 'But we need to do a bit of repair work to make sure the way's safe for Lord Franklin's horses. It'll take us ten, perhaps fifteen minutes—no more.'

The moment he'd disappeared, Ellie leaned forward. 'Miss Pringle?'

'Yes?' Miss Pringle had got out her smelling salts and was sniffing vigorously.

'I think I will take advantage of our halt to get a little fresh air.'

'But you took a walk less than an hour ago, Elise, when we last stopped to change the horses! And very soon, we'll be at Bircham Hall. Can you not wait? Besides, I'm not sure it's safe for you to wander hereabouts, I'm really not sure at all.'

But Ellie had already opened the carriage door and was jumping down to the road, with her cloak wrapped tightly around her.

Although it was not yet four, a fierce chill was starting to pierce the air. And the mist! The mist she'd seen out at sea was rolling in across the land now, blanketing the woods that surrounded them with its clammy and sinister air. Though if she looked hard, she could still just see the road ahead. Could see, too, where the left-hand side of the road's stony surface had fallen away, into the verge that bordered it.

That, Ellie, is the problem with insufficient drainage, she could almost hear her father saying. *And look at the lack of proper foundations! You cannot build a road for heavy traffic merely by throwing a haphazard layer of rocks on top of mud. And of course the Romans knew it was often necessary to dig deep ditches on either side to take away the winter floods...*

At least Lord Franklin's two grooms were well equipped for emergencies like this. Her father would have approved of *that*. The grooms couldn't see her, standing as she was in the shadows beyond the coach; but she could see that one of them had an axe to hew down the nearby saplings, and as fast as he felled them, the other was spreading them across the damaged part of the road to create a surface that would—at least temporarily— bear the weight of Lord Franklin's coach and horses.

And as she watched them working, she realised what they were saying.

Pretty little piece, isn't she, the girl? And she speaks good English, for a Frenchie.

Well, her mother was English, I've heard. An English trollop, who ran off with a Frenchman.

I wouldn't mind running off with that *one...*

Ellie's cheeks burned. So often. She'd heard the same vitriolic gossip so often. Head high, she walked away from them, back down the road they'd come along—and only when she was completely out of sight of both the carriage and the grooms did she stop, realising that her eyes were burning with unshed tears.

It is the cold air, that is all, she told herself fiercely, dashing them away with her hand. *The cold.*

She walked on, remembering seeing the sea and that fishing village. In what direction, she wondered suddenly, did the coast of France lie? South? East? Almost instinctively, she reached deep into the capacious pocket sewn to the inside of her cloak to pull out a small leather box.

And jumped violently as a tall figure loomed out of the shadowy woods ahead of her. The box fell to the ground, somewhere in the undergrowth beside the road.

'If I were you,' the man was saying calmly, 'I wouldn't run. There's really not much point, I'm afraid.'

What he meant was that there wasn't much chance of escape. From *him*. Ellie fought her stomach-clenching fear. This man was tall. This man was powerful. Hampered as she was by her heavy travelling clothes, she'd never make it back to the carriage before he caught her. What was he? A highwayman? One of the local smugglers, perhaps, that Miss Pringle had fretted about?

He certainly didn't look like a law-abiding citizen. His long coat appeared to have been mended over and over again; his leather boots were spattered with mud, as if he'd walked a long way. Stubble roughened his strong jaw, and his dark wavy hair was unkempt, but his eyes were bright blue and knowing.

A man to be afraid of. Her heart was already pounding wildly; but she forced herself to speak with equal calmness. 'You may as well know,' she said, tilting her chin, 'that I have nothing about me of any value. If you're intending to rob me, you're wasting your time.'

His eyes glinted. 'I'm not here to rob you. I'm merely curious. I'd heard that Lord Franklin has a new ward— and you must be her.'

What was it about his voice—his deep, husky voice—
that sent fresh pulses of alarm tingling through her veins?
And how had he heard that she was coming to Bircham
Hall?

'I am not Lord Franklin's ward,' she answered. *Keep
your breathing steady, Ellie. Look at him with the dis-
dain he deserves.* 'But there is a family connection. My
mother was his relative…'

He came closer. Panicking, she took a step back. 'Indeed, *mam'selle*,' he said softly. 'to find yourself suddenly
in the care of a rich and aristocratic Englishman must
have seemed like a fairy tale come true. Lord Franklin
is said to be a great collector of foreign *objets d'art*. And
what could be more fitting than for him to return from
the Continent with a pretty French girl in his care?'

She felt her breathing coming tight and fast. She had
been a fool, indeed, to have wandered so far from the
coach. *Play for time*, she told herself. *Play for time.*

'You are mistaken,' she said steadily, 'if you think
that I would allow myself to be…*collected.* Lord Franklin took me in his care out of duty, that is all. In other
words—no fairy tale. And unless you wish me to assume
that your own intentions are unworthy, *monsieur*, I would
ask you to let me pass—this minute!'

She'd already started to move. But he was quicker,
stepping sideways to block her path, intimidating her
with his height and the breadth of his shoulders.

'Did you realise,' he said, 'that Lord Franklin was a
relative of yours before you met him, I wonder?'

She was momentarily overwhelmed by the hard, purposeful set of his face. By the brightness and intensity of
those blue eyes. *No. No, she didn't.*

Memories whirled around her. Memories of a badly

furnished attic room above a bread shop in Brussels. Memories of her father lying on a narrow mattress while she bathed his forehead, desperate to cool his fever. The bread-shop owner, the Widow Gavroche, hurrying upstairs to her. '*Mam'selle, mam'selle*—there is an English gentleman here to see you! His name is Lord Franklin Grayfield and he is very fine!'

Ellie had been alone, with no friends and no money. In danger there. She had thought that she'd left danger behind her now that she was in England—but this tall man who'd come prowling out of the mist reminded her otherwise.

She had to get away. But that little box…

Letting her eyes sweep downwards, she spotted it suddenly in the undergrowth. She made a swift move towards it, but he was quicker, and before she could stop him, he had stooped to pick up her small leather box for himself.

Ellie felt the blood leave her face. 'That is mine. Give it back to me!'

He gave her a curious half-smile—and ignored her. Her heart was hammering so hard against her ribs that it hurt. He'd picked up the box with his left hand, she noticed—held it there in his palm, while with his right hand he was turning it slowly.

He wore a black glove on his right hand. And there was, she realised, something odd about it. Something wrong with it. *The first two of his fingers were missing.* But he had no trouble opening the box. And Ellie felt slightly sick, as the brass casing of her father's compass gleamed in the half-light.

'A pretty trinket,' he was saying approvingly as he gazed down at it. 'It must be worth something.'

'Perhaps it is. Perhaps it isn't.' Ellie was sliding her hand into the folds of her cloak. 'But, *monsieur*, if you've any sense at all, you will return it to me—*immédiatement*—or I swear you will regret it.'

His eyes gleamed. 'You're going to make me?'

For answer she lifted the small pistol she had in her hand and released the safety catch. She was pointing it straight at his heart.

His body tensed very slightly, but his eyes still glinted with mockery. *'Mam'selle,'* he reproved. 'Really. To go to such extremes... I take it you know how to use that thing?'

His voice. The rich, velvety timbre of it. Every word he spoke made something shiver down her spine in warning. Made her grip the pistol even tighter. 'Do you want to find out?' She forced her voice into absolute calmness. 'Give me the compass back. Or I shoot.'

He watched her, his eyes assessing her. Then suddenly he laughed and held the compass out with a small nod. Ellie grabbed at it, her pulse pounding.

'An unusual object,' he said calmly. 'A valuable object, I would venture to say.' He swept her a mockery of a bow. 'Our meeting has been interesting—but I'll make no further effort to detain you. And I hope your stay at Bircham Hall is a pleasant one. Your servant, *mademoiselle*.'

And he was gone. Into the mist and woodland. As suddenly, and as silently, as he'd appeared.

She found she was gasping for breath, as if the air had been kicked out of her lungs. She remembered the gleam in his blue eyes as he gazed at the compass. *Dieu.* Had he had time to look at it? To *really* look at it?

With an enormous effort at self-control, she secured

the safety catch on her pistol, then slipped it and the compass back into the pocket inside her cloak.

She hurried towards the carriage, willing her heart to stop thudding. Please God, the compass had only attracted his attention because he thought it was something he could sell. But surely he was no ordinary roadside thief. Who was he? And how did he already know so much about her?

She drew a deep, despairing breath. The answer to that was easy. Bircham Hall, Miss Pringle had frequently pointed out, was the largest and most prestigious house in this part of Kent. The staff would all have been warned of Ellie's arrival and they would doubtless have spread the news around the neighbourhood.

That was how he knew. And he'd been watching for the coach, guessing it would have to stop there; hoping for a chance perhaps to rob its occupants. She'd provided him with the perfect opportunity, by wandering away down the road.

A common thief. That was the obvious answer. And yet she had a feeling that his intentions were somehow far, far more dangerous than that.

She could see Miss Pringle now, standing outside the carriage, visibly fretting. She let out an exclamation when she saw Ellie. 'There you are. I've been imagining all sorts of terrible things…'

'I'm all right, Miss Pringle,' Ellie soothed her. 'Really I am.'

Just at that moment a groom came up to inform them that the carriage was ready to set off again. And for the remainder of their journey to Bircham Hall, Ellie closed her eyes and pretended to be asleep.

But she couldn't erase the image of the man with the

maimed right hand and the dangerous blue eyes. Something strange and unfamiliar tingled through her body. Fear? No—she'd known fear often enough, and fear didn't make your pulse race at the memory of a man's face, of his dangerous smile. Fear didn't make you notice a man's thick dark lashes. Didn't make you remember the magical curve of his lips when he smiled and make you wonder how many women he had kissed.

She would be safe at Bircham Hall, she told herself. She would have no friends, but she would be safe. And the man was surely nothing but a lowly ruffian.

Then she shivered. Because she was remembering that the stranger in the long, patched coat had spoken not like a ruffian, but like an English gentleman—and his voice had melted her insides, even though every word he spoke was either a veiled insult or a threat.

Sharp waves of panic were clawing at her throat. She'd thought she would be out of danger, when she reached England's shores—but clearly, she could not have been more wrong.

Chapter Three

The dusk always fell swiftly along this part of the coast, blurring the lonely expanse of gorse-topped cliff and the miles of shingle beach. There were still ghostly reminders of the now-ended war with France, for in the distance was a rugged Martello tower, built in case of a Napoleonic invasion, and sometimes soldiers rode out from Folkestone to patrol the coast; though they were more likely nowadays to be hunting for smugglers rather than invaders.

Just enough light lingered for Luke to see that both headland and beach were deserted, though he could hear gulls crying out above the waves. Still on foot, he had left the woods and the road well behind him now, taking instead the ancient paths used by local fishermen and farmers until he came at last to a rough track that led to a solitary house looming up from behind a thicket of wind-stunted sycamores.

The house was said to have been built on the site of an ancient long-vanished fortress, constructed over a thousand years ago to protect this coastland from Germanic invaders. Now wreaths of mist shrouded it, whispering of past lives and of ancient battles. The locals said it was

haunted; said that the fields which surrounded it, blasted
by winter winds, were good only for the most meagre of
crops and the hardiest of sheep. But Luke loved this landscape with a passion that was ingrained in his very being.

He loved the winters, when frost and snow shrouded
the bare countryside, and howling winds blew in from
the sea; winds so cold they might have come straight
from the freezing plains of Russia. He loved the sum-
mers, when the fields were filled with grazing sheep and
lambs, and birdsong filled the nearby marshlands from
dawn till dusk.

His brother, Anthony—two years younger than he—
had loved it all, too.

Anyone seeing the house from a distance would think
it derelict, but the locals would tell a passing stranger
that it was the residence of Luke Danbury, a spendthrift
and a wastrel who had once been a captain in the army
in Spain, but who had now mortgaged his family estates
to the hilt and was anyway absent for much of the time,
doing God knew what.

Making madcap, mysterious sea voyages, he'd heard
people say. *Up to no good. Away as often as he was
here. Gambling, probably, and women,* they muttered
knowingly. *Once he was engaged to an heiress—and
didn't she have a lucky escape! He's let all his farm-
land, once so prosperous before the war, go to waste.
And his missing brother's a disgrace as well. The family name is ruined...*

The track led up to the front gate of the house, which
stood permanently open. Indeed, such was the tangle of
undergrowth—old, half-wild shrubs and ivy growing all
around—that Luke doubted it could ever be shut. The
house itself looked uninhabited; no lights shone from any

of the front windows, and wreaths of sea fog crept around the gables and turrets. But Luke pushed his way through the wreck of a garden and past the twisted sycamores, towards the courtyard and stables round the back—and there, glowing lantern light welcomed him.

There, the cobbles were well swept, with stacks of logs for burning, and bales of hay for the horses, all neatly piled under shelter. Several farms belonged to the estate, and the equipment for the usual winter jobs had been gathered there also for his tenants to collect: tools for fencing and ditching work, shovels and pickaxes.

He noted it all automatically; yes, this what he had to concentrate on now. Saving the estate. Saving the livelihoods of the men, and their families, who depended on him. But all the time, he was thinking, too, that the rumours were true—that Lord Franklin Grayfield had returned from abroad with a French girl. An orphan, they said, and a distant relative, whom Lord Franklin had taken into his care.

But Lord Franklin, as far as Luke knew, was not a man given to sudden, sentimental gestures of generosity. So why go to the trouble of bringing this girl—this relative—back to London? And why did Lord Franklin almost immediately decide to banish the girl to the Kent countryside?

Of course, there would be gossip aplenty for Luke to listen to and sift through for himself, in the taverns of Bircham Staithe harbour, or in the larger ale houses of Folkestone a few miles away. There always was gossip about a rich, clever and ultimately mysterious man like Lord Franklin. There was already gossip about this girl, too—Luke had heard from people who'd glimpsed her in London that her name was Elise Duchamp and that she was pretty, in a French sort of way. But they hadn't told him that she went around carrying a pistol in her pocket and quite clearly knew how to use it. No one had mentioned *that*.

And as for 'pretty'—was that the way to describe her rich dark curls, her full mouth and slanting green eyes? Was it her mere *prettiness* that had sent a jolting kick of desire to his blood—and had urged him, with age-old male instinct, to draw her slender body close, so he could feel the feminine warmth of the curves he just knew would lie beneath that old, shapeless cloak?

She was intriguing, in more ways than one. There was considerably more to her than met the eye. Take, for example, that compass.

Luke Danbury let out a breath he hadn't even realised he was holding. He was passing the stables now, mentally registering that the horses were secure for the night. A couple of them gently whickered as he paused to stroke their noses, murmur their names. A moment later he was opening the stout door that let him in to the back of the house, inhaling the familiar scents of stonework and smoke from the fires as he walked through the flagged hall to the low-beamed dining room at the very heart of the old building.

The sound of cheerful voices told him before he even entered that Tom, the two Watterson brothers and Jacques had settled themselves extremely comfortably around the vast oak table, eating Mrs Bartlett's hot beef stew and drinking some red French wine.

Eagerly they welcomed Luke and pulled out a chair for him, while Mrs Bartlett, Tom's wife, came hurrying from the adjoining kitchen to ladle out a dish of stew for him. Jacques poured Luke a glass of the wine.

'What detained you, my friend?' asked Jacques curiously. 'We were beginning to think you might have gone into town, to find yourself a pretty girl.'

Tom was blunter. 'Did you find out if Lord Franklin was in the coach?'

'He wasn't.' Luke drank half his wine and put his glass down. 'Apparently he's still in London.'

'Then who were the girl and the old woman?'

'The girl's a relative of Lord Franklin's. The other one's her companion, I believe.'

Tom nodded wisely. 'Ah. The orphan he's said to have taken into his care—which must have been a surprise to everyone, cold-blooded fish that he is. I heard rumours that she's pretty. Is she?'

'She certainly does her best *not* to be.' *No more. No need to say any more.*

'She's French, they say,' announced Josh Watterson eagerly. 'That's interesting.'

'Maybe.' Luke poured himself more wine and the others concentrated again on their food—all except for Jacques, who was watching him sharply.

Monsieur Jacques, Luke's men called him. He'd been a soldier, captured by the English and condemned to rot as a prisoner of war—until Luke freed him. 'And I pay my dues,' Jacques liked to explain to Luke's companions. 'I help my friends as they help me.'

It was to pay back his debts that Jacques now ran his small sailing ship with skill and bravado between the coasts of France and England on dark and misty nights such as this. But Jacques was frowning in puzzlement as he pushed his empty plate aside and said, 'Why, my friend Luke, would Lord Franklin suddenly discover a young French relative? Why didn't he know of her before?

Surely, wealthy families such as his have their ancestry well documented for generations back?'

'That's true.' Luke paused in eating his meal. 'Their family lines are guarded as thoroughly as their fortunes, to prevent interlopers from getting any of their money.'

'That's exactly what I thought. Has the girl taken his fancy, do you think?'

Luke let out a bark of laughter at that. 'Highly improbable. They say Lord Franklin hasn't touched a woman since his wife died ten years ago—and he wasn't over-fond of *her*, by all accounts.'

Jacques smiled. 'So a liaison of some sort is out of the question. But why did he go to the trouble of bringing her to England? And why—having claimed her as his responsibility—would he banish her to Bircham Hall?'

'When I have the answers, I'll be glad to share them with you.'

'Indeed,' the Frenchman said. 'So you're going to make enquiries, are you? Should I perhaps begin to wonder if this French *demoiselle* of Lord Franklin's is more interesting than you say?'

Luke savoured his wine before putting the glass down. 'Totally uninteresting,' he said. 'Too young and too proud, I imagine. Besides, I have more than enough to deal with at the moment.'

'With your estate and your farms? I hope I sense optimism?'

Just then Mrs Bartlett came bustling in to clear away the used dishes, and Tom and the Wattersons stated their intention of carrying out their usual evening tasks. Luke sat back in his chair and took his time answering Jacques's question. 'I'm not sure if it's optimism, or foolishness. I've found some new tenants for the farms—but do you know how much the price of English grain has dropped in the last year? I'll be keeping the men busy, it's true, but it might all be for nothing.'

'You're not wishing you'd married your heiress?'

'Hardly. That ended almost three years ago. She's marrying someone else in spring—someone her father considers far more suitable—although my tenants might wish I had her money to throw around.'

Jacques shook his head. 'You're giving them something better than money, Luke. You're giving them hope, and you've got to remember that.'

Luke looked around bleakly. 'I'm postponing bankruptcy, that's all. I must by now have sold off everything of value that's ever belonged to my family.'

'You can still fight for your family's honour. Not with sword or pistol, it's true—but you know as well as I there are other ways. I'm going back to France tomorrow—and if your brother's still alive, I will find him, I swear.'

Tom Bartlett came in, with more logs for the fire. 'You're talking about the captain's brother?' he said eagerly. 'Who knows—he might even turn up here one day, right out of the blue. I can just see it, Captain Luke—he'll ride up the track, bold as ever, and tell us all his adventures, just like he used to.'

Jacques nodded approvingly. 'That's the spirit. Let's raise our glasses to the captain's brother. Let's wish him a safe journey home!'

'To Anthony,' they echoed. 'A safe return.'

Gradually, the fire died down. Midnight came and went; they talked of battles they'd fought and comrades they'd known until at last, knowing they must rise well before dawn, they went off to their beds.

All of them except Luke.

The big house was quiet enough now for him to hear the whisper of the wind in the trees outside and the faint hiss of the waves breaking on the long shingle beach below the cliffs. Somewhere in the distance a nightbird called.

He went to stir the embers of the fire, lifting the metal poker with his maimed right hand by mistake. *Fool. Fool.* The heavy implement clattered on the hearth. He picked the poker up almost savagely with his left hand and jabbed at the logs until they roared into life.

Damn it. He was of no use to *anyone*, least of all to himself. He ripped off the black leather glove and stared at the two stumps where his fingers had been. The scars had almost healed, and as for the ache of the missing joints—well, he was used to it.

What he could not grow used to was the feeling that his younger brother—who'd relied on him, who'd *trusted* him—was lost for good. Was dead, like the others. By hoping that Anthony had somehow survived, he'd made the final blow ten times as bad for himself.

Again and again during these last few months, he'd cursed his injured hand, because it had stopped him sailing to France with Jacques and hunting the coast for clues or answers. He couldn't use a pistol, or a sword; wasn't even much use at helping sail a ship. But perhaps Fate was telling him that he should turn his mind to other matters.

Perhaps Fate was reminding him that the answers he was seeking could also lie here, in England, not in France at all. Perhaps Fate was telling him that *here*, he could find out what had really happened to Anthony and his brave comrades. Why they had been betrayed—and by whom. Even though such secrets were as closely guarded as rich men's fortunes.

He thought again of Lord Franklin Grayfield, a rich widower in his late forties; a remote, clever man who had a son out in India whom he hadn't seen for years. Lord Franklin Grayfield, who cared far more for his art collection, it was said, than for female company.

Yet he'd claimed an unknown French girl as his relative—the girl Luke had met that afternoon. Harshly, he dismissed his memory of the light lavender scent that emanated, ever so faintly, from her creamy skin. Harshly, he thrust aside his awareness of her downright vulnerability and the haunting sadness in her eyes. Instead, he told himself to remember the pistol she'd handled so deftly and so purposefully—as if in mockery of his own injury.

Caroline used to squeal in girlish horror at any mention of the war and weapons. But the French girl had that dainty gun and looked as if she knew how to use it. What kind of life had she led, before coming to England? And if the pistol had startled him, what in God's name was he to make of the compass she'd dropped?

Once again Luke remembered the astonishing inscription that he'd seen engraved upon its side—he found that his heart was speeding at just the thought of it. He also remembered the look on her face as she'd snatched it from him. *No wonder she was so eager—so very eager—to get it back.*

Who was she, really? And what in hell was she doing here, under Lord Franklin's so-called protection?

Chapter Four

Ellie, too, was still awake, sitting alone by the window in the icy spaciousness of her bedroom in Bircham Hall. It was past midnight. But she couldn't sleep, because this was a day she would never, ever be able to forget.

After the repair to the road, Lord Franklin's carriage had made swift progress, its driver no doubt eager to make up for the delay. They'd left the main road to pass through some gates by a well-lit lodge, after which they followed a long private drive; Ellie had seen how the carriage lamps picked out clumps of winter-bare trees set amidst grassy parkland.

And as they crossed the bridge over a river, she had her first view of the Hall—stately and foursquare, with flambeaux burning on either side of the huge, pillared entrance, as if in defiance of the January night.

Lord Franklin's country residence. It was magnificent. It was haughty and forbidding. 'Oh, look,' cried Miss Pringle, who was peering out of the window, too. 'Here we are at last, Elise. And I see—goodness me!—that all the staff are outside, waiting to greet you!'

Indeed, Ellie had seen them all there in the cold: the

maids in black and the footmen, straight as soldiers, clad in Lord Franklin's livery of navy and gold.

All waiting for *her*. Ellie's heart sank.

But Miss Pringle practically bubbled with excitement. 'Such an honour for you!' she murmured as the grooms hurried to hold the horses and lower the carriage steps. 'Such a very great honour! And look—here is Mr Huffley, his lordship's butler...'

'Miss Pringle. *Mademoiselle*.' The butler made a stiff bow to them as they descended from the carriage. 'It is my pleasure, *mademoiselle*,' he went on to Ellie, bowing again, 'to welcome you most heartily to Bircham Hall. Allow me to present our housekeeper, Mrs Sheerham. Our cook, Mrs Bevington. The senior housemaid, Joan...'

The maids curtseyed to her, the footmen bowed their heads to her; all politeness, all decorum, despite the fact that their breaths were misting in the chilly air. For their sakes Ellie got through the ceremony as quickly as she could, then followed Mr Huffley up the stone steps to the house.

And only then did she remember that there was somebody else she had yet to meet.

'Lady Charlotte will be expecting you,' Miss Pringle was whispering at her side. 'I declare, I cannot *wait* to see her ladyship again.'

The entrance hall was huge and cold, its walls hung with coats of arms and stags' heads. All kinds of statues stood on either side of the hall: reclining figures of smooth white marble, stone busts set on pillars, precious relics that must, Ellie realised, have come from the ancient civilizations of Greece or Rome or Egypt.

It was a *proud* house, thought Ellie to herself with a

shiver. All these priceless objects from the past seemed to be there to declare the history, wealth and importance of those who dwelt there. And in the midst of all this, as if claiming her own right to be a part of the grandeur, was a lady in her early seventies, with a lace-trimmed cap perched on her iron-grey hair and a gown of black. She sat in a bath chair. Two footmen were on either side of her, standing stiffly to attention.

'Your ladyship...' breathed Miss Pringle to her, sweeping an extravagant curtsey.

And Ellie was suddenly dry-mouthed as she made a low curtsey also. Nobody had told her about the bath chair. Nobody had told her...

She rose from her curtsey, aware that Lady Charlotte was raking her with hard eyes. 'So you must be Elise Duchamp,' she said, distaste for the foreign name etching every syllable. 'I am Lord Franklin's mother. I gather he has decided to banish you to Bircham? So much, I imagine, for your hopes of trapping my son into marriage.'

Ellie was shocked not just by the nature of the attack, but by its vicious suddenness. Never—*never* had she thought of Lord Franklin in that way. *Dieu du ciel*, he was surely over twice her age! 'I do assure you, my lady, that *nothing* could be further from the truth!'

Lady Charlotte wheeled herself close, forcing Ellie backwards. 'Are you really telling me that you never intended to make him your prize? Some people might—just *might*—believe you. I don't, as it happens. Just remember, Elise—I shall be watching you.'

Her ladyship glanced up at Miss Pringle. 'It's almost five o'clock. I hope, Pringle, that you've shown some common sense for a change, and told the girl that we dine at six? We do not indulge in town hours here.' She beckoned to the two footmen, who throughout all this had stared blankly ahead. 'Take me to my room. *Now.*' And Ellie watched speechless as the footmen wheeled the elderly lady away.

How could she have allowed herself to be brought here—*trapped* here like this? Why had she entrusted herself to these people?

Yet how could she have resisted her father's last desperate plea as he lay dying? *You must go with him, Ellie, to England. You must.*

'Papa,' Ellie had argued. 'We don't know him. We cannot be sure.'

But her father had insisted. *Lord Franklin will keep you safe, as I have never been able to,* he'd said. *Promise me...*

Miss Pringle still hovered, all of a flutter. 'What an honour for you, Elise,' she was saying brightly. 'How wonderful to be welcomed to Bircham by Lady Charlotte herself.'

But her hands were trembling, and Ellie realised that Miss Pringle was afraid of Lady Charlotte. Terrified, in fact. And then the housekeeper was there—Mrs Sheerham—saying to Ellie, 'May I take you to your room, ma'am?'

Ellie followed her, quite dazed.

She found that she had been allotted a spacious suite on the second floor. Her trunk and valise had already been brought up and placed in the bedroom that adjoined the private sitting room.

She went over to them quickly, to check that the valise was still firmly locked. Looking round, she noted that thick curtains were drawn shut across all the windows; fires had been lit in both rooms and a dozen or

more wax candles banished the darkness. The luxury of
it all stunned her.

'I hope everything is to your taste, ma'am?' Mrs
Sheerham was still standing by the door.

'Yes. Thank you, it's—it's wonderful.'

'Very good, ma'am.' Mrs Sheerham's expression softened just a fraction with the praise. 'You'd no doubt like
some tea and someone to help with your unpacking? I'll
see that a maid comes up to you shortly.' She left and
Ellie began to slowly remove her cloak.

Lady Charlotte hates me. She never wanted me here.

She'd barely had time to lay her cloak on the bed, when
there was a knock at the door, and a girl in a black dress
and white apron entered hesitantly.

'My name is Mary, miss!' She bobbed a curtsey. 'Mrs
Sheerham, she asked me to come up and see to you. And
I've brought tea for you.' Mary darted out again and came
back in with a tray of tea things, which she set down on
a small table in the sitting room, while Ellie stood back,
hoping the girl wouldn't guess that—before being taken
under Lord Franklin's wing—she had never had a personal maid in her life.

'Now, while you drink your tea,' Mary went on, 'I
shall start to unpack your clothes, shall I?' Her eager eyes
had already settled on Ellie's trunk and valise, then fell
a little. 'But is that all?'

Ellie knew that most ladies of quality travelled with
so much luggage that often a separate carriage was re-
quired for it. 'There's only the one trunk, I'm afraid,
Mary,' she answered quickly. 'And, yes, I'd be grateful
if you would unpack it.'

'And what about the bag—?'

'No,' Ellie cut in. Mary was staring at her in surprise.

'I mean,' Ellie hurried on, 'that there's very little in the valise. My clothes are all in the trunk. So if you would put them away, I would be most grateful.'

'Of course, miss!' Briskly Mary set about unpacking Ellie's clothes and hanging them in the wardrobe, or folding them into the various chests of drawers that were ready-scented with sprigs of dried lavender. As she did so, she exclaimed over the silk gowns, the velvet pelisses, the exquisite underwear. 'Oh, miss. Are all these from Paris?'

Ellie shook her head. 'They're from London. Lord Franklin was kind enough to arrange for a modiste to make them for me.'

Mary gazed longingly at a rose-pink evening dress. 'I don't know when you're going to wear these things here, miss. It's a cold house, is Bircham Hall. And Lady Charlotte, she doesn't have many guests or parties, exactly...'

'It doesn't matter,' Ellie said quickly. 'I've never been interested in parties or clothes.'

'No, miss? But it's such a shame that you're going to be so quiet here. Now, if you'd stayed in London... Mr Huffley told us that in London there are lots and lots of French people like yourself, who had to run for their lives when that monster Napoleon became Emperor of France. Napoleon sent armies marching all over Europe, didn't he?'

'Yes.' Ellie's voice was very quiet. 'Yes, he did.'

Mary had paused to admire an embroidered silk chemise before folding it meticulously in a drawer. Then she nodded. 'But now, Napoleon's locked up good and proper, on that island in the Mediterranean. Miles from anywhere. And our clever politicians and Lord Wellington will see that he never, ever gets free. Are you quite sure you don't want me to unpack that valise for you, miss?'

'Quite sure. And I think that is all, for now.'

But Mary's eyes were still scanning the room. 'Your cloak!' she said suddenly. It was still on the bed, where Ellie had laid it. 'It will be dusty after your journey. Shall I take it downstairs and brush it out for you?'

'No!' Ellie had already taken a step forward, to stop her. 'No. That will be all, Mary.' She forced herself into calmness. 'Thank you so much.'

'You're very welcome, miss. You've not drunk your tea yet! Never mind, I'll collect the tray later.' Reluctantly, Mary took one last look around. 'It'll be time for you to go down to dinner soon. You'll hear the bell ringing downstairs, ten minutes before six. Oh, and her ladyship doesn't like anyone to be late.' Her bright voice dimmed, just a little. 'Most particular, her ladyship is. *Most* particular.'

Mary let herself out. And as soon as her swift footsteps faded into the distance, Ellie leaned back against the closed door and thought, *I should never, ever, have allowed myself to be brought here.* She hurried across to her cloak and, reaching deep into the inside pocket, drew out her pistol and the compass in its box.

She clasped them to her.

The man. The man, on the road... She could still remember how she'd felt, standing there with him so close, so powerful and dangerous. She would perhaps never forget the way her pulse had pounded when he smiled at her.

She *had* to forget him. As she hoped he would forget her. *You will never see him again. You must erase him from your mind.*

Drawing a deep breath, she laid the pistol and compass

on the bed. Then she unfastened the silver chain round her neck, feeling for the small key that hung from it, and with that key she unlocked her valise. In it were several maps and charts, carefully folded, and below them were more objects, each in black velvet wrappings. She opened them one by one.

A surveyor's prism. A miniature folding telescope. A magnifying lens, with an ebony handle. A tiny geologist's hammer.

She wrapped them up again and put them back at the bottom of the valise. Put the pistol and compass in there, too, then the documents on top of them all.

She knew she ought to lock the valise again and hide it from sight, but instead she withdrew one of the folded documents and spread it out, carefully.

She translated the title into English, under her breath. *A map of the valley of the Loire, showing its geology. Devised and drawn by A. Duchamp, Paris, in the year of Our Lord 1809...*

She picked up the map with her father's signature on it and held it close to her breast as the memories flooded back.

Chapter Five

Ellie's father, André Duchamp, was a geologist, surveyor and map-maker. He had lived with his wife and daughter in Paris, close to the church of St Denis in an apartment off the Rue Tivoli, which had a little balcony from where Ellie could look out on to the main street. She remembered being enthralled as a five-year-old child to one day see ranks of soldiers marching by, their tricolours held aloft, and two years later she'd seen Napoleon himself, the newly crowned Emperor of France, ride past at the head of his cavalry on a prancing white horse, acknowledging the cheers of the crowds who'd gathered to see him.

'He is a great man,' her father used to say. 'He will bring peace and prosperity to France again.'

Their apartment was small, but even so, a whole room was given up to her father's work, and he used to let Ellie watch him while he drew his maps. She was fascinated, too, by the telescopes and star charts he had in there, for he was a keen astronomer. 'Why should I only map the ground beneath my feet?' he would say. 'When there are also the heavens above us to explore?'

Best of all, she loved to gaze at the array of geological samples he kept in a glass cabinet in that room. To Ellie they were as beautiful as any jewels, and her father would tell her about each one.

'These pink crystals are feldspar, Ellie. Such a delicate colour, don't you think?'

'Oh, yes! And the green one, Papa?'

'That's olivine. And here's a piece of hematite—such a dark, deep red that it's almost black.'

Ellie nodded eagerly. 'And that one must be gold!'

'Fool's gold, alas.' Her father smiled at her excitement. 'It's called pyrites and it's tricked many a fortune-hunter.'

She'd gazed at him earnestly. 'You know so much, Papa.'

He'd ruffled her hair. 'Ah, but there's always more to learn, little one.'

'Is that why you go travelling?'

'It's my job, Ellie. I'm lucky to have a job that I love.'

She was always sad when her father was away. He went travelling for days—sometimes even weeks—at a time and only later in her childhood did she realise why he was so busy. It was because his expertise in both geology and map-making meant that he was invaluable in the planning and the physical creation of new roads that were intended to connect all of the cities and ports of France for travellers and traders.

When he was away, Ellie would gaze down the street from her window for his return, waiting for him and missing him. She was only vaguely aware of the wars the Emperor Napoleon was waging on France's borders and beyond. But as the years went by, her father was away more and more often, for longer periods of time, and when he returned, his mood was often heavy, sombre, almost—though he always smiled to see his daughter.

When Ellie was seventeen, her mother died. She'd been ill for only a short while, and her father was brokenhearted. And that was truly the end of their old, familiar way of life, because one night, a few weeks after the funeral, Ellie found her father packing all his precious things into his leather valise. She saw how his face was etched with grief, how his hands trembled as he put them on her shoulders and said, 'Ellie, my darling, we must flee Paris, you and I. This city is no longer safe for us.'

It made her almost smile to remember how in Brussels Lord Franklin had expressed his fear that the journey to England might exhaust her, because Ellie was used to the kind of journeys Lord Franklin probably couldn't even imagine. She was used to travelling under a false name, and often by night; sometimes in mail coaches if they had the money, and in farm carts or on foot if they hadn't.

They'd headed for Le Havre first, where her father had once had relatives—only to find that they'd long since disappeared, in the upheavals of revolution and war. After several cold and lonely weeks, her father came home one day with the heavy news that they were still being pursued—and so their travelling began again and they headed north.

If they felt they were safe—if they'd gone for a day without suspecting anyone was on their tail—they would treat themselves to a room in an inn for the night, even if the room was flea-ridden and furnished only with a couple of lumpy, straw-filled mattresses. More often they had to sleep in barns, or ruined cottages—places left derelict by years of war.

And Ellie had to be the strong one, because already her father's health was failing. She had to do things she'd not have believed possible—become a liar, a thief, a fighter, even. Her father had taught her to use that small but lethal pistol, and though she'd never been forced to fire it, she'd made it plain to anyone who threatened their safety that she would—and could—shoot to kill.

She'd had to plan their route, make the decisions, and find—or steal—medicines for her ailing father, who was becoming weaker and weaker each day.

'Soon we will be safe, Ellie,' he would murmur each night, as he carefully unpacked his valise and checked his precious instruments. 'Soon we will be able to stop running at last.'

For her papa, the running had indeed ended. He was dying of pneumonia in Brussels when Lord Franklin came to them—Lord Franklin Grayfield, a wealthy middle-aged English aristocrat who travelled abroad a good deal, he told Ellie in fluent French, because he was fascinated by European culture and art, and was eager to add to his collection of paintings and sculptures. To his great regret, he had been thwarted in his travels by the long war. 'But now,' he told her, 'I am making up for lost time.'

He was clearly rich. He was also ferociously clever. And never in her life had Ellie been so astonished as when he told her, in the Brussels attic where she lived with her dying father, that her mother was a distant relative of his.

Ellie had been astounded. A relative? But her mother had told her that her English family had disowned her completely when she told them she was marrying a French map-maker.

'How I wish I'd known this earlier,' Lord Franklin

said earnestly. 'I'm afraid it's only a few weeks ago that I was making some family enquiries and learned your mother had died; learned, too, that she had a daughter. I vowed to find you, although I wasn't sure how. But my search for antiquities happened to bring me to Brussels. And you can imagine my surprise, to find out by chance in the marketplace that living here was a gentleman from Paris called Duchamp, whose wife was English and who had a daughter.'

Ellie had listened to all this with her heart pounding. Since arriving in this city, Ellie and her father hadn't troubled to change their name, Duchamp, for it was common enough; but they'd done their utmost to conceal the fact that they were from Paris. And Ellie couldn't recollect telling anyone, not even Madame Gavroche, their landlady, that her mother was English.

Lord Franklin was kind. He paid for an expensive doctor to visit her father, although it was far, far too late for anything to be done. He paid for the funeral and the burial, and afterwards he had taken her hand and said kindly, 'You must come with me to England, Elise. And I promise I will do my utmost to make up for the dreadful grief you have had to face, alone.'

He never once asked her why she and her father had left Paris. He was thoughtful, he was generous; but she was wary of his generosity, and of *him*. Her strongest instinct was to stay in Brussels, in the little apartment above the bread shop, where Madame Gavroche and her son had been so good to her. But her dying father had pleaded with her to let Lord Franklin take her into his care.

What else could she do, but agree?

* * *

And so Ellie travelled to England—first in an expensive hired carriage to Calais, and then on Lord Franklin's private yacht, across the Channel to Tilbury. And from there, they went on in Lord Franklin's own carriage to his magnificent house in London. The city astonished her with the magnificence of its buildings, and she was overwhelmed by the elegance of the Mayfair house on Clarges Street in which Lord Franklin resided. And there, every possible comfort was offered to her by her new protector.

She was given her own maid. She was visited in rapid succession by a hairdresser, a modiste and a mantua maker. Soon a selection of expensive and fashionable gowns began to arrive for her. But Lord Franklin seemed—despite his generosity—to be reluctant to let her meet anyone, or to let her go out anywhere. Once, she had asked him if he was in contact with any of her mother's other relatives, and he replied, 'Oh, my dear, most of them have died, or live somewhere in the north. No need to trouble yourself over *them*.'

Ellie was surrounded by a luxury she'd never known, but she hated being confined in that big house. Nevertheless she was determined to keep her promise to her father. *Lord Franklin will keep you safe, as I have never been able to.*

But her trust in Lord Franklin was badly shaken when one day she returned to her room after lunch and realised that, in her absence, someone had made a very thorough inspection of all her belongings.

She felt sick with the kind of shock and fear that she'd hoped never to feel again. To anyone else, certainly, there were no outward signs of disturbance—but she, who was used to running, used to hiding, could tell straight away.

Someone—surely not her maid, who was a young, shy creature—had been through everything: every item of clothing, every personal effect in her chest of drawers and wardrobe. Ellie even felt sure that each book on her bookshelf was in a different place, if only by a fraction of an inch.

With her pulse pounding, she'd pulled out her father's old black valise from the bottom of her wardrobe.

The lock was still intact—but if she looked closely, she could see faint scratch marks around it. Someone had been trying to get inside.

She went downstairs to find Lord Franklin. He was out a good deal of the time, either at his club or attending art auctions; but from the housekeeper she learned that, as luck would have it, he was in his study, talking to a man called Mr Appleby, who was, the housekeeper informed her, the steward at Lord Franklin's country home, Bircham Hall.

Ellie had knocked and gone in.

'Elise!' Lord Franklin had turned to her, with his usual pleasant smile. 'What can I do for you?'

Mr Appleby stood at his side; he was a little older than Lord Franklin, clad in a black coat and breeches, with cropped grey hair and with spectacles perched on the end of his nose. She glanced at him, then said to Lord Franklin, 'Someone, my lord, has been through my possessions. Has searched my room.' She'd meant to sound calm, but she could hear a faint tremor in her voice. 'I would be obliged if you would question your staff. I really cannot allow this.'

Mr Appleby had looked as shocked as if she'd challenged Lord Franklin to a pistol duel. Lord Franklin himself was frowning in concern.

'This is a grave allegation, my dear,' he murmured. 'But are you sure?'

'I am completely sure. My lord.'

'You perhaps doubt the honesty of my servants, Elise? You doubt their loyalty to me? Is anything actually missing?'

'No! But that is not the point...'

Lord Franklin had turned to his steward. 'Leave us a moment, would you, Appleby?'

'Now, Elise,' said Lord Franklin, when Mr Appleby had gone. 'I've been thinking lately that perhaps London does not suit you. I've been wondering if you might like to live in my country house in Kent for a while—it's in a peaceful area near to the coast and it will, I'm sure, be more restful for you than London, after the various ordeals you have endured. Do you have any objection?'

For a single wild moment, Ellie had thought of fleeing the Mayfair house, and of running back to...*to where?*

His lordship was already opening the door, to indicate their interview was at an end. 'Bircham,' he informed her, 'is barely sixty miles or so from London, which makes it an easy journey, if spread over two days. And you really will be most comfortable there.' He stood by the open door, waiting for her to agree. Her father's voice echoed insistently in her ears. *Lord Franklin will keep you safe.*

She had bowed her head. 'As you wish, my lord.'

And now, here she was at Bircham Hall. It was almost six o'clock and dinner would be served shortly. She paced her room in agitation. *It must be safer than France*, she kept telling herself. And safer than London, where someone had searched her room—she'd been sure of it. But here, she'd found danger of an entirely different kind.

Lord Franklin's formidable mother she felt she could deal with. But now, despite the heat of the room, she shivered afresh as she remembered the man on the road—the dark-haired man in the long coat, with the black-gloved hand—holding her father's compass so casually. *Lord Franklin is said to be a great collector of foreign objets d'art. And what could be more fitting than for him to return from the Continent with a pretty French girl in his care?*

Ellie gazed at herself in the mirror, seeing her face, with her wide green eyes and dark curls and even darker lashes. *Was* she pretty? She'd never troubled to think about it. She'd spent months hiding from men who might be hunting her, months concealing her feminine figure with drab clothing, keeping, always, in the shadows.

But now, she remembered the way that man by the roadside had looked at her. She'd been travel-weary and full of foreboding about her future, and the sudden and silent arrival of someone she realised instantly posed as strong a threat as any she'd yet faced should have set fierce alarm bells jangling in her brain. She'd behaved stupidly, by not running straight away, back to the coach—surely he wouldn't have dared to pursue her?

And yet, the very moment she saw him—yes, with his old, patched coat, his overlong black hair, his dagger-sharp cheekbones and his black-gloved hand—her heart had stopped and her breathing had quickened. Try as she might, she could not banish the memory of the way his blue eyes—his utterly dangerous blue eyes—had scoured her and seen through her, until her whole being had been infused with a sense that *here* was a kind of man she had never met before. The kind of man she had perhaps dreamed one day of meeting...

Fool. You fool. Even now, she shivered with something that had nothing to do with the coldness of the night and far more to do with the memory of his lean, powerful body and his husky voice. Drawing a deep breath, she looked around her suite of rooms. All quiet. All undisturbed. But what next? Whom could she trust? Could she even trust herself?

The dinner bell clanged loudly in the hall downstairs, and then Miss Pringle arrived to escort her to the dining room. To ensure that Ellie *remembered* to go down to the dining room, more like—and poor Miss Pringle, she appeared even more nervous than Ellie was. 'Such an honour,' she exclaimed, 'to be invited to dine with her ladyship. But...' She was eyeing Ellie's faded gown with obvious trepidation.

'Yes?' Ellie asked politely.

'I think—I think Lady Charlotte might expect you to wear something a little more *appropriate* for dinner...'

'I am perfectly comfortable in this dress,' Ellie said quietly but firmly.

'Yes, of course.' Miss Pringle nodded, wringing her hands a little. Then she led the way, along the corridor and down the stairs.

Dinner lasted over two hours. And at the end of the final course, Lady Charlotte expressed herself to be profoundly disappointed with Ellie's company.

'I thought the French were renowned for their wit and gaiety,' she said. 'I was going to invite you, Elise, to join me in my parlour; but I think it better if you retire to your room and count it your very good fortune that my son has taken you into his care.'

Thankful for her escape, Ellie went upstairs and closed her door. But she knew that sleep wouldn't come easily.

Had Lord Franklin really found her by chance? Why had her room in London been searched? And the man. The man on the road. He'd probably forgotten her already—but she already feared she would find it impossible to forget *him*.

Chapter Six

During the next few days, as the rain fell relentlessly outside and darkness closed in by four, Ellie grew quietly more and more desperate. Mealtimes with Miss Pringle and Lady Charlotte came round each day with monotonous regularity. Every evening at six, Ellie went down to the vast dining room whose panelled walls were hung with daunting portraits of Grayfield ancestors.

Lady Charlotte was invariably there before her—her ladyship was wheeled in by her footmen from her ground-floor suite at five minutes to six precisely. Once she was settled at the head of the table, she would watch with eagle eyes as the courses were brought in and served on fine china plates adorned with Lord Franklin's family crest.

Soon Ellie knew by heart the ancestral portraits that hung on the walls and the sculptures that adorned every alcove, every niche of the great house. *A nightmare for the servants*, thought Ellie. They must require constant dusting—something else for Lady Charlotte to complain about. And complaining was her ladyship's chief occupation, it seemed, especially at mealtimes.

Lady Charlotte criticised every course as it was served,

pointing out to the unfortunate butler Mr Huffley that the
soup was too hot, or the veal lacked salt. She never com-
plained about the wine, though; she was partial to Madeira
or sherry and liked her glass to be constantly replenished.

Miss Pringle didn't drink wine and she ate her food in
hungry nibbles, at the same time endeavouring to listen
intently to Lady Charlotte's every word. Lady Charlotte's
main topic of conversation, once the food had been criticised, was her son—she loved to talk of his travels and
his many illustrious acquaintances amongst the *ton*. But
she never, ever spoke of his dead wife, or of his son—
who Ellie gathered held some colonial post out in India.

Once, Miss Pringle timidly mentioned after dinner
that Ellie had told her she could play the piano.

'The piano? Is this true?' Lady Charlotte asked.

'Only a little, my lady,' Ellie replied. 'My mother
taught me to play in Paris and I—'

'I cannot bear the sound,' Lady Charlotte interrupted,
'unless it is played by a true musician. I know what I
shall do to entertain you this evening, Elise. You may
come to my private parlour to look at some miniatures
that a London artist painted of Lord Franklin when he
was twenty-one. They are very fine. Come in an hour—
I will have taken my rest by then.'

Ellie didn't think she was early, but she must have
been, because after knocking and walking into Lady
Charlotte's ground-floor suite, she saw Lady Charlotte
in there alone. And she was standing—*standing*—by the
sideboard, pouring herself a large glass of sherry.

Lady Charlotte heard her and spun round. With a
face like stone, her ladyship returned to her nearby bath
chair—walking with no obvious difficulty—and sat
down. She said, icily, 'Some days, I find that I can move

a little better than others. Mostly, of course, I am a complete invalid. Why are you here?'

It took a minute for Ellie to find her voice. 'You wished to show me some miniatures, my lady.'

'Ah. The miniatures. Pringle got them out for me—they're here, somewhere…'

Ellie looked around almost wildly for a servant or footman—for anyone else who might have witnessed the scene. Did anyone else *know* Lady Charlotte could walk?

Whether they did or not, Ellie knew she had to keep silent about this strange episode. *You're in enough trouble already. Quite enough.*

Lady Charlotte appeared to forget the incident altogether and continued to goad Ellie at every opportunity. 'I hear,' she announced one evening at dinner, 'that London has changed out of all recognition in the last few years.'

Miss Pringle looked up nervously, her eyes darting to Ellie; Ellie remained silent, aware now of Lady Charlotte glaring ominously at her.

'I have been reliably informed,' Lady Charlotte went on, 'that the city is becoming overrun with poverty-stricken vagrants.'

Miss Pringle was nodding. 'Oh, indeed,' she echoed. 'Overrun. Quite true.'

'In particular,' pronounced Lady Charlotte, 'one hears the most dreadful stories of foreigners who come over daily on the packet boats hunting for work, or more likely looking for mischief. The French, in other words. Now that the war is over, I hope that our prime minister and his government will send them all back to where they belong.'

Miss Pringle let out a little gasp. Ellie rose from her

chair abruptly and said, 'Please excuse me from the remainder of the meal, your ladyship.'

Lady Charlotte peered crossly at her. 'What? *What?*
It's really most irregular of you to retire before I have
even begun my dessert!'

'I realise that. But I feel particularly tired today and I
really need to go to my room. Pray accept my apologies—
Lady Charlotte, Miss Pringle.'

She made a brief curtsey and hurried from the dining
room. Just outside the doors stood the two footmen who
pushed Lady Charlotte around in her bath chair. They
had their backs to Ellie and were talking. And she felt
a sense of cold shock, as their topic of conversation became only too apparent.

'What do you make of the young French girl, then?'
one was saying.

'If you ask me, she's not as quiet as she looks. Got a
spark of liveliness in her eyes, most definitely.' The other
footman chuckled. 'A pity it's all wasted here. But perhaps she misbehaved in London…'

Ellie walked past them and past the antique statues to
the stairs, her cheeks burning as she climbed up to her
room on the second floor. And as she stood in her lonely
sitting room, trapped in that great, cold English mansion,
with the footmen's whispered vitriol and Lady Charlotte's
stark disapproval still echoing in her ears, she felt a hol-
low emptiness inside.

She'd been here nearly a week. The thought of another week was beyond endurance. *I cannot stay here
any longer*, she thought. *I cannot stay here, where I
don't belong.*

To leave would mean breaking her vow to her father—
her promise that she would come to England and be safe.

But it had been a huge, huge mistake to put herself at the mercy of strangers.

She had to get away, and Brussels was the only place she could think of: Brussels and the lodgings where she and her father had stayed for the last few weeks of her poor father's life. Maybe the kind landlady would allow her to rent her old room again, if it was still free? And surely she could find a job nearby—on a market stall, or in the baker's shop itself. Then she would be able to visit her papa's grave at the little church of St Marie every day.

She pushed aside the heavy curtains and gazed out of the window into the night. After days of heavy rain, the velvety sky was clear at last and far beyond the woods surrounding the Hall's gardens, she could see the moonlight reflected off the distant sea. Suddenly she remembered the small fishing port she'd noticed on her way here.

Bircham Staithe, Mary had told her it was called. It lay only a little way beyond the boundaries of Lord Franklin's estate—less than a mile, she guessed. And once there…

She had money. She could make up a story to some kind sea captain about how she had to return home now that the long war was over. Surely it would be straightforward to pay for a passage to northern France on a fishing vessel.

Already she was putting on her walking boots and her hooded cloak; already she was picking up her black leather valise, then she let herself quietly out of her room and stood there listening. The big house was absolutely silent. Making her way swiftly down the narrow servants' staircase, she slipped out of a side door into the enveloping darkness of the garden.

Freedom. She drew in deep breaths of the cold night air, but still hesitated before plunging into the shrubbery; because she knew that like most landowners, Lord Franklin kept half-a-dozen great mastiffs as guard dogs, which were let loose from their kennels by his groundsmen after dark.

Sometimes the dogs were released for only half an hour, though the timing of their outings was changed deliberately each night. But now Ellie reminded herself that she'd heard them in the grounds earlier, as dinner was being served, so surely they would be back in their kennels by now? She took the path through the shrubbery, aware of her pulse racing, but there were no cries of alarm from the house—neither dogs nor servants were giving chase. All was mercifully quiet.

Ellie had learned, during her travels with her father, to choose her route carefully, then follow it without hesitation. She'd noted on her first day here that beyond the shrubbery, smooth lawns and flowerbeds stretched to the boundary of Lord Franklin's estate, where the stone wall offered footholds in plenty for her to climb. From there she judged it was only a short distance to the road which led to the little port of Bircham Staithe.

She crossed the gardens and climbed the wall swiftly in the darkness. All that remained was to listen out for pursuers—and this was what troubled her now, as she hurried along the road that led down to the sea. She thought she'd heard muffled footsteps, in the woods to her right. She stopped, her breath catching in her throat.

Her thoughts flew to the man in the long grey coat, who'd held her father's compass in his hand and looked at her as if he could read her innermost secrets. Her heart hammered, but there was nothing now—no sound at all, except the whispering of the wind and the distant hiss of the sea. Perhaps it had been a small wild animal, or a bird scuffling in the undergrowth...

Four men loomed out of the darkness ahead of her. Four men dressed in the rough garb of fishermen, who'd spread out to bar her escape.

'Well, well,' the first one said, drawing closer. He wore a short serge jacket and strands of lank fair hair hung around his thin face. 'What *have* we got here? Looks like we've struck lucky tonight, lads.'

Chapter Seven

Luke Danbury was in a smoky tavern down by the harbour of Bircham Staithe, drinking rough ale and playing dice with a group of local fishermen. But his mind was miles away.

It was several days since Jacques had sailed back to France—heading south towards La Rochelle on the coast—and by now Jacques and his men would be searching. Questioning. Offering bribes, offering threats—all in the probably vain hope that Luke's brother wasn't dead, like the rest.

Suddenly he realised that one of the fishermen was nudging him. 'Your turn, Captain.' Luke nodded and gathered up the dice. He threw them awkwardly, of course. He did *everything* damned awkwardly with his left hand. He remembered the bleak night last autumn when the bandaging was removed for the first time and Luke—low in spirits after weeks of enforced inactivity—had said to Jacques, 'The next time, I will go to France with you. I cannot wait here any longer doing nothing, when my brother might need me.'

Then he'd seen the look on Jacques's face. And he'd known exactly what the Frenchman was thinking, even if he was too kind to say it. *You? With your crippled hand? What earthly good would you be to us? You cannot row a boat. You cannot wield a sword, or fire a gun.*

Luke's dice landed high and he realised that for once the pile of copper coins at his side was growing bigger. Well, there was a surprise. He ordered more ale for them all and muttered, under his breath, 'Anthony. If you're still alive, for God's sake let Jacques find you.'

And then, Tom Bartlett was at his elbow, with the Wattersons standing big and burly behind him. 'You're wanted outside, Captain.'

'Who by?'

'A bunch of local ruffians. And Sam Snaith is their leader.'

A hushed silence descended on the tavern. 'Why does he want me?'

'He says he's got someone interesting for you to meet. A girl—'

Luke was on his feet. He knew, without having to ask any more. He knew, as he strode around to the back of the tavern, where a dim light from a window illuminated the dingy courtyard.

Sam Snaith and his companions looked as disreputable as ever. They were all fishermen, supposedly, though he guessed they'd rarely brought in an honest day's catch in their lives. But this time, they'd actually caught something of value. Luke exhaled sharply.

Just as he'd suspected—there she was. The French girl who'd been heading for Bircham Hall in Lord Franklin's coach when he last saw her. The girl with the compass.

She'd been as haughty as hell with him, turning up her pretty nose in the air. And now that she'd recognised him, she was struggling even more desperately to free herself from Sam and his men, which they were enjoying, because it gave them all the more opportunity to manhandle her.

And he couldn't bear it.

'Stop,' Luke rapped out at them. 'Get your filthy hands off her. *Now.*'

They let her go, reluctantly. The girl lunged for a leather valise that had dropped to the ground and ran.

'Tom,' ordered Luke. 'Get her.'

The Wattersons went after her, too. The three of them brought her back, and this time she didn't struggle. But that leather bag, Luke noticed. She clung to it as if it meant more to her than life itself.

'So,' he said. 'We meet again. Having an adventure, are you?'

She threw him a look that expressed downright contempt, but even so, something smote him deep in his guts. *That wild dark hair*, he marvelled. *Those eyes.* Green, with flecks of amber that glowed brilliantly in the candlelight. She was proud, she was brave—and beneath that bravado he guessed she was absolutely desperate. *Whatever kind of mess she's in, it'll be all her own fault*, he told himself fiercely.

Tom nudged him. 'Captain, behind you—' and Luke was suddenly aware that Sam Snaith, all lanky hair and crooked teeth, was sidling up close.

'Now, look here, Captain,' Sam began. 'She was *our* captive first of all. And we trust you to treat us right for this. See?'

'Treat you *right*,' said Luke thoughtfully. 'Now, what do you mean by that, I wonder? Should I, perhaps, break every bone in your miserable body for attacking a de-fenceless girl?'

'Her? Defenceless? Ha! The wench knows how to put up a fight—you saw her!'

Tom and Josh were holding her by her arms, but she'd gone extremely still, as if her instincts told her he, Luke, was far more dangerous than Sam or his rogues. And by God, her instincts were right.

'You *told* us, Captain!' Sam was grumbling. He shoved his fists on his hips and stared up at Luke belligerently. 'You said there'd be a reward for any news about the girl staying at Bircham Hall. And we've done better than that, see? We've brought her to you!'

'Well—almost,' said Luke. 'Though I do believe I saw her a few moments ago giving all four of you the slip. Did you kidnap her from the house?'

'What—and take on Lord Franklin's men? No chance of *that*. But me and my lads, we were out on the Bircham road, minding our own business—'

'You'd been thieving, you mean? Or poaching?'

Sam scowled. 'Minding our own business, as I said— when all of a sudden, we saw the girl. She was scurry-ing along with that bag clutched in her hand, but Nathan here recognised her. Nathan said, "She's the new girl, at Bircham Hall! The French girl that everyone's talking about!" So we stopped her.'

Luke glanced at her, seeing the rapid rise and fall of her small breasts beneath her clothing, noting the fear that still shadowed those wide, alert eyes of hers. 'I imagine,' he said, 'that she was less than delighted.'

'We treated her well enough! We asked her, polite like—"Where are you going to, miss?"—and she said that she would give us money, good money, mind, if we

would find her a ship that would take her over to France!
But since you'd promised a reward, we brought her to
you, see?'

Luke turned and said to her, 'Is this true?'

Inside she must be terrified, he thought. Terrified. But
her voice was etched with icy scorn as she replied, 'Yes.
It is. And it's none of your business.'

'But it is, I'm afraid. Listen to me. You're wasting your
time and energy by trying to escape. Tell me why you
want to run and where to.'

She tilted her head defiantly. *'Je ne comprends pas,'*
she declared.

Luke sighed inwardly. She was telling him she didn't
understand—but he was pretty sure that she did. Every
single word. And now she was jumping away again, wary
as a wildcat, because Sam Snaith had drawn close, leer-
ing at her openly before saying to Luke, 'We thought
you'd be interested in her, Captain, and fair's fair. We
want that reward you promised—see?'

He held out his open palm, but Luke knocked it aside.
'I asked for news. Not a prisoner.'

'Oh, Captain,' said Sam softly. 'You're a proud one,
aren't you? And you know what they say, about pride.
Look around you.'

Luke looked, only to realise that more of Sam's comrades had come out of the tavern and were gathering in
the shadows—outnumbering Luke and his men by three
to one at least. *Damn.* He glanced quickly at the girl,
who'd gone very still.

And Sam was at his shoulder. 'If you're not going to
give us our reward—*Captain*—then we'll have the girl
back, if you please. We'll at least get a night's entertain-
ment out of her—'

The click of a pistol's safety catch being released echoed around the courtyard. Everyone stared in shock at the girl—because she had a pistol in her hand that was pointed straight at Sam's heart.

Luke groaned inwardly. *Oh, God.* He should have remembered. Most girls would have fainted—not this one.

'Back away,' she said to Sam Snaith. 'Back away *now*.'

Sam lifted his hands, but he was trying to sneer. 'You think you're frightening me? I'll wager it's not even loaded.'

She held the gun steady. 'Oh, I assure you it is. And it will take only one bullet to finish you off.'

And then—*as if that wasn't enough*, thought Luke as he braced himself—then they heard horses, clattering down the road towards the inn and the nearby harbour. More local men were pouring out of the tavern's back door and everyone was shouting at once. 'The Revenue men. Quick. Scatter.'

And Luke plunged towards the girl. Grabbed the gun off her and passed it to Tom, then seized her arm. Tom and the Wattersons were close behind him. *'Run,'* he whispered to her. 'This way.'

She tried to stand her ground. 'My valise...'

That leather bag of hers. It was lying on the ground. He grabbed that, too, and thrust it towards Josh. 'Here. Carry this.' By now, he could hear the government men pulling to a halt around the front of the inn; in no time they would be round the back, hunting for—what? Smugglers? Or were they looking for a runaway French girl, who was supposed to be dwelling in comfort at the country home of Lord Franklin Grayfield?

He, Luke, wanted a little time alone with her. He wanted to know what the hell was going on. Why she'd come to England, for a start—and why she was already trying to flee.

Luke pointed to a narrow alley that led away from the courtyard into the twisting steep lanes of the village. He tugged at the girl's arm. 'I said *run*.'

The first few riders were already jostling their way into the yard, peering around from their saddles in eager search of captives. This time she obeyed him. She ran.

For Ellie, the nightmare had begun when those men had appeared out of the darkness, on the road down to Bircham Staithe. She'd thought at first they might be Lord Franklin's men after her; but the way they spoke soon dispelled that notion—as did the way they leered at her, before asking insolently what her business was and where she was bound.

'I'm on my way to the harbour,' she'd answered. She'd tried to keep her voice calm. 'I need a ship, to Calais or any part of the French coast. I can pay you—'

They'd stared, incredulous. 'She's French,' they'd said. 'It's the little French missy from Bircham Hall. And we know there's someone not far from here who might be willing to pay a fine fat reward for her, lads.'

They'd grabbed her so swiftly that she hadn't had chance to get her gun. They'd marched her down to the harbour and the inn. *They don't know that I've got my pistol*, she kept telling herself. *They don't know.*

But her heart had really started beating hard when they reached the inn yard, and the man strolled out. The man in the long patched coat, who wore a black glove on his damaged right hand. His voice, as he spoke to her, had been cool and controlled and almost amused. His blue eyes had gleamed with some knowledge she couldn't begin to guess at.

Having an adventure, are you? he'd said. And she'd felt as though she was on the brink of hurtling down a bottomless abyss.

She would never, ever admit how vulnerable—how *scared*—she felt. She'd rather die than let him know it. But she knew, in that moment, that he was the most dangerous of them all.

She'd foolishly hoped that producing her pistol would help her get away from the lot of them, but the arrival of the riders—Revenue men, she heard the others call out—had put paid to her plan. And now she'd lost her gun, one of his accomplices had her valise and the man they called the captain was dragging her away from the village, into the blackness.

'Come,' he was saying harshly.

It was either him or the Revenue men.

His three henchmen were just behind them, running, too. One held her valise and the other one—stocky, with spiky black hair—had her pistol. But it was the captain's strong left hand that still grasped her wrist.

They were heading away from the harbour, she realised, towards a rough track that led up the headland; so that as they climbed, she could see the black surface of the sea stretching out below her, its softly churning waves painted silver by the moon. A salty breeze caressed her face and teased her with its hint of freedom.

What now? she was thinking desperately. All right; so *Captain Luke* had rescued her from the ruffians who'd captured her on the road. But wasn't this man—this cold, forbidding man—even more dangerous than they were?

He knew she was in Lord Franklin's care. He knew, now, that she'd run from the Hall tonight.

And it was clear that he didn't intend to let her return there. Perhaps he wanted a ransom, she guessed suddenly—but she was pretty sure that Lady Charlotte would pay him to *keep* her. She felt a bubble of sudden, rather despairing laughter rising up and stumbled slightly over a stone.

The man intensified his grip on her wrist. 'Keep up,' he rapped out. 'They could still be after us.'

'I'd go faster, if you weren't…*dragging* me!'

'Very well. I'll go a little slower.'

She shook her head. 'No need. Just—don't *touch* me.'

He nodded, his face expressionless. He let her go—and *Dieu*, for a moment her body craved the strong comfort of his hand around her wrist… Fool. Fool. She drew her cloak more tightly around herself and hurried after him.

Be calm, she told herself. *You've travelled through half of France, fleeing from your enemies, and you managed not to show your fear then.*

But she was feeling something else, as well as fear. Yes, her heart was hammering as she followed her guide, Luke. The captain. Yet she couldn't help but notice that tall and strongly built as he was, he moved with a kind of lithe grace that made her think of pictures she'd seen of exotic hunting beasts, untamed and dangerously, savagely beautiful.

She felt a plunging sensation in her stomach, as if she'd missed her footing. *He's your enemy. Remember he's your enemy. Concentrate on what's happening. On where he's taking you.*

The village was out of sight now and they were following the path along the top of the cliffs. Below, she glimpsed the long line of the beach, with its wet shingle gleaming in the darkness; though up here the springy turf was dotted with clumps of gorse and sea thrift. And ahead...

She felt her breath catching in her throat. Ahead, looming up before them, she could see where the moonlight shone on the gaunt roofs and turrets of the old, mysterious house she'd seen on her journey to Bircham Hall.

It stood there, so lonely and desolate that it appeared to be daring any intruders to approach it. *What views it must have by day!* she thought. But it looked half-ruined—surely it must be uninhabited.

The captain touched her arm. She jumped. 'Follow me,' he said softly.

With his men bringing up the rear, he kept to the path that left the clifftop to weave between the tangle of trees and overgrown shrubs that almost surrounded the house. He strode on, round to the back—and here, Ellie realised, everything changed. Here was a courtyard, freshly swept. Here were stables, which smelled sweetly of hay. All of it was lit by a welcoming lantern hanging by the door, and yet more lights shone from the windows.

The captain turned to his men. 'Keep watch,' he told them tersely. 'Look out for any unwanted visitors.'

'Aye, Captain. We will.'

The three men disappeared into the darkness—and her bag had gone with them. Before she had time to protest, she realised that the back door to the house was opening and a small middle-aged woman dressed in a faded black frock and long white apron stood looking anxiously at them all—especially at Ellie. 'You've brought another visitor, Captain. Goodness me. Oh, goodness me...'

Ellie's captor stepped forward. 'It's quite all right, Mrs

Bartlett. We do have an unexpected guest, but there's no cause for alarm.'

He spoke almost gently to the woman, but the moment he looked back at Ellie, his features were hard again. 'This way,' he said. Already he was leading Ellie inside the house, while the woman Ellie assumed was the house-keeper followed them.

'I trust, Mrs Bartlett,' Luke said, turning to her, 'that there's a fire lit in the dining hall?'

'Of course. Of course, sir. Do you require anything else?'

'I'll call you if I do.'

'Very well.' And after another quick, frightened glance at Ellie, Mrs Bartlett hurried away. The captain's hand was on Ellie's arm again, and once more she tensed— she *shivered*—at his touch.

Pull yourself together. Concentrate on where you are. On what's happening.

He was, she realised, guiding her along a stone-flagged passageway to a huge old oak-beamed dining hall, where the only light came from a pair of candles set in wall sconces and from the remains of a glowing log fire. Then he closed the extremely solid door and stood with his back to it.

Life had taught Ellie that whenever she felt herself to be in danger, she ought to look for any means of escape. Because there always was one, wasn't there?

Not here, apparently. *Not here.*

Chapter Eight

Ellie saw that the room was thirty feet long at least and twenty wide, while the fireplace was large enough to take a pig on a spit, and the dining table, roughly hewn of oak, was surrounded by a dozen or more chairs and assorted benches. On the table's surface sat a variety of half-full liquor bottles and glasses.

There were no carpets and no ornaments, although shadowy marks on the limewashed walls showed where once paintings must have hung and furniture stood. The candles were of tallow and the candlesticks plain pewter. Whereas Bircham Hall shouted aloud its pride and wealth, this house betrayed nothing but its owner's poverty. And yet once, she thought, it must have been so fine. Was this his house? Did he live here? It was a suitable abode for him indeed. Wild, untamed, untameable.

Her eyes flew back to her captor, who was unbuttoning his coat, shrugging it from his broad shoulders and laying it over the back of a chair. The movement was without any kind of vanity, yet beneath it, his loose white shirt, paired with a horseman's buckskin breeches and black leather riding boots, drew her eyes compellingly to his utterly masculine figure. He moved without any demonstration of strength or bravado, yet she felt a slow rhythm of warning pumping through her veins and her mouth was dry.

He glanced at her. 'You might be more comfortable if you took your cloak off,' he said.

'You think so?' She clutched it tighter.

His lips thinned a little. 'Have you any objection to sitting down?' He was pointing towards a chair set close to the fire. 'I really would prefer it if you didn't faint on me.'

After a moment's hesitation, she sat down—and he sat on a chair opposite to her, leaning forward to gaze at her.

In his power. The thought almost felled her. Yet instead of summoning a plan of escape, of resistance even, all she could see—all she could think of—were those hooded, dangerous eyes of his. And that mouth, those cheekbones...

He was still watching her and she felt her pulse hammering.

'Tell me,' he said, 'did you really want the Revenue men to find you?'

'I would have preferred nobody to find me. Least of all you!'

He went on as if she hadn't spoken. 'I wonder—what would the Revenue men have made of you? That was just a routine raid of theirs, by the way; they like to show their strength now and then, in their hunt for smugglers. Though if they'd found a young French girl on the run— now, *that* would have provided them with some excitement. Although I think you'd probably have been better off with them than with Sam Snaith and his comrades.'

'I had my pistol to protect me from Sam Snaith and his comrades!'

He nodded. 'And you told me you know how to use it. Would you have killed him?'

She moistened her dry lips. 'I only meant to threaten him. So I could get away…' Her voice faded.

'You put yourself in an impossibly dangerous situation,' he said quietly. 'Don't you realise you were an absolute fool to be out alone at night?'

Her heart turned over, because she knew he was right. But he didn't know how desperate she was. She found herself trembling slightly as he leaned nonchalantly across the table and pulled over a bottle and two glasses, with his left hand—*Jésu*, she realised, that hand. Of course he had to do almost *everything* with his left hand.

And now he'd filled two glasses and was pushing one towards her. 'Brandy,' he said curtly. 'It's good for shock. It will steady you a little.'

She tore her eyes from that black glove. 'Thank you. But I don't want it.'

He drank his own in one. Then he set his glass down and went over to the large fireplace to lay another log in the grate. *What had happened to this man?* she wondered. *What was he doing in this amazing but half-derelict old place?* He must be a smuggler. But how many smugglers walked with such arrogant confidence and spoke like a gentleman?

He'd come back now from tending the fire and was sitting opposite her again. 'So,' he said. 'You don't drink.'

She sat very straight. 'I don't need alcohol,' she answered calmly. 'But I do think it would help—*Captain*—if you and I were honest with one another.'

He looked almost amused. 'Honest,' he echoed. 'Very well. You first.'

'I came out tonight,' she began, 'because I want a sea passage across the Channel.'

He leaned back in his chair, studying her. 'You surprise me, *mademoiselle*. In my experience, most French exiles, both male and female, are only too glad to seek refuge in England.'

It occurred to her suddenly that he was doubtless experienced in all kinds of things, especially where females were concerned, and she felt something tighten inside her. But she forced herself into calmness. 'I've realised,' she said steadily, 'that I made a mistake in leaving my home.'

'So you're rejecting the generous hospitality of your relative Lord Franklin?' His voice was etched with sarcasm. 'But couldn't you just explain to him that you're not happy here, and let him arrange for you to travel home in comfort? Now that the war's over, there's surely no danger involved in returning to France. Providing,' he added, 'that you have friends, and a home, awaiting you there?'

She caught her breath. 'Of course I have.'

'Of course,' he echoed politely.

'But for reasons of my own,' she went on, 'which I don't wish to go into with *you*—I prefer to leave without the knowledge of those at the Hall. Quite simply, I need to get back to my home and I doubt that you have any right to stop me, since I can only suppose that you are some kind of smuggler—'

He let out a burst of laughter at that. 'A smuggler. You're quite sure of that, are you?'

She was stammering a little. 'Of course! Why else should you be hiding in this old house by the sea? Why else should your men call you "Captain"?'

'Perhaps because I was in the British army?'

He saw her composure fracture slightly. 'But if you're not a—*malfaiteur...*'

'A wrongdoer,' he said softly.

'If you're not a wrongdoer, then why were you so frightened of the Revenue men?'

'I'm not frightened of anybody,' he said. But his eyes had gone very dark and rather cold.

'But you *ran* from them,' she persisted. 'You must be a smuggler. I've heard how men like you fight with rival gangs. With people who must in the past have got the better of you—'

'How do you know?'

She should have stopped then. She should have seen how his expression became infinitely more dangerous. But instead, like a fool, she blundered on. 'Your hand. You have fingers missing...'

She saw the look in his blue eyes and her voice faltered.

'Go on,' he encouraged softly.

She shook her head. 'No.'

He nodded. 'I'm afraid you jump to rather too many conclusions, *mam'selle*.' His mouth was a thin, hard line. 'I assure you that it's not wise to do so, with me.'

She tried to shrug. 'Whatever you've done, *monsieur*, I assure you that I really don't care. It's what happens next that concerns me. Clearly, you are resourceful. So am I.'

'So I've noticed,' he said thoughtfully. 'You have a pistol. You also, if I remember rightly, have a rather intriguing compass.'

Dieu, she'd hoped to God he'd forgotten the compass. She looked round instinctively for her valise, but of course his men had taken it.

And then her heart started to beat very fast again; because he'd stood up and was walking towards her.

'Oh, *mam'selle*,' he said. '*Mam'selle*, I find myself giving you credit for somehow worming your way into Lord Franklin's household. For enticing him into taking pity on you and bringing you here to England.'

He folded his arms across his chest and put his head a little to one side, allowing her to see that his eyes were glinting with calculation. 'Yet now—you feel free to end your brief stay under his protection. Why?'

She shrugged, though her heart was hammering so painfully that she thought she might be sick. 'Perhaps England isn't what I hoped it would be.'

'Very well.' His voice was cold now and sharp. 'But surely—*surely* you realise the absolutely reckless position you were putting yourself in, by running away tonight? What do you think those men would have done to you had you actually gone aboard their fishing boat?'

She tilted her head to meet his eyes, striving with every ounce of her being to remain calm. 'Then perhaps,' she said, 'it's as well you came to my rescue, *monsieur le Capitaine*. And perhaps you yourself might take me to France.'

What made her say it? *Dieu*, how could she have suggested such a rash, such a crazy thing? Was she mad?

He clearly thought so, judging by the way his dark eyebrows shot up. 'So what kind of reward are you offering?'

'Your reward, Captain, is one well worth having. I would be convinced, you see, that you are indeed an honourable Englishman. And you would have my eternal gratitude.'

He laughed. He actually laughed. 'Your gratitude!

Mam'selle, you are priceless. You also appear to be forgetting—deliberately, I suspect—that you have something other than *gratitude* that you can offer me.'

And just as the heat was flaring in her limbs at the dark insinuation of his words—just as she felt her cheeks burn at some hidden, lethal meaning—he went to open the door and called out, 'Tom? I want milady's bag.' A moment later, his henchman came in with her valise, put it on the table and left. The captain closed the door again. 'Do you have the key to your bag, *mam'selle*?'

She felt the dull thud of another kind of panic. 'No! I...'

'Then I'll just have to force it,' he said calmly, picking up a corkscrew that lay amongst the bottles and holding its point a mere inch from the lock.

'Stop!'

He stopped.

With a feeling of utter doom, Ellie reached for the silver chain around her neck and detached the key for him. Rigid with apprehension, she watched him withdraw the contents and lay them out, one by one. The spare chemise and shawl that she'd packed for her journey. Her father's maps, carefully folded; he lifted those out, too. Then he came to the small case that contained her father's precious instruments. The theodolite. The prism. The magnifying lens. The pocket telescope.

And—within its own little box—the compass.

Of course, he'd already seen the compass.

Luke glanced at the girl. Her eyes—*God*, he realised suddenly, *he'd never seen such amazing green eyes*—were, like his, fixed on the objects being laid out one by one on the table before her. He saw how white she'd gone.

How tensely she held herself, with her hands clenched at her sides.

He felt a sudden, unexpected rage at her for bringing all this on herself. Surely she realised what kind of fate would be meted out to her on her madcap journey by any ruffian she might encounter on her way?

All right, so she'd tried her hardest to disguise her all-too-feminine figure with that shabby old cloak. She'd pushed back her swathes of soft black hair under her bonnet. But she was still every bit as…breathtaking, that was the word, there was no denying it, as he'd first registered, when he met her on the road to Bircham several days ago, on her way to Lord Franklin's.

He'd glimpsed then—as he was glimpsing now—a kind of raw vulnerability and courage that churned him up inside. What secrets lay in her past? Why, having so recently arrived at Bircham Hall, was she now hurrying *away* from there, in desperate flight?

Luke's hand drifted over the compass. Stopped and moved on. He would leave the compass till last. Instead, he picked up one of the half-finished maps and held it out to her.

'This is a map of northern France,' he pointed out. 'And the roads leading to Brussels have all been carefully marked. Why?'

'The maps are mine.' She stepped forward. 'I will need them for my journey home—'

She lunged to grasp at it, but he lifted it beyond her reach and heard her soft hiss of despair. He held her gaze. 'They're exceptionally well-crafted maps. Aren't they? Good maps are precious, especially in a time of war. As valuable as a thousand men in certain circumstances, I've heard military experts say.'

Again he heard the sibilant sound of her indrawn breath. He put the map back on the table, then turned to her and said, very softly, 'Whose side were you on in the war, *mam'selle*? More to the point—whose side was your father on?'

He saw the signs of her distress straight away—the pulse point that throbbed in her slender throat, the flicker of outright fear that rippled through her body. But she replied almost instantly. 'He was on nobody's side, *monsieur*! My father was a good man, who wanted peace above all! And I want to return to Brussels because it's the place where my father is buried, so I can pay honour to his memory...'

Her voice trailed away. Because Luke had put the maps down and was picking up the small box that contained the compass.

'You have many interesting objects here,' he said. 'But *this* is the most intriguing of them all.'

He saw the enormous effort at calmness that she made as she reached out her hand. 'That is my father's compass,' she said steadily. 'One of his favourite possessions.'

'I'm not surprised.' Luke had calmly lifted the compass out of its box and was turning it in his hands. Cruelly letting her *hope*, just for a moment, that perhaps he hadn't been able to translate the French inscription that was engraved on the side of it.

'I don't suppose,' he went on, 'that your father would want anyone to know that he was a devoted servant to Napoleon. A mapmaker to Napoleon. I don't suppose that *you* would want anyone to know that either—'

He broke off as she lunged for it. He held it high beyond her reach and translated from memory the words inscribed on it. '"*To my devoted servant, André*

Duchamp—my creator of maps. A gift from Napoleon Bonaparte.'" He looked straight at her. 'And this was—your father's?'

The flush of colour in her cheeks had drained away, leaving her skin white as porcelain. Her dark-lashed eyes were green as deep pools, wide and anguished.

'You have no *right…*'

He was still holding the object high. Tormenting her. 'Of course,' he said, 'you'll remember that I saw this compass when your carriage was halted by the landslip. I read the inscription then.'

She was trembling slightly, he saw. 'You—you *did*?'

'At first,' he went on, 'I could hardly believe my eyes. But there it was. Plain as daylight. *"A gift from Napoleon Bonaparte."'* As he spoke, he was casually slipping the compass in his pocket, then he proceeded to pick up another folded map. Only this time, it was a half-completed one, with notes and measurements written out below it, in French.

With care, Luke translated it aloud.

"'From Reims to Dinant. Total distance: one hundred and twenty kilometres. The River Aisne must be bridged at Rethel. The route is detailed below, with areas of rock, clay and marsh depicted accordingly. The road must be made with a subbase of larger stones, covered by smaller ones. No substance that could absorb water and thus lead to frost damage should be incorporated…'"

Luke skimmed the rest of the paper to read aloud the signature at the bottom. *"'Written by André Duchamp, Paris. April 13th, 1810.'"*

He looked at her. 'Your father would have made a better job, wouldn't he, of constructing that road to Bircham, where your carriage was halted by the landslip?'

She appeared calm, defiant almost, but he saw her breasts beneath her cloak rising and falling, rising and falling. Saw her eyes sliding towards the door.

She's ready to run, he acknowledged. *Ready to make a break for it.*

And he was ready to stop her.

'He drew maps for Napoleon,' Luke went on, almost in wonder. 'He designed roads for Napoleon. Your father. Your father.'

Chapter Nine

For a moment, the silence hung so heavy that Ellie realised she could hear the waves in the distance, rolling
up the desolate beach. The candle shimmered in a sudden draught, and she thought, *This man must be able to
hear the pounding of my heart.*

'My father worked for France,' she said at last, holding her head up proudly. 'For the good of all of France's
citizens. He was employed by the state, as so many
were—'

'Dear God. Do you take me for a fool?' he cut in impatiently. 'Are you trying to make out he was a government clerk? Even *I* have heard of your father. André
Duchamp was one of the foremost cartographers of our
age! I've heard it said that it was his mapping skills that
made Napoleon's new roads the marvels that they were.
Roads that permitted Napoleon's soldiers to march out
of Paris and across France—into Prussia, into Italy and
Spain and almost all of Europe. To defeat army after
army—'

'My father is dead!' Her voice was tight with emotion.
'And Napoleon is a prisoner! The past is behind us...'

'The past has a nasty habit of leaping out at us, *mam'selle.*' Luke's lip curled as he said it. 'Does Lord Franklin know who your father worked for?'

'What business is it of yours?'

'*Does* he?'

Slowly she shook her head. He paced the length of the room, then swung back on her, pressing on without pity. 'Your recent history, *mam'selle*, is, to an outsider like me, somewhat confusing. You grasped gratefully, it appears, at Lord Franklin's offer of hospitality—but now I find you fleeing from his house by night and declaring, to anyone except *him*, your fervent wish to put England behind you. I can think of only one explanation.'

He picked up one of the maps again and put it down with a snap. '*Mam'selle*, I am forced to assume that you are spying for Napoleon.' He heard her let out a low gasp. 'I am forced to assume you are serving him,' he pressed on, 'perhaps as loyally as your father did. I have to conclude that you wish to return across the Channel because somehow, during your sojourn in England, you have discovered something vital and you wish to convey it to Napoleon's secret supporters in France—of whom, as we both know, there are still many.'

She was shaking her head. He saw how her lips were parted, how her breath was coming short and fast. 'Napoleon has surrendered. The war is over…'

He was flicking through the rest of her father's maps. 'Don't pretend to be stupid. No one expects Napoleon to stay cooped up on Elba for long. The French people are already growing sick of fat King Louis, who's been thrust on them by the British and their allies. You know that, *mam'selle*. Don't you?'

She stared at him, speechless, then slowly nodded.

'A large proportion of the French populace,' he went on, 'are eagerly starting to wonder how long it will be before their Emperor Napoleon returns once more. And— let me see—if he were to set sail from Elba, he might land—where?' He was gazing down at the maps, leafing through them. 'Well, he might land at Nice, perhaps. Yes—Nice, why not? Then he could gather men—gather an *army*—and travel north towards Paris, marching by way of…Lyon? Clermont? Your father would have known which roads the Emperor's army ought to take. Since he doubtless helped to *build* them.'

She lunged towards the table in a desperate attempt to grab the maps, but in doing so, she stumbled and knocked over one of the heavy chairs. He grabbed at it as it fell with his right hand—the hand in the black glove—and she heard him suppress a hiss of pain.

He was gritting his teeth as he slammed the chair upright again and nursed his right hand with his left. She backed away, horrified. A recent wound, then. A still painful wound… A moment later his men were charging through the door into the room, grasping her roughly by the arms.

They must have heard the chair fall. Heard his exclamation of pain and guessed that she'd hurt their captain. They wouldn't forgive her easily for that, oh, no.

She struggled as she spat out words at them in French. 'You can have my things,' she called to the captain. 'The theodolite alone is worth fifty livres. You can have it, if you'll take me to France. You can have everything…'

'Everything except the compass, I presume?' he said softly.

Luke had recovered his composure now. Had recovered from the red-hot stabbing pain that had shot through his crippled hand as he grabbed for the chair. He ordered his men to leave the room again and once they'd departed—they were reluctant to go, he saw how they still shot warning glances at the girl—he turned to her again and said, flatly, 'I'm afraid, *Mademoiselle* Duchamp, that I've absolutely no intention of helping you to leave the country. You see, you're far more useful to me here.'

She went very still. And then she shrugged. Oh, Luke admired her for that. That casual gesture of indifference, even though he could see the enormous effort she was having to make to hold herself firm.

She gazed up at him, and he let his eyes wander over her face—which was shadowed with outright fear, yet still defiant. And those full lips... *Not a chance*, he warned himself. *She's far too dangerous.* Besides, she despised him.

'So I am to be—useful. Is that it?' she said quietly. '*Monsieur*, whatever your intention is, I will make very sure that you regret this day. I will not be an easy captive, I assure you. And when Lord Franklin finds out...'

He almost laughed. 'Oh, so Lord Franklin is being named as your saviour now, is he? Would he be flattered? I'm not sure. Please, *mam'selle*, don't let your imagination run away with you. You see, I've no intention of keeping you captive here.'

She stepped back. 'You—haven't?'

'On the contrary. I'm going to send you back to Bircham Hall.'

Her face expressed her sheer astonishment. 'Back to Bircham Hall?'

'Exactly.' His voice was businesslike. 'Will anyone have realised yet, do you think, that you've gone?'

'No. No, they won't. I told them all that I was tired and was retiring early for the night.'

'Very well. Now, listen carefully, *mam'selle*. You're not going to say one word of what's happened tonight—of your flight, or of your encounter with me. But you *are* going to stay on at Bircham Hall, as if nothing at all had happened. And you're going to do something for me. Clearly, you're resourceful and I'm sure you're observant. Have you noticed Lord Franklin's private library?'

She nodded, looking absolutely bewildered.

'In that library,' he was continuing, 'are stored many of Lord Franklin's private papers—including his correspondence and his diaries for at least the last five years.'

'How do you—?'

'It doesn't matter in the slightest how I know. Now, listen. I want you to get into the library—and to bring me anything you can find, any papers, documents or letters that relate to the autumn of 1813 and a place in France called La Rochelle. Do you understand me?'

For a moment there was complete silence except for the crackling of the logs on the fire. 'I thought you might be a smuggler,' she said, gazing at him steadfastly. 'Now I realise you're most likely just a common thief. And what you suggest is laughable. The library is always, always locked.'

'Wherever there's a lock, there's a key,' he said with an air of imperturbability. 'I believe that with your considerable spirit of enterprise, you can get inside that room for me, *mam'selle*. And in the meantime—just to make sure you cooperate—I'll keep this compass.'

'No...'

'I'll keep it.' He stood up. 'I'm going to let you go

now. But you must do exactly what I say, do you understand? And you must not breathe a single word of our meeting to *anyone*.'

She stood, too. She said, very quietly, 'And if I disobey you? If I escape some other way?'

He was turning the compass thoughtfully in his hand, but suddenly he looked straight at her with those chilly blue eyes. 'If you disobey me—if you run again—then I'll make sure that a description of you, and this compass, reaches the port authorities forthwith—do you understand what that means? It means that this part of the coast will be crawling with men looking for you. And if you're caught, you'll find yourself thrown into prison, for being a spy for Napoleon. Prison isn't much fun for a girl. I'm sure you can imagine some of the things that might happen to you, although some things I truly hope you *can't*.'

There was a long silence. She appeared to be examining a fastening on her cloak and when she looked up again, her face was pale but calm. 'Do you know,' she said, 'when I left London, I had no idea I could cause such *excitement* in a desolate backwater like this. What a very interesting diversion I must provide, for you and your friends—'

She broke off with a low cry, as he took two steps towards her, cupped her chin with his left hand and tilted her face up to his.

Oh, God, thought Ellie in desperation. His clothes were shabby, even for a smuggler. His dark hair couldn't have been cut for weeks and looked as if he'd tried to tame it with his fingers rather than a comb. He had at least two days' worth of beard growth. She realised with a stab of warm shock that he was brushing his knuck-

les very softly across her cheek—how *dare* he?—and
yet she was aware of feeling an unbelievable storm of
emotion. Of yearning. For what? For *him*? Impossible.
Impossible…

He bent his head a little closer to hers. 'You are un-
wise, *Mademoiselle* Duchamp,' he murmured, 'to defy
me so.' His blue eyes were scorching and his voice was
a rough caress, making her shiver as much as his fingers did.

She felt his free hand slide around her waist, pulling
her just a little closer to him—or was that her, leaning
into his tempting strength, his warmth? Was he going to
kiss her? Every muscle of her body tensed in anticipa-
tion, and she felt a strange ache blooming into life low
in her abdomen. And his mouth was curving into a half-
smile, a knowing smile…

He brushed the pad of his thumb lightly across her
lips, and a deep shudder ran through her. Then he let his
hand drop. She almost fell.

'Are you after Lord Franklin?' he asked softly.

'What?'

'Was it a part of some scheme of yours, to come to
England to seduce him? To become his mistress?'

Her cheeks were burning. '*No*. There has never been
anything like that. Never.'

'But it's what people are whispering.'

She forced herself to shrug. 'He's rather *old* for me,
don't you think?'

'If you say so. Most women I know aren't too choosy
about age, if there's a title and plenty of money involved.
And I would guess that you know how to use your femininity as well as you know how to use that gun of yours.'
He bent a little closer and gave her a thin smile. 'But—a

word of warning, *mam'selle*. I would advise you *not* to try to use your charms on me.'

She stood gazing at him, quite speechless, aware of the thundering of her ragged heartbeat.

He went to fetch his coat from the back of his chair. Shrugged it on, then walked over to where her valise and her father's instruments and maps lay on the table and started gathering everything together, putting them back in the valise. 'Here you are,' he said, handing it to her. 'You really had better be getting back before the Hall is locked up for the night. And the next time we meet, I expect you to have some information for me. You'll remember, I hope, what I want?'

She heaved in a steadying breath. 'You want anything about La Rochelle.'

'And the date?'

'September 1813.' She intoned the words without expression.

He nodded. 'Good.'

But her father's compass still lay on the table.

'The compass,' she said. 'I must have it.'

'Oh, no.' He shook his head. 'I will keep that.' He was already heading for the door, which he opened to call out, 'Tom? Tell Josh to get two horses saddled, will you? One for him and one for *mam'selle*.'

'You expect me to ride?'

'Why, yes. You've walked all the way from the Hall and you must be tired—best if you ride back. You *can* ride, I take it?'

'Of course I can!'

'Then I'm sure you'll agree that the sooner you get back to the Hall, the better.'

It was as if he was *bored* with her, she thought with

incredulity. Having put her through this torment—these insults—he was *bored* with her. Holding the valise tightly, she followed him out through the house, wishing she could ignore his broad back, his powerful shoulders. Several French insults rolled off her tongue—inaudible to him, she thought, until he called back over his shoulder, 'I can hear you. My French is far from perfect, but I do know what you're saying.'

Then he carried on leading the way to the stables.

Luke saw with approval that two horses were waiting out there—one of them was for big, curly-haired Josh Watterson, and there was another, smaller one for the girl. Luke watched as, disdaining Josh's help, she used the mounting block to settle herself expertly in the side saddle; then she took up the reins and was almost out of the yard before Josh, muttering to himself, could spring on to his own big horse and catch up with her.

Luke was amused. Tom, who'd come out to stand at Luke's side, was watching with his arms folded. 'She's likely to be a damned nuisance, that one,' Tom said flatly. 'I do hope, Captain, that you haven't let your wits be set wandering by a pretty little French face—'

Luke cut in. 'Do you really think she's pretty, Tom? Because I don't.'

Tom coughed and muttered something about some jobs that needed doing, and as soon as he'd disappeared inside, Luke paced the courtyard, then turned to look up at the house. The moon rode high between windswept clouds, and the chimneys and turrets of the old place were black against its silvery light. He could hear the sound of the waves sucking at the shingle beach below, and somewhere a nightbird's call pierced the darkness.

When Luke and Anthony were boys, they'd sometimes gone sea fishing after sunset, rowing out so far that they'd imagined they could row all the way to France and back. Once, though, a vicious current had swept them beyond the headland and Anthony, only eleven, had tried not to show his terror as Luke struggled to hold the boat firm and get them back to safety.

Had his brother been afraid, when he and his companions faced betrayal and captivity in France almost a year and a half ago? If Luke had been there, would he have been able to save Anthony?

So much to think about—and now there was the girl. Luke's hand closed tightly around the compass. He remembered how, as he'd caressed her cheek, he'd heard a soft catch in her breath. Remembered how her lips had parted in invitation, whether she realised it or not. As he'd leaned his head towards hers, he'd seen those amazing green eyes cloud with uncertainty. And with need…

He didn't think she was pretty. He thought she was beautiful. Stunningly beautiful. But he had to make use of her, he had no choice—because she'd given him the chance he'd long been waiting for, to discover the truth of what had happened to his brother.

In silence, Ellie followed Luke's man Josh Watterson back to Bircham Hall. He knew every inch, it appeared to her, of the paths and byways around here, even in the black of night. Knew how to avoid any farms or cottages and knew how to travel the road quietly, always on the lookout for any other travellers, until they came at last—it was a journey of a mile, no more—to the boundary wall which she'd climbed earlier—so long ago, it seemed.

He tethered the horses in the woods outside the wall, then, after scanning the dark expanse of Lord Franklin's gardens, he offered to help her over. 'Looks all clear, ma'am.'

'The dogs,' she reminded him sharply. 'Sometimes the dogs are let out after dark.'

He shook his head. 'They won't be out again till after midnight. We're quite safe.'

She stared at him. How could he possibly know? But she let him assist her over the wall, then he escorted her with the utmost confidence through the shrubbery to the far side of the house, until they reached a door that Ellie had noticed before, on one of her walks round the garden.

'It will be locked...' she began.

But Josh was already reaching for the handle purposefully. Opening it, and holding it wide for her. 'In you go, ma'am. Quietly now.'

She obeyed, only to pull up jerkily as she realised that one of Lord Franklin's footmen was standing in the shadows beyond the door.

Her heart pounded against her ribs. *Joseph.* That was his name, Joseph. She'd noticed him at mealtimes—he was one of the youngest of the footmen, polite and deferential. Surely, as soon as he saw her rough companion, he would raise the alarm!

But he merely said to her respectfully, 'You've been out for an evening stroll around the garden, have you, ma'am? I'm afraid the weather's a little chilly, even for this time of year.' He went to exchange a few words with Josh, then he came back to her. 'Now,' he said, 'let me just lock this door. And then, by your leave, I'll escort you upstairs.'

She followed him, stunned.

Joseph left her outside the door to her room. She went inside and sat on her bed. *Jésu.* He must know the man called Luke. He must be in Luke's pay.

Chapter Ten

Ellie was appalled at everything that had happened to-night. Her attempt to escape had ended in abject failure and meant that she was now in a far worse mess than she was before.

That man. The captain. He and his colleagues were quite possibly smugglers—she knew that this part of the English coast was riddled with them. They landed the contraband goods—brandy and tobacco from France, wines and silks also—on secret shores by night, to avoid paying the taxes that English law demanded.

But why had the captain insisted that she look for those documents in Lord Franklin's library? A thought struck her. Could it be because Lord Franklin perhaps had records of the local smuggling gangs? Possessed, in his library, some incriminating evidence that the captain was intent on destroying?

Yet the captain had specifically mentioned the town of La Rochelle, which she knew was a seaport on the south-west coast of France—and too far away, surely, for English smugglers to travel to! So what was its significance? Why did he need to know about it?

Captain Luke. He exerted his authority over his gang of ruffians with a mere glance—and even though his right hand was maimed, no one with an ounce of sense in their heads would ever dream of doubting the real threat he posed.

He was a threat to her especially, because she'd been fool enough to challenge him. And what was even worse was that when he'd put his arm round her, when he'd touched her face, she'd felt the astonishing urge to know what his mouth might feel like, pressed against her skin, her lips...

Alone in her bedroom at Bircham Hall, she held her hands to her cheeks and felt her stomach twist with heated shame. Never—*ever*—had she thought that a man could affect her like that. And if the captain realised it, she would be in even worse trouble than she was already.

Slowly she changed into her nightdress and climbed into her big bed, shivering as she remembered the cold calculation with which he'd studied that fateful compass. Ideas born of desperation scurried through her mind. What if she spoke to Lord Franklin as soon as possible about all this? She could set off to London tomorrow and there she could tell him—tell him...

Tell him *what*, precisely? She tried to picture herself facing Lord Franklin in his exquisite Mayfair drawing room. She tried to picture his aristocratic features darkening with incredulity as she blurted out, 'My lord, I really ought to have told you this from the beginning. You see, my father worked for the Emperor Napoleon. He drew maps for him and helped to design and build roads, so that his armies could march from Paris and threaten the whole world...'

Lord Franklin would be furious. 'Why didn't you tell me this? You have endangered my reputation; my entire standing in society.'

She wouldn't be able to sleep tonight. How could she? Wearily Ellie got out of bed and went to draw back the curtains, seeing that the night clouds had drifted away to reveal a sparkling canopy of stars overhead. She remembered her father's astronomy books and the sky charts he loved to draw for himself; how he would often take his notebook out at night and walk beyond Paris's walls to the countryside that lay not far from the city. From when Ellie was seven, he'd taken her with him, especially in winter when the dark came early.

'Papa's star walks,' Ellie used to call them, clapping her small hands in delight as her mother wrapped her up warmly.

Ellie's mother never came with them on those star walks. Already she was showing signs of the illness that would one day claim her—the thinness, the pallor, the constant cough. But Ellie wasn't aware of that, in those days. And her memories were still precious, of the winter evenings she and her father spent beyond the city walls and market gardens of Paris, as he pointed out the constellations sparkling high above them.

Ellie's mother died in the late spring of 1813, when Napoleon was sending out his ragged and hungry troops to march against the combined armies of Britain and Austria, Prussia and Russia. And little more than a month after her funeral, Ellie's father came home from work and told her they had to leave their home.

'I cannot work for the Emperor any more,' he'd said. 'He is sending thousands of men to their deaths on the very roads I helped him build. Your mother's frail health kept me here till now. But I've made up my mind that I will help no more with the Emperor's plans to ruin the entire world with his constant waging of war. His endless ambition.'

Of course, Ellie knew even before then that if you weren't on the Emperor Napoleon's side, you counted as his enemy. And so began their journey, their flight, until at last they'd reached what they'd hoped was the safety of Brussels; but even there, Ellie had still been terribly afraid—not only because her father's health was rapidly failing, but because she was sure that there was a pursuer on their trail.

She felt she was still under surveillance, even when she went out on as simple an excursion as to buy food from the market. *Napoleon's spies*, she had whispered in fear to herself. *Napoleon's men have tracked us down. We are not safe even here.*

Several times she glimpsed the same man—he was easy to remember, because he had strangely pale eyes and pale hair. Sometimes she caught sight of him walking down the crowded street, or saw him standing outside the wine shop just over the road where the locals gathered to drink. He never approached her. She never even saw him actually watching her. Perhaps, she told herself, it was only her imagination that made her think he was on her trail.

Shivering, she dragged herself back to the present, to Bircham Hall and her failed attempt at escape. Certainly, there was nothing imaginary about Captain Luke—who was possibly the most lethal enemy she had faced so far.

As she and her father made that last, desperate journey out of France and towards safety, she'd had to confront men who thought she would be an easy target. Innkeepers, coach drivers, other travellers on the road—she had had to assume they were all her enemies and had to become adept at showing—if not actually firing—the little pistol her father had taught her to use.

She was accustomed to dealing with enemies, but the captain posed an altogether more formidable challenge. She curled herself up in an armchair by the window, her hands across her breasts. Take his voice, for instance. Despite his shabby clothing, he possessed the voice of an English gentleman and his husky enunciation made something curl warmly—dangerously—at the pit of her stomach. As for his face, and the enticing curve of his mouth…

She'd wanted him to kiss her and he knew it. His touch had set her blood on fire—oh, how that would make him laugh, how he would despise her for her weakness! She was aware of cold despair wrapping itself around her like a cloak, yet still she imagined she could feel the lingering heat of his body, so close to hers.

She was a fool. Not only was she going to have to guard herself from a new enemy, but from new and treacherous emotions. She was in his power and she was terrified.

Luke sat in the dining hall, turning the compass thoughtfully in his left hand as the fire in the hearth slowly died. But he was on his feet the instant he heard Josh Watterson stride into the house and swiftly he went to meet him. 'Did you get the girl into the house safely?' His voice was sharp.

'Aye, Captain.'

'Did you meet anyone?'

Josh was fumbling in his pocket. 'I met Joseph at the

house. He's a wise lad, that one—he'd realised she'd gone and reckoned you'd return her safely one way or another, so he was watching out for us. And then, on the way back here, I met Davey Patchett.'

Luke nodded—Patchett was a local fisherman and smuggler, who often sailed over to France by night for illicit liquor.

'His boat got into Bircham Staithe earlier this evening,' Josh went on. 'Davey's been over to Calais. And he was about to set off up *here*, Captain, because when he was in Calais harbour, someone came up to him and asked him to deliver a letter to you. I said I'd bring it.'

Davey sometimes brought messages to Luke from Jacques—it was nothing unusual. But this time, Luke felt a coldness at his chest. A premonition. He held out his hand and Josh gave the letter to him; it was sealed and salt-stained. His pulse racing now, he tore it open.

Luke's eyes scoured Jacques's familiar, scratchy writing.

Mon ami,
I have learned for certain that your brother was on the run for only a few weeks after the betrayal at La Rochelle before he became a prisoner of Napoleon's men. After that—no news at all. But we have met someone who knew your brother well. And I hope to be with you in person, very soon.

Luke read the letter again, as if reading it could alter the contents. Anthony taken prisoner? There was little hope for him, then. Luke knew the kind of atrocious conditions that an Englishman suspected of being a spy would be kept in.

'Is it bad news, Captain?' Josh's enquiry was hesitant. Tom was there, too, hovering in the shadows.

Luke suddenly realised how every muscle, every sinew of his body was taut with the shock of the news. 'I don't know,' he said. 'Jacques writes that my brother was taken prisoner.'

Tom spoke up. 'Then he might still be alive somewhere?'

Luke didn't reply. *But I will not give up hope*, he vowed under his breath. *Never will I give up hope.*

Josh and Tom had quietly left him, realising, he guessed, that he needed solitude. Luke went back to the dining hall to pour himself more brandy—and all that kept him company in that big, lonely room was this letter and the delicate lavender scent that lingered from the girl who'd been there a short while ago.

Elise. Elise Duchamp. He swallowed some brandy. She was another weapon in his hand, that was all—another possible lead to follow. If her father was Napoleon's man, it meant nothing to him. During Luke's years in the British army, he'd seen countless men on both sides die terrible deaths, and for what? His mouth curled cynically. Was there really so much difference between Napoleon's grand ambitions to expand his empire and Britain's ruthless will to keep its control of trade and sea routes?

It was justice for his brother that mattered to him now. Nothing else. Which was precisely why the girl must mean nothing to him—especially since she was clearly deceiving Lord Franklin, and would no doubt deceive him, too, if he gave her the chance.

He had to make use of her, that was all. He had to shut his mind to that reckless, desperate bravery of hers that tugged at some emotion deep inside him; because, quite simply, it was an emotion that he could not afford to indulge.

Chapter Eleven

During the next few days, Ellie watched from her bedroom window as the iron-hard frosts of late January took Bircham Hall in their grip. She saw how the lawns and neatly clipped hedges shimmered with delicate ice crystals all day long; saw how the sun scarcely seemed to rise above the bare woods beyond the garden and how, as twilight gathered, great flocks of geese would fly overhead in immaculate formation, making for the marshlands for the night, while the sun sank into a fiery red sky.

Ellie continued to join Lady Charlotte and Miss Pringle for meals, at which Lady Charlotte dominated the conversations, always. Miss Pringle ate as quickly as she could and nodded her agreement with all of her ladyship's outrageous opinions, while Ellie remained as silent as possible.

'Clearly,' Lady Charlotte said to her, 'no man is going to marry you for your conversation, Elise.'

Every afternoon, Ellie went walking in the gardens, in spite of the bitter cold that clawed at her gloved fingers, and she thought of the man, Luke. What was his story? He'd told her himself that he'd been a captain in the army and she had to assume that his hand was injured in some battle in Spain—but why his acute interest in the French port of La Rochelle, which was far away from any fighting involving the British ?

There were other issues that she tried, for now, to push aside—such as the fact that he had offered her a starkly undeniable male challenge at that meeting, as if he was staking some kind of claim.

He was making her his spy, she reminded herself bitterly. That was all. The instant he touched her, she should have slapped his hand away—but she hadn't, and the memory of his touch still burned inside her veins, long and slow and deep. What a fool she was.

Quelle idiote.

She was becoming accustomed, now, to the clockwork routine of the household, which was strictly run by the housekeeper, Mrs Sheerham. She was all too aware of the early hour at which the servants had to start their work; was familiar now with the arrival of the maid Mary at seven every morning to light a fire in her bedroom. Mary always carried out her work cheerfully even though her poor fingers were painfully red and chapped.

'I have some woollen mittens you may borrow, Mary,' Ellie said to her once. Mary was lighting the fire and was visibly shivering; Ellie had already risen from her bed and was wrapped in her dressing robe. She went to fetch the mittens from a drawer. 'Here. Please take them. And I can lend you this chemise, made of flannelette—it's not right that you should suffer so in this cold weather.'

Mary's face brightened as she looked at what Ellie was holding out. But then she shook her head. 'Thank you, miss! But Mrs Sheerham says we must never accept any gifts from his lordship's guests.'

'Then tell Mrs Sheerham that I was going to throw the gloves and chemise away,' said Ellie. 'If you are asked.' She thrust the items into Mary's hands. '*Please* use them. I really don't need them.' And Mary accepted, gratefully.

I would gladly, thought Ellie, *give her, too, the gowns and pelisses that Lord Franklin bought for me in London*. But of course Mary would have even less use for them than she did.

Mary was still disappointed by Ellie's refusal to wear any of the lovely gowns. Sometimes, when she was fetching one of Ellie's old dresses from the wardrobe, she would gaze longingly at the London clothes, made of satin and silk in colours of pink and turquoise and pale green.

'You could wear one of them to dinner with her ladyship, miss,' Mary said hopefully. 'It seems such a shame to leave them untouched.'

Ellie almost laughed—to dress in silks and satins for Lady Charlotte, who thought her a jade anyway, was surely the height of folly. She shook her head. 'I'm quite comfortable in my old gowns,' she told Mary gently.

She continued to walk around the grounds without fail every afternoon, despite the bitter chill. She noted that every few days Lady Charlotte was driven out in her carriage to visit friends in the neighbourhood—she saw her being assisted out to the carriage, swathed in furs, with a groom carrying a hot stone bottle to place by her feet. On these occasions, Lady Charlotte made more fuss than ever to anyone within hearing about her lack of mobility and the pain she endured.

'Especially in the cold weather,' she would say. 'I am a martyr to my health.'

Ellie could not forget the time she'd seen her on her feet and pouring herself some sherry before walking back to her bath chair. She wondered if the servants knew of Lady Charlotte's duplicity, though all of them appeared to bear her complaints with stoic endurance. But Ellie also noticed that the atmosphere in the house changed markedly on the afternoons when her ladyship went visiting. Bircham Hall, without her acid tongue and her judgemental eye, was to Ellie a much kinder place.

Although Ellie herself was still filled with tension. *Any day now*, she kept reminding herself, *the man called Captain Luke will find a way to remind me that I must get into Lord Franklin's library. Or else...*

Or else he would let Lord Franklin—and possibly the whole world—know that her father once worked for Napoleon.

Would Luke dare to approach Lord Franklin himself? She doubted it. She felt sure that he had spent part of his recent life at least tangling in some fashion with the law, and he would surely tread carefully where Lord Franklin was concerned.

But there were plenty of other ways in which he could expose her—for instance, he could ensure that the compass was seen by curious observers, or he could set rumours in motion. Once the secret of her father's past was out, Ellie knew there would be no refuge for her here in England.

And if you're caught, he'd warned, *you'll find yourself thrown into prison, for being a spy for Napoleon*. She pressed her hands to her cheeks. If only she'd never let him see the compass! But it was too late, now, for that.

It was too late also to think of running—she'd already tried it and failed.

Yet what else could she do? How else could she escape the threat the captain posed? Not by visiting him in person, that was sure. Because the effect he had on her was quite possibly the biggest threat of all to her safety. Just one touch. Just one *look* and she'd felt herself under attack; felt heat racing through her veins and her blood pound.

Guard yourself, you fool. *Guard yourself.*

Ellie had already met Lord Franklin's steward Mr Appleby in London, and here at Bircham Hall she came across him quite frequently. He had a comfortable house in the neighbourhood, he told her with some pride, and his own office in the Hall, close to the housekeeper's rooms. His job was to manage Lord Franklin's vast Kent estate, dealing with taxes and salaries and collecting in the rents from the tenanted farms.

'There couldn't be a fairer landlord in all of England than Lord Franklin,' he remarked when he invited Ellie into his office one day to enquire after her well-being. 'It really is a privilege to work for him. I call here at the Hall often, mainly to update the accounts. And of course, I regularly visit all of the tenant farms, also—but last week I travelled to London to see his lordship, who asked me to keep an eye on you particularly and to let him know if there is anything at all you need.'

If Mr Appleby remembered anything about Ellie's protest to Lord Franklin that her room had been searched, he made no reference to it.

'Yes,' Mr Appleby went on, adjusting his spectacles, 'and if you do have any requests, I will gladly convey your wishes to his lordship once he's returned from his travels.'

'He's going to Paris, isn't he?' Miss Pringle had told her that.

'Indeed, yes. Of course, you probably know the city, *mam'selle*?'

'I grew up there.' Her voice was almost a whisper, because it took a great effort to push aside the haunting memories of childhood happiness. 'Is Paris restored to normality then, Mr Appleby?'

'Yes, thank goodness! And Napoleon Bonaparte is confined on the last kingdom he'll ever rule—the island of Elba. Don't you worry, *mam'selle*—the Corsican monster is beaten for good and Paris, they say, is a city full of parties and gaiety again. Although as you'll probably know—' he chuckled '—his lordship is not much of a one for partying, since his true passion is fine art. Doubtless he'll be looking for more exceptional items to add to his collection. I've heard that now peace has come, many paintings and sculptures that were hidden away at the time of the Revolution—well before you were born, of course!—are coming to light again. Ah, Paris. A lovely city. And some day—who knows?—you may be able to go back there.'

She remembered Paris with a sudden vividness that wrenched at her heart. Remembered the Palace of the Tuileries, where her father once took her to see Napoleon himself holding court. The glorious celebrations that accompanied Napoleon's wedding, when the public fountains ran with wine and the city was bright with fireworks and flowers.

Mr Appleby talked on, but Ellie, in her heart, was far away.

* * *

The February days went by slowly, marked by grey
skies and bitter cold—and Ellie heard nothing more from
the captain. Perhaps he'd gone away? Perhaps he was
afraid she might have reported his threat?

She couldn't imagine him being afraid of anything or
anyone, but even so, she allowed herself the luxury of
hope. Until, one day after breakfast when sleet was battering at the window panes of her private sitting room,
there was a quiet knock at her door.

Ellie was curled up before the fire reading a poetry
book of her mother's. Slowly she put the book aside.
Mary? Miss Pringle? Poor Miss Pringle—she regularly
came to Ellie's room to keep her company, Miss Pringle
explained, but really Ellie guessed it was to escape her
ladyship's constant harrying.

But it was neither Mary nor Miss Pringle, because after
the knock, Ellie heard a man's voice. 'I've brought coal
for your fire, ma'am.'

She was already on her feet. 'Come in.' It was Joseph. She'd seen him in the distance often enough, but
he'd never before tried to speak to her, never made obvious in the slightest way his connection with the captain.

She stood there, her heart thudding as he carefully
refilled the coal scuttle on the hearth. Then he turned to
her and said quietly, 'The captain asked me to tell you
that he is waiting to hear from you, ma'am.'

Fierce rebellion suddenly burned in Ellie's heart. What
right had he? What right? Joseph meanwhile made his
bow and was about to go—clearly he didn't even expect
a reply. But she called out to him, 'Wait. I will write to
your captain! Wait there.'

She hurried to her little desk where her writing things

lay. Just for a moment, she gazed out of the window at the bare trees and the lowering sky, watching the sleet lashing in rods across the bleak foliage of the garden and remembering the months that she'd spent fleeing from France with her father. It was true that she'd lost everything—but she wouldn't submit to the dangerous man who was Joseph's master.

It's impossible, she wrote to Luke swiftly, her pen scurrying across the paper, *for me to achieve what you demand. And I must insist that you return what is rightly mine.*

She would never forgive herself for allowing him to take possession of her father's compass.

Sealing the letter carefully, she gave it to Joseph. 'Please deliver this to your captain.'

And Joseph—surprisingly polite, surprisingly calm—gave her another bow as he took it. 'Be sure that I will, ma'am.'

He left her and she sank into her chair again, picturing Luke's expression as he opened and read her letter. *Not good enough, I'm afraid*, she could almost hear him saying. *Mam'selle, I really expected more of you than this.*

That night, it began to snow. It snowed so heavily and lay so thickly that going for her usual walk the next day was impossible. Ellie gazed out of her window and thought of Luke in that strange old house overlooking the shore and the sea. Why his interest in the French seaport of La Rochelle? He would have fought in Spain, not France. Why had he left the army to live in such isolation with his friends?

Was he dismissed because the injury to his hand meant he was of no use any more? She could well imagine that such a fate would have made him full of bitterness. Full of the need for revenge.

Had Joseph delivered her message? She expected every hour, every minute almost, to be contacted anew by Joseph's secret master. She struggled with the dawning awareness that in him, she'd met someone who had invaded her life. Could *control* her life.

By the next day the snow had stopped, but the temperatures remained bitter. Lady Charlotte had been due to visit a friend in Hythe that afternoon, but the visit had to be cancelled, and Lady Charlotte decided to retire to her room—though not before reminding Ellie that she really ought to take up some ladylike diversion to occupy her time.

'You could work on some embroidery, Elise,' had become her repeated refrain. 'Or how about music? You play the pianoforte, you told me.'

'Yes, I did. But...' *You told me you couldn't bear the sound, unless it was played by a true musician.*

'But what? There is a perfectly good instrument in the music room. You really should be able to demonstrate to Lord Franklin, when he next honours us with his presence, that you have been using his hospitality to advantage.'

Indeed, that afternoon Ellie went to play the pianoforte by herself, but it was badly out of tune—and after only a few minutes, she bowed her head over the keys, remembering how sweetly her mother used to play.

Suddenly she was so homesick that she could scarcely breathe.

Hurrying from the music room, she went up to her room to put on her cloak and her little laced-up boots. By now it was late afternoon and almost dark, thanks to the lowering clouds, but she was beyond caring—she had to leave the confinement of this place, if only for an hour.

Avoiding the servants, she left the house by the back door and followed the snow-covered path to the shrubbery. It was a path she took often, knowing it led to an ornamental pavilion well away from the house where she could sit in peace. Sometimes, too, she brought crusts of bread she'd saved from the dining table to feed the birds, and often a bright-eyed robin would be watching out for her from the nearby branches.

Already a full moon was rising above the trees. Behind her the lights from the house glittered in the frosty air and her breath misted. Nearby was a stone birdbath, where she headed now to break the ice for the birds. But she never got there.

Because she'd heard a muffled movement behind the trees.

She remembered her fear in Brussels, her belief that someone was still after her. She remembered the man with pale hair and pale eyes, whom she'd kept glimpsing in the crowds that filled the square by day or gathered outside the local tavern by night.

And then she realised that someone was coming towards her from the darkness behind the pavilion. A nearby jay clattered out its alarm call, making her jump and drop the bread; the shadows shifted, and an all-too-recognisable figure stepped forward.

It was Captain Luke.

Chapter Twelve

He was dressed in his usual long coat and shabby boots, but even they couldn't detract from the obvious strength of his powerful figure. And the way that he moved—graceful, purposeful—somehow reminded her of an animal stalking its helpless prey. *Her.*

For a moment, Ellie felt her heart drumming so hard she thought it might burst. She took a step backwards, her eyes fastened on that blue, knowing gaze, the slanting cheekbones, that wickedly distracting mouth. He came a little closer, in a series of easy, lithe movements that belied the harsh strength of his body.

Her hand flew to her throat. If she tried to run back to the house, he would catch her almost instantly. *He is too dangerous for me*, she acknowledged in despair. *Too dangerous.*

He bowed his head curtly. '*Mam'selle*,' he said. 'I startled you. I'm sorry. But I need to talk to you.'

'How did you…?' She was going to ask him how he'd known she was here, but she stopped herself. *Joseph, of course.* Joseph must have told him she came out here often; Joseph had quite possibly arranged some signal to let him know when she left the house.

'I assume,' she said, 'that you received my correspondence. My letter.' She meant her words to sound defiant, but it all came out wrong—somehow she lost her breath completely and her words tied themselves up in knots.

His head was a little to one side, as if he was considering carefully what she'd said. 'I did get your letter,' he answered calmly at last. 'And I'm afraid that what you wrote just wasn't good enough.'

As he spoke he was moving towards her, all the time. Somehow she held herself steady, although she couldn't help but feel her heart constrict at his nearness. A sharp jolt of awareness imploded quietly yet devastatingly inside her—awareness of what, exactly? Of his pure and utter masculinity, that was what. She found herself thinking, in one wild, crazy moment, that all kinds of women would seek to keep him company. To seek his kisses and to share his bed…

'I cannot do it,' she whispered. 'I cannot gain access to the papers you require.'

He arched his dark eyebrows. 'I don't recall giving you a choice—*mam'selle.*'

She made a sudden, involuntary move towards the path that led back to the house, but even more quickly, he blocked her way—and put both his hands on her shoulders.

His touch burned her. *Dieu du ciel*—all of her burned. Surely, she told herself with a thumping heart, surely he wouldn't be intending to kidnap her? No—because she was of far more use to him *inside* Lord Franklin's home. And he'd come here, doubtless, to remind her of that fact.

She pulled herself, shaking, away from his grasp. He let his hands fall to his sides and gave a small sigh.

'I don't intend you any harm,' he said. 'But I wouldn't

advise you to try any tricks. And if you've got your pistol with you, you're certainly not going to improve your situation by firing it at me.'

She stared at him, white-faced. 'I haven't got it.'

'Good. Do I have your word that you won't run, or raise the alarm?'

He had her father's compass. He knew her secrets. 'What do you want?' she whispered.

He was watching her intently. 'What I want, *mam'selle*, is simple enough. Get those papers from Lord Franklin's library for me. That's all I ask.'

'And then?' She was breathless with emotion.

'Then I'll give you back your father's compass.'

Ellie squared her slender shoulders. 'Why not ask your friend Joseph to get into Lord Franklin's library?'

'Because,' he replied, 'I'm fairly sure that the documents I require may demand a knowledge of French geography, French vocabulary even—which Joseph, despite his many other skills, does not possess.'

'Who *is* Joseph? How much do you pay him to be your spy?'

'I pay him nothing. My grandfather, from whom I inherited the house where I live, took Joseph in from the workhouse as a youngster. He employed him as a kitchen boy—a lowly job, but my grandfather was good to him, and Joseph was grateful.'

'As I will be grateful to you—once you return what you stole from me. My father's compass.'

'You'll get it back,' he said softly, 'as soon as I get those papers.'

Already Ellie was shaking her head. 'It's impossible. The library is always locked...'

'And I'm very patient. You're not going to tell me that

you feel any particular sense of loyalty to Lord Franklin, are you? Not after your desperate attempt to escape?'

'Lord Franklin took me in when I was homeless!'

'Have you ever wondered why?'

'Because he is my *relative.*'

'And you accepted what he said, when he told you he was your relative? Turning up in Brussels, just like that?'

'Of course!' Her eyes flashed up to meet his. 'He is a generous man—although I can't imagine it's the kind of generosity that someone like you would ever feel!'

'It's rather rare in Lord Franklin, too, by all accounts.'

She couldn't answer, because deep down he'd voiced her own doubts. She couldn't trust Lord Franklin. She *didn't* trust Lord Franklin. She twisted her hands at her sides. *If only this man wouldn't look at her like that.* As if he could hear the wild pounding of her own heartbeat.

He'd folded his arms and was gazing down at her, impassive. 'You want your father's compass, don't you? Then you must find me the papers I need, from Lord Franklin's library.'

'How can I? The keys are kept in the steward's office.'

'Ah. Mr Appleby.' His eyes were knowing and shrewd. 'Surely, *mam'selle*, you can use your charms to distract him, somehow? I would guess that during your various adventures, you've learned how to use your femininity just as expertly as you learned to use that gun of yours—'

Her hand shot out to slap him; Luke caught her wrist just in time, forcing her hand away.

Damn it, he thought, *she was a little vixen.* She looked so physically fragile, so petite, and her defiance was hopeless—stupid—but she just didn't give up. The hood of her cloak had slipped back now and he saw how she'd tied back her long dark curls in a pale green ribbon, in the most simple and guileless of ways. His accusation about her using her charms had been unfair, he knew—she used no obvious arts or artifices, no face paint or jewellery. And as for her clothes, she wore the same old cloak over the same plain grey gown that she'd worn last time.

No vanity. That was only one of the things about her that stirred deep-seated emotions he'd forgotten he ever had. Brought to life his compassion, his respect—and another impulse that was far more dangerous. The desire to hold her in his arms and make her want him. Really want him, make her cry out his name, in need and passion.

Before he'd joined the army, Luke had built up a reputation for success with women—indeed, he'd had fashionable girls of the *ton* sighing for him and beautiful but bored wives of rich men eagerly competing for his attentions. He knew well enough how to keep them happy.

But—commitment?

Three years ago, he had entered into a romance—an engagement, no less—with Caroline Fawley. Her wealthy father had objected strongly; it had ended badly and Luke's name had been blackened. Now Luke knew he shouldn't lay a finger on the French girl standing before him in the snowbound garden, because he was damaged, body and soul.

But he needed, desperately, to find out what had happened to his brother. And this girl had to be a part of his plans—indeed, he was going to have to *force* her into cooperation if necessary. He wondered suddenly if she had anyone in the world on her side, now that her father had died.

He told himself it was nothing to do with him. It was none of his business—just as the slight quiver that he'd heard in her hitherto calm voice, betraying, he guessed, her desperate attempt to conceal her outright fear, was nothing to do with him either. Yet how old had she said she was? Nineteen? And without anyone in the world to trust, least of all *him*.

Luke thrust his hands harshly into his coat pockets and reminded himself to keep them where they belonged. 'I believe,' he said coolly, 'that you are completely capable of doing what I ask. You are trying my patience, Elise.'

'Ellie…' she breathed. 'My name is Ellie.' Then—before he could register her intention—she'd whipped round and was off, running. She managed to get several yards down the path before he caught up with her and turned her to face him.

'Let me *go*!' She struggled and he tightened his grip on her arms.

'So,' Luke said, 'you're still not going to cooperate.' *Ellie*. An English name—but of course, she had an English mother. 'Though really, you know—you haven't any effective way of fighting me.'

'Only because you don't play fair.' She was shivering a little, he saw, in this intense cold, but her voice was steady. *She was brave*, he thought again in wonder. Amazingly brave. Luke sighed. He'd been thinking about her far too much in the last few days and one of the reasons she'd haunted him was not just because of her remarkable obstinacy, but because of her outrageous—if useless—courage.

'*Mam'selle*,' he said, 'this isn't a game. And life isn't fair.'

'Do you think I don't know that?' Suddenly her eyes looked haunted—dark with unspoken grief. 'You've talked of justice, *monsieur*. Justice—and yet you hide away, in that half-ruined old house of yours. You openly

admit that you have spies everywhere. You're ashamed
to come out in the open, to ask Lord Franklin openly for
what you want, as other, *honest* men would—'

'Ellie,' he broke in. 'You talk a little too much.'

'And I won't allow you to silence me!'

'Won't you?'

She gasped. Because he was lifting the fingertips of
his left hand to let them trail across her full mouth, brushing away a tiny cold snowflake that had landed there—
then letting the pad of his finger travel on down to her
deliciously pointed little chin.

And he leaned in and kissed her.

Just a touch. That was all Luke ever intended. Just
one brief, sweet meeting of lips—but the joining of their
mouths, her soft skin against his, sent lightning bolts
through him, astonishing him. He saw that her eyes were
closed, he realised that her lips were slightly parted and
his heart drummed, his loins pounded. She was wonderfully sensual—and she was an innocent. *Stop there*, Luke
ordered himself. God help him, everything about her
shouted a warning for someone like *him* to stay well clear.

But he didn't. Instead, he wrapped his other arm
around her narrow waist, which meant that her slender
body was up against his, fitting so sweetly that his pulse
jolted with lightning desire. He gazed down at her. Her
green eyes, flecked with amber lights, were wide open
now, half in fear, half in longing. He drank in her dark
lashes, her creamy skin, her full mouth and he kissed
her again.

Only this time his lips stayed there. He heard her
moan softly, felt her press herself closer in, her mouth
opening shyly under his. She tasted of honey and melting snowflakes, and Luke deepened the kiss, at the same

time strengthening his grasp on her narrow waist and holding her closer, harder, exploring the inner softness of her mouth with his tongue, until he felt her hands twined urgently round his back, until all he knew was the drumming of his blood in his ears and the heat engulfing his loins.

And then she pulled away. She wrenched herself from his arms, her hand to her throat, and he saw that her eyes were dark with shock.

'Stop,' she whispered. 'Please stop.'

Luke sighed and dragged his hand through his hair. He moved away resignedly, willing his pulse to return to normal. He shouldn't have done what he did. Shouldn't have *touched* her, much less kissed her. 'That's a pity, *mam'selle*,' he said coolly. 'I thought perhaps we'd found a way of resolving our differences. But I'm afraid that your father's compass stays in my hands until you've got yourself into Lord Franklin's library and found those documents for me.'

She looked devastated. All the colour had drained from her face, except for her lips, which were still rosy and swollen from his kiss.

'You are hateful,' she whispered. 'Hateful.'

His face never changed. But raw emotion hit him in the gut. She was right—he was. But his brother. His brother, who might still be alive...

He reached down to the floor to pick up the delicate green ribbon that had fallen from her hair. 'You know,' he said quietly, 'green suits you. You should wear more of it. It matches your eyes.'

Without a word, she snatched the ribbon from him and thrust it into her pocket. *What did you expect, you fool? That she might like your flattery? Beg you for more?*

'I think it's time for you to go,' he said. 'Joseph should be nearby. I'll check with him that it's all right for you to return to the house.'

'There's no need to check. Let me go *now*. I often go out walking in the garden—the staff won't be at all surprised to see me going back in. They're used to me...'

Her voice trailed away as she felt his eyes raking her. 'Not looking like that, they're not,' he said softly.

Her hands flew to her long hair, which fell in disarray around her face and shoulders.

Without another word, Luke left her, heading out beyond the pavilion. Ellie realised that though it was scarcely five o'clock, darkness had engulfed the garden and it had started to snow again heavily. She sat on the stone bench in the shelter of the pavilion and gave way to sheer, raw hurt.

Her cheeks burned from the memory of his kiss. From the warmth of his lips on hers, the strength of his lean, hard-muscled body pressed against hers. All a joke, a cruel joke on his part, because it was absolutely clear now that he never intended to give way on *anything*. He'd been pretending that he desired her, coaxing her sweetly with his touch and his caresses—all the better to make it quite clear that he despised her.

She hated him. So why, then, did the heat flare in her blood and an ache of need squeeze at her chest when, a few moments later, she realised that her tormentor was on his way back?

His dark hair and his shoulders were covered with snow. His face, as he entered the pavilion, was expressionless. She rose to her feet and drew her cloak around her like armour, meeting his gaze defiantly. 'So can I go?'

'I'm afraid not.' He was knocking snow off his coat and boots. 'The dogs are out.'

'No!' She couldn't hold back her obvious dismay. 'No, it's too early…'

'Perhaps they've scented an interloper. You'll have to stay here for a while, I'm afraid—' He broke off, because the dogs were barking closer now, drowning his words. He, like her, listened in silence to the blood-chilling baying.

'Might they find us, Luke?' she whispered.

His name. She'd used his name, he realised, for the first time. He sat down on the stone bench beside her and said calmly, 'I doubt it, because this fresh snow will mask our scent and our footprints.'

She nodded. She'd clasped her hands together and he saw something else.

She was *terrified.*

She'd been so full of defiance on the day she'd travelled to Bircham Hall, when she'd wandered from the coach and he'd waylaid her by the roadside. It had been the same again on the night Sam Snaith had brought her to him, in that tavern by the harbour—he remembered with fresh incredulity how she'd insisted she was going to make the journey back to France, alone. But now he saw that she was shaking. 'Are you afraid of dogs?' he asked quickly.

'Of dogs like them. Yes. Yes…'

And suddenly he guessed. He *knew.* 'You've been hunted by dogs, haven't you? Some time in your past?'

Again, she whispered, *'Yes.'*

'You'll be safe,' he said. 'I give you my word.'

She nodded, but her skin was paper-white. The dogs were still howling in the distance and he saw how, as she listened to them, every inch of her conveyed her battle with overwhelming terror. Hunting dogs had been set after her? For pity's sake, what other secrets did her past life hold? What other terrors? *Talk to her, Luke, for God's sake*, he urged himself angrily. *Take pity on her. Distract her. She's only a girl, after all. You must stop her listening to those damned great brutes...*

He lifted his hand, to point to the falling snow. 'It's lethal. But it's beautiful, too, isn't it?' he said quietly. 'It reminds me of the Spanish Pyrenees, the winter that we crossed the mountains with Wellington in the snow.'

She gazed up at him, her eyes wide with wonder. 'So you *were* in the army? I heard your men call you "Captain", but I wondered if it was—if it was...'

'A joke?' He met her gaze steadily. 'No joke—it's true that I was an officer.'

Her eyes widened a little, then travelled to his gloved hand. 'But you were injured.'

He exhaled sharply. 'Put it like this. One way and another, the army didn't have much use for me any more.'

She sat very still. Good. He had her attention now. Which was as well, because confident as he'd tried to sound about the dogs, they were damnable beasts and even this snow might not be sufficient to put them off the scent of humans lurking in the garden.

'Luke...' He saw that she was struggling for the right words. 'I'm sorry about your hand. But you were an officer. You must have held responsibility. People must have trusted you. Yet you...'

'Became a wastrel.' He kept his voice light. 'An outcast from society. That's what you think, isn't it?'

She got to her feet and started walking to and fro. 'I

don't understand why you live as you do. Can't you lead a life more worthy of yourself somehow?'

Well, thought Luke drily, this was certainly better. The colour had come back to her cheeks, and she was back to insulting him as normal. He gave her a cool smile. 'You think that I got up to no good after leaving the army. That I'm a free trader—a smuggler—at the very least. Don't you?'

She drew a deep breath, then she said, very quietly, 'Perhaps. Luke, why are you so desperate for me to get those papers? Are you facing some kind of prosecution—prison, even? Are those papers some kind of evidence against you?'

He rose to tower over her. Saw the fear flicker in her eyes again, even though she stood firm. 'Ellie,' he said, 'I cannot give you any reasons. Not yet. All I can tell you is I have a brother. He was in the army, too. Whether he's alive or dead, no one's sure. And I need you to find those papers.'

'They're something to do with your brother?' She was struggling to understand. 'And yet they're in Lord Franklin's house?'

'I can't tell you any more,' he said. 'But I will have to insist on your obedience in this matter, I'm afraid—'

He broke off, because outside the pavilion a figure emerged from the whirling snow. Luke's hand was on her arm, reassuring her. 'It's Joseph. No need to be afraid.' He was already stepping forward to exchange a few words with his henchman.

Then he turned back to her. 'The dogs have been returned to their kennels. So you're safe to go back to the house now.'

Safe? She almost laughed. Wrapping her cloak around

herself, she stepped out into the wintry darkness, holding her head high, and Luke followed her. At the last minute, she whirled round on him, the fast-falling flakes whitening her shoulders and hair.

'You ask too much of me, *Capitaine*,' she whispered, 'in many ways. In fact, in most ways.' She clutched at his arm. 'Please let me have my father's compass back. I beg you—'

Again, the emotions rolled through him—waves of bitter regret and of self-loathing. He had no option. He'd never had any option. *Anthony, I'm doing this for you.*

He pulled his hand away almost sharply, and said, at last, 'You will have the compass back once you've done exactly as I asked. You're quite clearly a resourceful person, *mam'selle*. I'll give you a week to complete the task. No more.'

Chapter Thirteen

The big clock in the hallway was striking six by the time Ellie reached her room. She heard it reverberating all around the great, proud house that was packed with priceless art treasures.

She would be late for dinner. She didn't care.

Slowly she took off her cloak and boots, which were damp from the snow. Then she sat on the bed and put her hands to her cheeks.

She'd known from the very first time she met Luke— the captain—that she ought to be afraid of him. She remembered how in the moment before he kissed her in the pavilion, there had been no tenderness in his eyes, only a look of harsh challenge. She shivered as she remembered the way his mouth had curved into a slight smile— a *knowing* smile—as he pulled her steadily into his arms.

She also remembered how every nerve ending in her body had been crying out a warning. *Be careful. Be careful.* But then he'd touched his lips to hers and his mouth had been warm and sweet and wonderful. Her legs had threatened to give way, her heart had pounded like a drum and without thinking, she'd let her fingers tighten round the hard muscles of his back and found she was letting her tongue twine with his, letting him taste her fully in a way she'd never dreamed of.

She'd hardly been able to *stand*. He'd thought her a fool. A stupid little fool, and who could blame him?

There was a knock at the door and Mary came in. 'Miss, dinner is about to be served...' Suddenly, she saw Ellie's wet cloak and boots. 'Oh, miss! You've been out in all this snow! But the dogs were let out earlier—didn't you hear them? One of the groundsmen thought he glimpsed an intruder... Your hair's all damp and your stockings are wet—I would have lit a fire for you if I'd known. Here, let me help you.'

Swiftly Mary set about drying her hair, finding her fresh clothes, helping her change her shoes.

'Mary,' Ellie interrupted her as she helped her into a clean gown. 'Mary, there's a big old house, on a head-land overlooking the sea. It's less than two miles from here and it looks half-derelict.'

'Oh, you mean Higham House, ma'am! The Danburys' family home!'

Ellie's heart was beating a little faster. 'Tell me about Higham House. Tell me about the Danburys, Mary.'

'Well, there was old Mr Danbury, who owned the place when I was a little girl—there are farms, too, you know, not just the house, though the last year or two have been bad ones for harvests, I believe. Old Mr Danbury, he died back in 1810, leaving his grandson as his heir.'

'Luke Danbury?'

'That's right. Luke Danbury's father died some time ago, you see, and his mother even longer ago. So Luke Danbury inherited the estate. There was a younger brother, Anthony, but he went off to Spain for a soldier and never came back. Whether or not he died in battle, no one's ever said for sure, miss—his body's never been brought home. And people whisper things.'

I have a brother. He was in the army, too. She remembered Luke's expression. 'What do they whisper, Mary?'

'Oh, miss.' Mary looked distressed. 'There's talk that Anthony Danbury was a traitor.'

'A traitor?'

'Yes, although I don't know a thing about it, I must say. All I know is that now the big old house—so beautiful, it once was!—has gone to rack and ruin, and the farms are scarcely any better.'

'But Luke Danbury still lives at the house?'

'He does now, miss—though he joined the army, too, in 1812, a while after his brother did. Some were surprised that he went, leaving the place without a Danbury in charge. But there was a woman, you see, an heiress— her father owned land in Hythe and she was ever so beautiful. She and Luke Danbury became engaged, but she broke it off, they say, and he was so bitter that he turned his back on his estate and went off to join the army in Spain.'

Ellie was reeling. Luke Danbury had been engaged to an heiress. He'd had a love affair that had ended with such bitterness that he'd gone to be a soldier.

She remembered the hundred secret things he'd made her feel with his lips and hands, just in those few moments in the snowbound pavilion. 'When did he come back from the army, Mary?' She was surprised by how calm her voice sounded.

'He came back nearly a year ago and, to be quite hon-

est, miss, no one knows quite what he's up to these days
because he doesn't mix with society. Mrs Sheerham, she
says he's gone and mortgaged that lovely old house and
sold off everything he could from it, for gambling and
bad company. Not only that, but when he first came back
early last year, he was forever sailing off to France by
night—or so the locals said.'

Ellie tried to keep her voice cool. 'His fiancée perhaps
had a fortunate escape.'

'Oh, yes, indeed! Her father in particular was ever so
relieved. Luke Danbury is unpopular with all the landed
gentry around here.'

'Because he's a rogue?'

'Well, no.' Mary hesitated. 'Truth to tell, miss, he's *not*
exactly a rogue to the local people. He treats his tenants
and his labourers better than any other landlord. Pays
them as much as he can for the work they do—and often
you'll see him out there in the fields himself, helping his
men with the lambing and shearing and harvesting, and
working harder than anyone. The other landowners, they
don't like it. They don't like *him*. They say that he gives
the working folk ideas. So I think, miss…' Mary hesitated '…that perhaps you'd be well advised not to mention Luke Danbury to Lord Franklin, when he arrives
here tomorrow.'

Ellie stood up slowly from her chair. 'You say that
Lord Franklin is arriving *tomorrow*?'

'Oh, yes. You didn't know? Everyone's in a flurry, of
course, but he likes to arrive all of a sudden from time to
time, does his lordship. Cook says he does it to keep us
on our toes. And Mr Huffley says he comes to admire
all his paintings and statues—Cook believes that he cares

more for those cold, dead things than he cares for any living person—'

As if realising she was saying too much, Mary broke off mid-sentence. 'Anyway, a messenger arrived from London this afternoon, to say he'll be here after lunch tomorrow, in spite of all this snow. You'll find that her ladyship is very excited, for of course she dotes on her son. And while you're having your dinner, miss, I'll sort through those lovely new clothes of yours that you've never yet worn. Because with Lord Franklin arriving, you'll surely want to look your very best...'

After leaving the girl, Luke walked swiftly through the darkness to the boundary wall of Lord Franklin's estate and climbed it with ease. *No guard dogs, no groundsmen and this falling snow will cover my trail.* Soon afterwards he reached the clearing in the woods where he'd tethered his mare, Diablo, who whickered gently when she saw him, nuzzling at his coat pocket for treats.

'At least someone's glad to see me,' Luke murmured as he fondled the mare's neck and brushed the snow from the saddle. It would take him some time to erase the memory of the look on the French girl's face as he emerged from behind the pavilion. It had been a look of downright fear—and quite probably he deserved nothing less.

His mouth was set in a grim line as he mounted Diablo and rode onwards to join the coast road. The snow had almost stopped now, but the track was crisp and lethal underfoot and Luke kept Diablo to a walk, following the road beneath the many stars that were beginning to come out. After a while, he turned off down the narrow, overgrown lane that led to the top of the cliffs, where a tiny church overlooked the sea.

The girl—Ellie—would be back indoors by now, he thought. Back at Bircham Hall, hating, no doubt, what he was forcing her to do—to betray her protector, Lord Franklin. Hating him, Luke. And yet…that kiss.

It was meant to subdue her. To chasten her. He hadn't been prepared for her response, or for his own hunger for more. He could have sworn that her lips parted of their own volition under his; could have sworn that, as he held her closer and caressed her inner mouth with his tongue, her hands had tightened around his back and she'd let out a low, husky sound of desire as her lips clung to his and her soft breasts pressed against his chest…

Wrong. It was all wrong—yet her slender but sensual body had made him think of things that were forbidden, things he should have banished to the back of his mind. Instead, he'd been a fool, allowing himself to be swept by a kind of madness that had taken him well beyond the limits of his usual iron self-control.

Yet she'd seemed *unaware* of her own allure, and her apparent innocence haunted him. He bit out an oath and rubbed his hand over his face.

He was using her. He deserved every bit of her contempt.

He'd reached the church now, the small Saxon church with its graveyard surrounded by ancient yews. Luke dismounted, aware that the snow had altered everything, painting the landscape a stark white that contrasted almost eerily with the black sky and sea. He knew his way well enough through the graveyard and he went to stand at the place where a marble memorial thrust its way up out of the snow.

He reached out to push some of the snow crystals away and, as a sudden shaft of moonlight lit up the inscription, he read aloud, *Here lie, united in death, John Danbury Esquire and his wife Elizabeth Danbury. Dearly loved parents of sons Luke and Anthony. At peace, thanks to a loving God. A just God.*

At peace? His mother, he scarcely remembered—she'd died giving birth to Anthony twenty-six years ago. His father had died when Luke was ten and Anthony eight— the two boys were at boarding school by then, but Luke had vivid memories of his father as a big, loud man, a drinker and a braggart.

Next to the memorial was another gravestone, belonging to his grandfather. Edward Danbury had died five years ago and it was to him that Luke owed everything. Edward Danbury had been a man of integrity, who'd done his best to safeguard the estate and had given both Anthony and Luke the stability they needed, while their father led the life of a wastrel in London.

Luke glanced again at the memorial to his parents. A loving, just God? No—not by his reckoning. Or Anthony would be here. Anthony wouldn't have been branded a traitor.

He still had Jacques's letter in his pocket—the one brought to him by Davey Patchett, the fisherman—but he didn't need to look at it again, because he remembered every word. *I have learned for certain that your brother was on the run for only a few weeks after the betrayal at La Rochelle before he became a prisoner of Napoleon's men. After that—no news at all.*

Luke gazed out to sea, remembering how Anthony had been an officer in the army, and served bravely for years in the Peninsula. But then he'd been summoned to

London—and was asked to work for British intelligence, in France. 'It's because I speak French so well,' he'd said to Luke lightly when he came to tell him. 'That's all.'

'It will be dangerous,' Luke had warned.

Anthony shrugged. 'More dangerous than a battle-field? I doubt it.'

By then it was 1812 and Luke had joined the army, too, fighting under Wellington in Spain. Their home leave coincided only one more time, in the summer of 1813, and they'd walked along the miles of shingle beach talking of old times, of old friends, until Anthony had said at last, 'There's something different coming up, Luke. Something's being planned, down in the south-west of France. It's risky, but we're well prepared. And I'll tell you all about it, when I next get home.'

But Anthony never did come home.

And once Luke was free of the army, he'd never stopped seeking news of Anthony and his comrades. Had never stopped trying to uncover, one way or another, what he bitterly suspected was the truth—that Anthony and his friends had been betrayed and abandoned by their superiors, because some people high up in government had changed their minds and decided they were no longer useful.

Luke left the churchyard at last to go back to his horse. As he settled in the saddle, he recalled that some of his tenant farmers had been to see him today, asking for the payment of rents they owed to be postponed. This freezing weather, they explained, meant they were running out of fodder for their animals, and they feared they would have difficulty buying their seed corn come spring.

'Forget about your rents for a while,' Luke had said. 'You can pay me when the harvest is in.'

But what, he wondered now, if it was a bad harvest locally, like last year? What if the price of wheat continued to calamitously fall, as it had ever since Napoleon's surrender?

Somehow Luke would manage—he had to, for all their sakes. The only regular income he'd had for the last year or so was the rent paid on a small London house his grandfather had left him, but the current tenant had recently announced he was leaving, and the place badly needed doing up. With a wry twist to his mouth, he recalled his staunch old grandfather's advice as he lay dying. *There's nothing for it, Luke. You'll have to find yourself an heiress. But for God's sake, make sure she has a gentle heart.*

Caroline had possessed a heart, of sorts, but she'd been proud, too, proud as sin. And her father, the wealthy Kent landowner Sir Graham Fawley, had wreaked his own kind of revenge on Luke while Luke was away in the army, by instructing the local bankers to call in all the Danbury loans. Another bad enemy to make.

He would fight on, though. He would fight them all. But how he wished that he hadn't had to involve a courageous young French girl, whose lips had parted so sweetly to his kiss. Whose haunted green eyes had almost begged him to tell her that she could trust him.

It would have been better for her, he thought grimly, if she'd never set eyes on him, with his estate heading for destruction and himself quite possibly heading for the kind of hell he deserved.

Luke rode on to his house on the headland that as usual looked shuttered and apparently abandoned; though round the back, the yard had been swept clear of snow and lanterns glowed brightly. He found his spirits lifting, just a little. Maybe the old place *could* be restored. Maybe Anthony would some day return.

Josh Watterson was there rugging up a horse, but he turned as soon as he saw Luke. 'Monsieur Jacques has arrived, Captain!'

Luke swiftly dismounted, handed the reins to Josh and strode towards the back door.

Inside the large dining hall, a fire burned in the hearth, illuminating the faces of the men who sat round the big table—Tom Bartlett, Pete Watterson and their guest, Jacques. They were looking at maps, Luke saw, which were spread out across the table. The remnants of a cold repast—bread and cheese, and a joint of ham—had been pushed to one side.

'Luke, *mon ami*.' It was Jacques who saw him first, jumping to his feet and coming over to grip Luke's left hand firmly. 'Here I am, as I promised. And I'm so sorry I didn't have better news for you in my letter. But there is something else which I only half-told you. Something very important...'

Already he was looking towards the open door. 'I found them,' Jacques went on, 'living in a small town ten miles inland from La Rochelle. You will realise that they are exhausted by their voyage here, but I assured the lady—her name is Monique—that you will be able to offer them both a refuge. And—'

He stopped. Because in the doorway had appeared a beautiful young woman swathed all in black, clutching a small boy tightly by the hand.

Luke gazed at them, emotion punching his ribs.

'Anthony's wife,' Jacques told Luke quietly. 'And Anthony's two-year-old son.'

And the thought struck Luke like a fresh hammer-blow. *My brother must be dead. He must have been executed by the French, or killed in captivity, because, one way or another, he would have fought to the death to be with these two. He would never, ever have abandoned them.*

Chapter Fourteen

When Ellie rose the next morning, Mary poured out her tea, then opened her wardrobe and pointed eagerly to one after another of the expensive gowns. 'Perhaps you'll wear one of these today, miss? Lord Franklin will be arriving, Mrs Sheerham said, this afternoon around two. Might you like to wear the blue gown, miss? Or the green one is very pretty!'

Mary chattered on, as Ellie sat in a silk wrap in front of the dressing table and let Mary brush her hair. *Green suits you*, she remembered Luke saying softly. *You should wear more of it. It matches the colour of your eyes...*

Ellie moved suddenly and Mary's brush dropped on to the dressing table with a clatter. 'I'm sorry,' Ellie said. 'I'm sorry. And I'll wear my grey day dress, Mary.'

Dieu, she thought distractedly, this was almost worse than the long weeks of flight with her father from Paris. Of knowing that dangerous pursuers would always be on their trail.

Here she was in as much danger as ever—from Luke Danbury, the stranger with the dark hair and intense blue eyes, who had said to her yesterday afternoon, in the snow, in his lethally polite voice, *I will have to insist on your obedience in this, I'm afraid.*

And, oh, that kiss. The memory of his lips touching hers continued to haunt her, yet to him it would have meant nothing at all—she knew that. Even as she'd melted to his touch, she'd registered that the kiss was merely another way for him to assert his power over her—and she'd been a fool to submit to it as she did, because it had made her terribly vulnerable. It had filled her with a rush of pleasure she'd never known and a disturbing sense of exhilaration, and afterwards she ached with longing somewhere deep inside.

Ellie bowed her head and closed her eyes. She didn't want to feel like that ever again. She couldn't *afford* to feel like that again.

'Miss?' Mary was saying. 'Miss, which ribbon did you want in your hair?'

She realised Mary was holding several velvet ribbons out to her. 'Any,' she said quickly. 'I really don't mind.' She pointed to one. 'Black will do.'

'Oh, miss. No one will even *see* it against your dark hair...'

'Black,' she repeated.

A week, Luke Danbury had given her. One week, to do as he asked. Or he would tell Lord Franklin Grayfield that her father once worked for Napoleon Bonaparte.

Lord Franklin arrived in his carriage shortly after two and Ellie, in her second-floor room, heard his horses rattling up the drive at speed—clearly the wintry weather hadn't presented any problems at all to his coachman. Her sitting-room window overlooked the front courtyard, which had been swept clear of snow earlier, and she saw that four grooms were waiting to tend the horses, while Mr Huffley the butler and three footmen stood stiffly to attention by the great front door.

Mr Huffley strode forward, bowing as Lord Franklin stepped down from the carriage. And Miss Pringle was knocking on Ellie's door. 'Elise!' she exclaimed as Ellie opened it to her. 'Elise, his lordship is here. You are coming down to welcome him, aren't you?'

Miss Pringle was nervous, yet terribly excited. A few minutes later Ellie descended the main staircase to see that Lady Charlotte was already positioned in the great hall with her two footmen standing to attention behind her bath chair, while Miss Pringle hovered close by and watched the main doors eagerly.

And then Lord Franklin swept in. Bluff and hearty, wearing a caped greatcoat and highly polished boots, he looked as if he'd stepped out of his Mayfair house for a drive in the park, rather than having just completed a long journey on winter-bound roads. He bowed over his mother's hand and Ellie could see that Lady Charlotte was nearly bursting with pride. Then he stood up straight and let his eyes wander around the great hall; taking in the paintings and the statues. And his eyes rested, finally, on Ellie.

The last time she had seen him was in London on the morning of her departure for Bircham Hall. He had been chilly with disapproval, because of her accusation that someone in his house had searched her room. 'You perhaps doubt the honesty of my servants, Elise?' he'd said. 'You doubt their loyalty to me?'

Yes, Ellie had wanted to reply. *Yes, I do.* Thank goodness her father's valise had been safely locked; but the knowledge that someone in that Mayfair mansion had been through everything else she possessed—her clothes, her books, her pitifully few personal effects—had shaken her profoundly.

That was when he'd announced he was sending her to Bircham Hall. It was banishment, in effect. Yet now he was coming towards her to rest his hands briefly on her shoulders and smile down at her.

'My dear Elise!' His warmth was almost effusive. 'This is a brief visit only, I'm afraid. I've been obliged to come and attend to some affairs of the estate with Appleby. But I must say I was extremely glad to take the opportunity to see you. My mother writes to me that you have settled in well.'

It was as if he was once more the generous benefactor who'd taken her under his wing in Brussels; assuring her constantly that, as her relative, he felt it his absolute duty to take her into his care.

'I am most comfortable here at Bircham Hall, my lord,' she said quickly. 'Thank you.'

All the time, she was aware of Lady Charlotte's sharp eyes on her. And now her ladyship said pointedly, 'I rather think, my dearest Franklin, that Ellie finds our company here a little tedious after the excitement of foreign cities.'

Lord Franklin had been handing his coat and hat to his valet, but now he turned back to Ellie. 'So you find life here tedious? Indeed, I am sorry for that.'

'I am glad of the peace and quiet,' she assured him quickly.

'You've had no problems with the staff?'

There it was. The subtle reference to her complaint in London that her room had been searched. He'd not forgotten.

'No problems at all.' She gave him a swift, bright smile. 'In fact, my lord, everyone has been exceptionally kind.'

'Good,' he replied. 'Good.'

And then Mr Appleby was joining them. 'Ah, Appleby,' Lord Franklin said affably, shaking him by the hand. 'We'll look through the household accounts shortly, shall we? Always something to keep us busy. And while I was in Paris, I bought several fine paintings that had come on the market there; I've brought some of them with me and I'm thinking of having the gallery on the first floor rearranged a little, to accommodate them...'

He guided Appleby aside to continue the conversation, and already Lady Charlotte was commanding her footmen to wheel her away. Ellie was about to leave, too, but Lady Charlotte spoke sharply to her over her shoulder.

'Ellie? You will come with me to my room—I wish to talk to you. But first I want you to fetch my shawl from the dining room—I must have left it there, after lunch.'

'My lady.' Ellie dipped a curtsey and hurried to the dining room for the elaborate cashmere shawl, which was draped across the arm of a chair. But as she headed back towards the door into the hallway, she realised that Lord Franklin and Mr Appleby were talking still, in low, grave voices, but she could hear every word they said.

And she froze, because they weren't talking about art at all.

'You're quite sure, Appleby,' Lord Franklin was saying, 'that he's been brazenly roaming the area again? That the fellow is actually daring to show his face, along with his band of renegades? I'm very glad you wrote to me about it and that's why I've come. To have Danbury at large, especially in the present circumstances, is intolerable. Something must be done…'

Already they were moving away, heading for Mr Appleby's study. Ellie stood there for a moment, allowing the shock to ripple through her.

She knew already from Mary that the local landowners didn't like Luke Danbury. *They say that he gives the working folk ideas*, her maid had said. *So I think, miss, that perhaps you'd be well advised not to mention Luke Danbury to Lord Franklin.*

But Mary had not mentioned that Lord Franklin *hated* Luke Danbury. Ellie felt very cold all of a sudden, and the marble statues in the great hall seemed to be staring down at her. Mocking her.

For nearly an hour, Ellie had to sit with Lady Charlotte and hear yet again about Lord Franklin's prodigious intellect, his academic attainments at Eton and Oxford, and his renown as a collector of art from the Continent. Miss Pringle was there, too, scurrying about at Lady Charlotte's beck and call. Ellie bore it all in silence, until relief came at last because it was time for Lady Charlotte to take afternoon tea with her son.

Ellie went up to her own room, hardly touching the tray of tea that Mary had brought her, trying to make sense of the strength of Lord Franklin's words. *To have Danbury at large, especially in the present circumstances, is intolerable.*

Why the great enmity between the two men? Ellie wondered again if perhaps the papers Luke wanted her to get from Lord Franklin's library contained evidence that Luke—or his missing brother—was guilty of some kind of wrongdoing.

But Luke didn't seem *afraid* of Lord Franklin. He gave the impression that he cared not one jot for society or society's opinion of him—in fact, only once had she seen his cool façade fracture a little, and that was when he spoke of his lost brother. He'd talked in calm, measured tones, without emotion, but she could tell by the shadows in his eyes and by the way his injured hand clenched at his side that the unspoken grief was there always, tearing at his mind. Colouring his every action.

Even that kiss that had shaken her so. Even that kiss had seemed almost like an act of revenge.

During dinner Lady Charlotte positively sparkled in her son's company. Ellie was dressed in sober grey, but her ladyship wore an elaborate brocade gown and a quantity of jewels, and she almost flirted with Mr Appleby, who had joined them for the meal and spoke to her with obsequious flattery.

It was hard to believe, thought Ellie, that this was the same woman who was normally so abrupt and unpleasant. Her son was clearly the light of her life. Miss Pringle was there as well, but apart from the odd rebuke from Lady Charlotte, she was left free to concentrate on the succession of rich delicacies that Cook had prepared in honour of Lord Franklin's presence.

Ellie's appetite, however, was small. And she stopped eating altogether when Lord Franklin began to describe his recent visit to Paris.

'Ah, Paris,' he said. 'I think it is my favourite city in all of Europe.'

'Thank goodness,' said Lady Charlotte, 'that the French have recovered their senses and rid themselves of that monster Napoleon Bonaparte. I trust, Franklin, that he is still a prisoner on the island of Elba?'

'Most definitely,' Lord Franklin assured her. 'And now the city is just as it used to be, with King Louis back on the throne and all of France at peace again!' He turned to Ellie. 'You grew up in Paris, didn't you, my dear? Did you or your father ever meet Napoleon, I wonder?'

Ellie's pulse almost stopped. 'As you will know, my lord,' she answered at last, 'Napoleon kept a very grand court at La Tuileries. But I never visited there. My family lived a secluded life in Paris.'

'And you lived where, exactly?'

'In the Rue Tivoli, my lord. Close to the church of St Denis.'

'Ah,' he said. 'I know it. Not far from the new main road that Napoleon ordered his engineers to build from Paris to Orléans.'

Ellie dropped her fork and heard it clattering to her plate.

Lord Franklin gazed at her a moment longer, then started speaking to Mr Appleby about some matter of the estate. And for the rest of the meal, Ellie was scarcely able to say a word.

Her father had drawn up the designs for the Paris to Orléans main road. But surely—*surely* Lord Franklin couldn't know that? Surely, if he'd any idea that her father had worked for Napoleon, he would have wanted nothing at all to do with her, despite his connection to her mother?

Dieu. She should never, ever have come to England with him. And yet, she had made that solemn promise to her dying father...

More than ever, she felt a great sense of dread. And even when the meal was over, there was to be no escape, for as they rose from the table Lady Charlotte tapped her son's arm and declared, 'Elise plays the piano, you know, Franklin, after a fashion. She might entertain us in the music room for a while.'

'The piano is a little out of tune...' Ellie began.

'You are making excuses, I believe.' Lord Franklin turned and smiled at her benignly. 'Some music would be delightful—I'd no idea you were so talented.'

She bowed her head, recognising defeat. 'I will have to fetch my music.'

She went slowly upstairs.

When she headed down again, she saw that both Lord Franklin and his mother were outside the music room waiting for her. But they'd not seen her and she halted on the stairs when she realised that their topic of conversation was—*her.*

'The girl really is most tiring, Franklin!' Lady Charlotte was declaring crossly. 'So *slow.* She'll be deliberately wasting her time and yours with it. There's bad blood in her. I told you it was a mistake ever to bring her into your household—'

She broke off as Lord Franklin raised his hand in sharp warning. 'That is the last occasion,' he said, 'on which you will refer aloud to the girl's ancestry. Remember that she truly believes she's related to us.'

Ellie stepped back into the shadows, stunned. *She truly believes she's related to us?*

Meaning that—she wasn't?

Somehow she carried on down the stairs. Somehow she played the piano for them, to Lord Franklin's enthusiastic applause, although Lady Charlotte merely gave a disdainful nod at the end of each piece. As soon as she could, Ellie retreated to her room and sat on her bed. And suddenly, in her solitude, it was as if the terror-filled days and nights of desperate flight from Paris with her father—of being pursued, for mile after mile—were upon her again. She felt as alone and as frightened as she'd ever been in her life. This house, which ought to have been a refuge, seemed darker. Colder.

Then she thought—*the man called Luke knows something*. Each of his words came back to haunt her. She remembered his incredulous comments. 'And you accepted what he said? That he was your relative? Turning up in Brussels, just like that?'

It appeared that Luke quite possibly knew more about Lord Franklin than she did. If that was the case, she had to see him again—even if it meant that she had to do what he wanted. Had to gain access, somehow, to Lord Franklin's library.

That night she lay in her bed, listening to the wind in the trees. Remembering how she'd felt when Luke had held her and had kissed her. Imagining what it *could* have been like, if she'd pulled him closer and let herself be ruled by her instincts, let him do the kinds of things she knew he would do so well.

Her whole body was trembling, perhaps because her clamouring senses realised—even if her brain didn't—that she couldn't bear the thought of *not* seeing Luke Danbury again.

Chapter Fifteen

Lord Franklin stayed at Bircham Hall for three nights, and with the snow thawing rapidly, he rode out each day with Mr Appleby to survey the estate. Afterwards he was closeted with him to discuss business. In the library.

Ellie saw Lord Franklin every evening at dinner, when his manner to her was unfailingly courteous. But Ellie felt she could trust him with nothing now. Felt she could tell him nothing about herself, without fear of betraying her secrets.

Why had he made up those lies about being her relative? Why had he brought her to England? She felt sure, now, that Luke Danbury could have told her, that Luke knew many things he'd not revealed. She wanted—she *needed*—to talk to him again. She longed above all to be in his arms again, and that, she knew, was the most dangerous longing of all.

On the day of Lord Franklin's departure, his carriage and horses were ready in the courtyard by ten. Lady Charlotte bid him a fond farewell, then almost immediately she summoned the butler and the housekeeper to give them a precise summary of all the staff's failings during her son's visit. It was Mary who told Ellie this, just before lunch.

'Tore into them both, her ladyship did,' Mary said sadly. 'Some of us heard her. Don't know why they put up with it, I really don't.'

For the next few days, Lady Charlotte harried the staff at every opportunity. The atmosphere at the Hall was forbidding, and Ellie saw some of the maids in tears. On the fourth day, during lunch, Lady Charlotte rounded on a nervous young footman who had dropped a serving spoon and Ellie broke in, saying, 'I'm sure he did not do it intentionally, Lady Charlotte.'

Everyone in the dining hall—Lady Charlotte, Miss Pringle, the hovering staff—looked at Ellie in astonishment. Lady Charlotte turned puce, then summoned her two footmen to take her to her room. 'Enough,' she said dramatically. 'I have borne enough.'

Word came soon that her ladyship had a headache and would remain for the rest of the day in her darkened bedchamber. Almost immediately Mrs Sheerham announced that she was due the afternoon off and would go into Folkestone in the barouche to visit her sister there, and Cook seized the opportunity to ride into town with her and do a little shopping.

Ellie was in the parlour when Miss Pringle came in to tell her this. 'Oh, dear,' Miss Pringle said. 'Oh, dear. I shouldn't be ungrateful. But how I wish…'

'That you, too, could have the afternoon off? Then do so, Miss Pringle! Do as you please!'

Miss Pringle's face brightened. 'I could walk to the

Vicarage, which was my childhood home. But what if Lady Charlotte needs me?'

'You're supposed to be *my* companion, not hers,' Ellie said gently. 'And I am giving you permission to go.'

And so Ellie was left in the parlour by herself. Thinking of Luke. Thinking of his command. *I'll give you a week to complete the task. No more.* But most of all— she was thinking of his kiss. He'd been toying with her, he must think her a fool and rightly so.

It was then that she realised Joseph had entered the room. He must have knocked, but she'd not heard him. 'Ma'am,' he said in his quiet voice. 'I've come to tell you that the library is unlocked for the afternoon.'

Her heart thudded. 'How do you know this?'

'Because,' he answered patiently, 'Mrs Sheerham has asked me to polish the brasses in there while she's out. She's given me her key.'

Ellie had already risen to her feet. *She* needed to know. *She* needed to discover what was going on. 'Give me five minutes, Joseph. And I'll be there.'

She went to check that Lady Charlotte was indeed still resting in her room; clearly she was, because the two footmen who attended her were dozing quietly in their chairs outside her door.

Ellie made straight for the library. The door was open; the lamps were lit and Joseph was already energetically polishing the brass surround of the fire. On seeing her enter, he came over to lead her towards a table at the far end of the room and said, in his quiet voice, 'I would estimate that you have an hour, perhaps a little more. Then Mr Huffley will require me for other duties and I shall have to lock the room again.'

He went back to his polishing and Ellie swiftly scanned

the room. Shelves full of books covered at least half of the wall area, but there were larger, deeper shelves that housed ledgers and files. *I want you to get into the library,* Luke had said, *and to bring me anything you can find, any papers, documents or letters that relate to the autumn of 1813 and a place in France called La Rochelle. Do you understand me?*

She moved closer to the thick files which, she saw, were arranged by year. Her hands fastening round the thick file marked '*1813*', she carried it to the nearest table, sat down and opened it.

There were pages and pages of notes and letters—private letters, addressed to Lord Franklin. And as she examined the addresses and the signatures, she realised that some of these letters were signed by the prime minister of England. Others were from the head of the Admiralty.

She felt her breathing almost stop. She'd had no idea that Lord Franklin was on close terms with men high up in the government. Was consulted by them, evidently, in matters of state and war. But did Luke know it?

She suspected he did. She suspected he would think her a fool for *not* knowing it.

The thick file was packed with letters. She looked through them as quickly as she could, aware of the clock out in the hallway striking the half-hour and then the hour. She was reaching for another sheaf of papers when a small bundle of letters, tied together with a ribbon, almost fell from the table—she caught it and saw that it was labelled '*Les Braves, Septembre 1813*'.

She pulled the ribbon aside and scanned the first one quickly.

My dear Franklin,
Further to our meeting in London about the British
landing on the west coast of France in September, I
would suggest that we proceed to give our instruc-
tions to the group known as Les Braves, although
all this depends, of course, on the cooperation of
the Foreign Office...

There were more letters—some of them in French—
giving names, places, dates. There were maps, of the
west coast of France and of the harbour at La Rochelle.
She studied them all with care. And again and again, the
same words kept cropping up.

Les Braves. The heroes.

'Ma'am?' She suddenly realised that Joseph was standing at her shoulder. 'Ma'am. I really ought to report to Mr
Huffley now and lock the room up again before he comes
looking for me. You had best put those things away, I'm
afraid, and get out of here before you're seen.'

Time had flown by. Swiftly Ellie tied the documents
together and thrust them back in their box. Joseph was by
the open door now, glancing alertly down the corridor—
she made for the door also. But Joseph put out a hand to
stop her. 'One last thing, ma'am. The captain wishes to
see you. Tonight, if possible.'

'With the papers? But I dare not remove anything—'

'He doesn't need papers, ma'am. He just wants to
speak to you. I will have a horse saddled ready for you—
at half-past seven, when dinner is over—and I will accompany you, of course. Lady Charlotte has already
announced that she will dine in her room.'

The captain would want to know what she'd found.
'But how will *you* get away, Joseph?'

'It's my evening off.'

She nodded slowly, her throat dry.

At the evening meal, Ellie could hardly eat a thing, but Miss Pringle was so relieved at Lady Charlotte's absence that she didn't notice. Nor did she comment when Ellie left early to hurry up to her room and put on her cloak.

In his usual quiet way, Joseph was waiting by the stables for her and managed to ensure that they left the house and gardens unseen. 'The staff are taking their time over their supper,' he told her, 'and enjoying a little peace since her ladyship is indisposed.'

Soon he and Ellie were riding swiftly through the darkness along the track to the headland, where Luke's home—Higham House—loomed ahead of them. From the front, it looked to Ellie as bleak and forbidding as ever; though when Joseph led her round to the back, she saw that lamps burned in the courtyard and lights blazed from the windows.

Joseph dismounted first and came to hold her pony for her as she eased herself from the side saddle. 'You ride well, ma'am,' he said admiringly.

I've had to, she thought. *I've had to learn all sorts of skills to save my life.*

Joseph hooked both horses' reins over a post and went to knock at the back door, which was opened by the middle-aged housekeeper Ellie had seen before.

'Joseph?' the woman said anxiously, peering out at them. 'Joseph, you've not brought more visitors? Goodness me!'

And the captain was there, behind her. 'Ellie,' he said in his calm way. 'Come in.'

Luke Danbury was leading her into the large dining

hall—the room that was almost filled by a huge old oak table and sturdy chairs and benches. She lifted her head to speak to him.

'You wished to see me,' she began. 'You no doubt know that I gained access to Lord Franklin's library—'

He'd put out a hand to stop her. 'I know,' he said. 'And we'll talk about that in a while. But there's another matter, Ellie. You see, I need your help.'

And something in the way he looked at her—something in the way the candlelight softened his hard features—made her suddenly breathless. In complete contrast to Lord Franklin's aristocratic attire, Luke's white shirt was made of coarse cambric, not lawn; his breeches were of well-worn buckskin, and his leather boots would never have known the tender care of a valet.

She remembered Mary saying, *Often you'll see him out there in the fields himself, helping his men with the lambing and shearing and harvesting, and working harder than anyone. The other landowners, they don't like it. They don't like him.*

They would be jealous of him, Ellie thought with a sudden surge of emotion, because he had the determination and the steadfastness so many of them lacked. And he'd said that he needed her help...

Suddenly she realised that he'd gone out into the hallway, and when he came back, she saw that he wasn't alone.

'Here are two people I'd like you to meet,' he said.

And Ellie saw that standing just inside the doorway was a young woman who held a little boy in her arms. The child would be scarcely two years old. '*Maman,*' she heard the boy whisper. He was tightly clasping the woman's neck. '*Maman.*'

The boy had blue eyes, Ellie realised. Blue eyes and dark hair, just like Luke's. For a moment, she felt such a fierce stab of jealousy that she could scarcely breathe.

The young woman cradled the child in her arms, murmuring words of comfort in French even though tears were sliding down her cheeks. 'There, my little one. There.'

'Ellie,' said Luke. She suddenly became aware that his hand was still on her arm. 'Ellie,' he went on, 'this is Monique. And this is her child, Harry. Monique speaks only French. She's recently endured a long and difficult journey and she's not been well.'

Ellie tried to nod, though confusion still racked her.

'She's anxious, above all,' Luke went on, 'for her child. I wonder if you might speak to her?'

Ellie whispered, 'So that's why you wanted me here tonight? It wasn't because you knew that I'd got into Lord Franklin's library?'

'That can wait a little while.'

Ellie looked at the woman again and there was one overwhelming question she wanted to ask—*Who are they?*

But there was no need; because Luke was already saying, 'They are my brother's wife and my brother's child.'

A mixture of emotions flooded through her—pity, sympathy, relief.

'*Mam'selle?*' Monique was saying hesitantly in French. 'You are from Paris? You speak my language? *Mam'selle*, I need your help…'

Luke saw Ellie go up to Monique without hesitation. Monique still had tears trickling down her cheeks, but as

Ellie spoke to her in fluent French, she gradually grew calmer.

She is so beautiful, he thought, gazing at Ellie. *I have used her badly.* She was all alone in a strange country— as far as he could make out, the girl hadn't got a friend in the world—and Luke had been as calculating to her as any of the enemies she must have faced so far.

Be careful, Luke warned himself grimly. *Remember you're no good for her.*

Ellie was young and alone and must surely be as afraid of him as she was of anyone, if she had any sense. Yet he couldn't stop watching her as she talked to Monique. He saw how the warmth and the caring shone from her, and how whatever she was saying made Harry smile through his tears and reach out to put his chubby fist in her hand.

Ellie was in her usual clothes, he saw, which were shabby and over-large for her petite figure, while her long dark curls were pulled back tightly in a plain band. She was neat and her hair shone, but she had no vanity. Luke thought of Caroline Fawley, and others like her, who were only too well aware of their own worth—but Ellie? She was different.

Ellie possessed courage, without a doubt; but she was also young, innocent and vulnerable. She'd clearly known nothing of sexual desire—and he had to make very sure that she didn't desire *him*. Yet in the soft candlelight, as she murmured in French to Monique, she looked more beautiful than ever.

And her lips had tasted so sweet...

He fought down the memory of that kiss in the snow-bound garden, seeing instead a young and brave woman tending to grief-stricken strangers, soothing their fears with kind words.

And who, he thought bitterly, had been there to comfort her, after she lost her father? Who had there been to soothe *her* fears with kind words, when she arrived in England, in an alien country? Who had there been to provide real, human warmth for a girl who'd lost her family and her home?

And what about himself? What part was he playing?

He was heaping on the punishment, by threatening to reveal her father's past. He'd been absolutely pitiless towards her.

She was coming towards him now, as calm and graceful as ever. The kick of lust hit at his stomach, and he wanted more than anything to take her in his arms, to kiss away the shadows of grief that marked the losses in her life that she tried to mask, always. He rebuked himself harshly. *It's up to you. Up to you, to stay away.*

She said to him, 'Monique told me they have come to you for refuge.'

He said steadily, 'That must astonish you as much as anything you've ever heard about me.'

Did he see her shake her head a little at that, as if to deny his own cynical self-contempt? She went on, 'She said that she feels safe here. But she is very tired from the journey with Monsieur Jacques.'

He nodded. 'They had a difficult voyage. There were navy boats off the British coast and both she and the child suffered bouts of seasickness. Mrs Bartlett has been doing her best for them, but the child won't eat.'

'That is what Monique told me—but perhaps you could explain to your housekeeper that Harry doesn't like milk or butter? But if she could prepare some dry toast and a little soup for him, Monique would be most grateful.'

Luke exhaled with relief. 'Of course. Poor Mrs Bartlett has been worried to death as to what to give the child. And though I can make some sense of written French, my vocabulary's deficient in the matter of children's appetites. Thank you, Ellie.'

'Il n'y a pas de quoi,' she replied softly. 'It is nothing.'

'On the contrary, it means a great deal. I'll take Monique and Harry to Mrs Bartlett, and explain—she's had four children of her own and has numerous grandchildren, so she'll know exactly what to do. But then I'll be back. And, Ellie, you must return to the Hall before you are missed—'

She stepped forward, a look of determination on her face. 'No! I have to tell you, Luke. Joseph helped me get into Lord Franklin's library today!'

He hesitated. Then he gestured towards a seat by the fire. 'Sit there,' he said. 'I'll be back as soon as I can.'

Chapter Sixteen

The room was very quiet once Luke had gone. Ellie sat by the fire and gazed into the flames. She'd thought he was her enemy—an enemy who was all the more dangerous because of the effect he had on her, whenever she saw him.

But she wanted, so badly, to *help* him.

Was she going mad? Had he cast a spell on her? Certainly, she couldn't forget how her breath had stopped in her throat when he'd suddenly appeared on the road to Bircham. How every instinct still told her he was possibly the most dangerous man she had ever met.

Yet Monique had said that she felt safe with him—and Ellie could well believe that if Luke was on your side, then you might indeed feel like the safest person in the world.

And now he was back, his shadow looming in the doorway. She found herself moistening her dry throat as he pulled up a chair to the fire. And she knew that, above all, she must fight down on the sudden, desperate yearning to trust him. The longing to be held once again in his strong arms.

He sat down opposite her—and smiled. Oh, his smile.

It sent heat swirling through all her nerve endings; it reminded her of how his lips had felt, caressing hers...

'Mrs Bartlett,' he said, 'is happily preparing toast and soup in quantities sufficient for a troop of soldiers. I must thank you again, Ellie.'

'As I said, it was nothing. Luke, how long do you expect Monique and Harry to stay with you?'

'For as long as they wish,' he said simply. 'For my brother's sake, I'll do everything—absolutely everything—that I can for them.'

'Of course.' She'd clasped her hands in her lap. 'And I'm so glad I was able to help. But I wanted to come to you anyway.'

'Lord Franklin's library,' he said.

'Yes! I got into the library as you asked. And I've not been able to actually bring you anything—but there are things you must be told...'

He was on his feet, rubbing a hand across his temples. She suddenly realised how tired he looked and wondered if he had slept these last few nights. 'I had no right,' he said almost bitterly, 'to order you to do such a thing. No right to put you in danger.'

'Danger...?' she breathed. '*Danger*, Luke? Who from?'

'You're cold. You're shivering.' He stood up. 'Wait a moment, while I put another log on the fire.'

'No, I'm all right! And I need to tell you—'

'Wait,' he repeated. 'The fire.'

And then something happened. Afterwards, Ellie tried to remember it but could never quite recall, because his back was to her. She knew that he'd gone over to the basket of logs to place a fresh one on to the fire using his left hand, but then—because the log rolled a little—he picked up the heavy metal poker that lay on the hearth—with his right hand.

Why his right hand? She didn't know. Did he forget it was injured? Whatever the reason for his mistake, he dropped the poker and the metal clattered harshly against the stone slab of the hearth. She saw him clench his gloved right hand and ram it against his other fist. And she saw the expression on his face.

It was filled with self-loathing. With despair, almost.

Some ashes and pieces of charred wood had scattered themselves across the hearth. Ellie, glimpsing a small brush and pan close by, hurried across to pick them up.

He almost pushed her aside. 'No need. I'll clear it up.'

'Let me!' She stood there, determined. 'Let me, *please*.' Without waiting for his answer, she knelt and started brushing up the debris from the fire. Felt the heat of the logs burning her cheeks, felt the unshed tears burning at the back of her eyes. She wondered what it must be like for a proud, strong man like him to be so injured.

Still on her knees, she said steadily, 'How was your hand injured, Luke? Was it in battle?'

He gave a harsh laugh. 'In battle? No—though I've often thought that would have been easier to endure.'

She caught her breath at his bitterness. *How, then?* she wondered. *A fight? Some crude punishment?* Standing up slowly, she said, 'You were lucky not to lose your hand.'

'I might as well have done,' he responded, 'for all the good my right hand is to me. You, for instance, can no doubt shoot a pistol far better than I can. I never quite got the trick of it with my left.'

She'd emptied the ashes into the fire and now she came to sit back on her chair, clasping her hands in her lap.

She always did that, Luke thought suddenly. Always.

Making herself look like some demure governess, as if she had no hidden past, no secrets to hide; instead of which her father had worked for Napoleon! And now she was caught between the devil and the deep blue sea—between Lord Franklin and him, in other words—though who precisely was the more dangerous for her, he really wouldn't like to say.

He sighed a little as he sat again in the chair opposite her and asked, 'Who taught you to shoot, Ellie?'

'My father. When I was seventeen.'

'Why?'

'So I could defend myself.'

Of course, Luke thought. *Stupid question.* This girl must have lived a life like no other. 'How old are you now, Ellie Duchamp?'

He saw her clasp her hands more tightly together. Her green eyes, as they met his, were dark with secrets.

'I'm nineteen,' she answered at last.

'In London,' he said, 'most girls your age have nothing more to fill their heads than pleasant dreams of ball gowns and dancing partners. Do you envy them?'

Her knuckles, he saw, were white with tension; but her answer betrayed none of it. 'Not in the slightest.' Her voice was quite calm.

'Do you ever let anyone see your true feelings?'

'Not if I can help it.'

'Do you trust anyone?'

She lifted her eyes to his. 'Would you? If you were in my position?'

'No,' he said quietly. 'And I was a brute to force you into entering Lord Franklin's library.'

She paused a moment, then said, 'What if I told you I *wanted* to do it for you, Luke?'

And Luke thought, *No. What have I done to her? I've made her trust me.* He stood and walked towards the window before stopping to face her. 'I want you to think very carefully about this, Ellie,' he said at last. 'I want you to think about the consequences of what you may have discovered.'

He thought he saw a flash of pain in her eyes. 'Did *you* think about the consequences, Luke? When you asked me—*ordered* me to get into Lord Franklin's library?'

'Not enough,' he said harshly. 'Not enough. You are right to blame me. All I wanted to do was to reveal a great injustice inflicted on my brother and his friends that should have been exposed long ago. But I had no right *at all* to involve you.'

And suddenly, something in his voice—some private anguish—smote Ellie so hard that she could scarcely breathe.

To the outside world, he—Luke—was the villain and Lord Franklin the shining knight who had rescued Ellie from poverty in Brussels. But she had been mistaken in Lord Franklin. The lies that Lord Franklin told her frightened her more than she could say.

And didn't Luke frighten her? Certainly, he ought to. Outwardly he was a rogue, an outcast from polite society, struggling to resurrect his failing inheritance in this neglected old house set high above the sea. She remembered the contempt, and the fear almost, with which Lord Franklin had spoken of Luke.

'You and Lord Franklin hate each other, don't you?' she whispered. 'Why?'

She saw how he clenched his left hand at his side. 'It's a long story,' he said. 'But I strongly suspect Lord Franklin's motives in bringing you to England. And I swear that I will do everything I can should you ever need my help.' He stepped closer. 'Tell me quickly, if you can, what you found in the library. Then I must get you back to the Hall—'

'Where you think I'll be safe?' she cut in, disbelief etching her voice.

'Safer than here,' he said bleakly. 'Believe me, safer than here.'

And then, as she thought wildly, *I so much want to trust him, to believe what he's saying*, the door flew open, and Tom rushed in. 'Josh has seen soldiers, Captain!' he gasped. 'A patrol of English redcoats climbing up the path from Bircham Staithe. And they're coming towards the house!'

Luke snapped out, 'You're sure?'

'Quite sure. Seems the soldiers have heard rumours that some Frenchies landed the other night. They've already questioned the fishermen down at the harbour and the redcoats have sworn they're going to search every farm, every house in the area—especially this one!'

And Luke had to think again, very quickly. Had to make a crucial decision again, very quickly.

'Put everyone on the alert, Tom,' Luke ordered. 'Get our men in here and bring a barrel of ale up from the cellar. Put out the cards and dice—we'll pretend we've been drinking together all evening.'

'And what about your guests, Captain?' Tom glanced worriedly at Ellie. 'As well as this young lass here, you've got the woman and her little one upstairs. If the redcoats search the house and find them—'

'I'll make sure everyone's safe. *Go* now. See that everybody knows what to do.' Luke swung back towards

Ellie. 'You heard what Tom said. I'm sorry, but this means you can't go back to the Hall yet.'

She'd risen to her feet when Tom came in. 'My maid will miss me, at Bircham Hall.'

'I'll send a messenger over there.'

'To Joseph? How can *he* prevent Mary from coming to my room?'

'Joseph has a younger sister who's a maid there. Her name is Sarah. Sarah can tell your maid that she's already attended to you.'

She caught her breath. 'How many spies do you have at Bircham Hall, Luke?'

He was silent.

She closed her eyes, briefly. 'So I'm to stay here. How long do you think all this will take?'

'I don't know.' He raked back his hair. 'Ellie, I can't tell you how much I regret putting you in this situation—but I give you my word that I'll make very sure they don't find you.'

'It's not that!' She'd stepped closer to him, her eyes suddenly wide with distress. 'I'm not afraid! I've faced soldiers before. I'm used to being pursued. But—oh, Luke, I've suddenly remembered something Lord Franklin said, when he was at the Hall, and I should have thought of it before. I should have told you *straight away*.'

He looked tense. 'Something Lord Franklin said?'

'Yes! I heard him say to his steward, *"To have Danbury at large, especially in the present circumstances, is intolerable. Something must be done."* Lord Franklin, of course, left the Hall days ago, but this could well be his doing.' She was clenching her hands in distress.

'Stop, Ellie!' He said it almost fiercely. 'Why should

you have told me? Why should you feel you owe me *any* kind of loyalty?'

She drew a deep breath. 'You know, my father used to say that I had an instinct for justice and for truth. Just as *he* did.'

'You're not saying—that you *trust* me?'

'I'm expressing regret that I failed to warn you,' she said. 'And what about Monique and Harry? Will they be in danger if they're discovered? Will *you* be in danger?'

She looked pale with apprehension now—not for herself, but for Monique, for Harry...and for him! Unbelievable. And so he lied, to protect her. He made light of a whole bunch of redcoats riding in his direction.

'This often happens,' he said swiftly. A complete falsehood—they were sometimes visited by the occasional group of Customs men after smugglers, but never the redcoats. 'Knowing in advance wouldn't have made any difference—we couldn't have stopped them coming. But it is just possible they might demand to search the house.'

Ellie listened with acute attention. 'Do they have the authority to do so?'

'They *always* have authority, I'm afraid. But they mustn't find Monique and Harry—and they mustn't find you here either. Ellie, I want you to do something for me.'

She nodded. 'Tell me.'

'Below this house are cellars. Beyond the cellars are some smaller rooms that can be sealed off—so even if the soldiers get into the cellars, they won't realise the hiding places exist. I must get Monique and Harry down there and I want you to go with them. They will be frightened, of course, and I want you to calm them. Comfort them.'

His eyes searched hers. 'I know I have no right to expect your help. But will you do this for me? For *them*?'

She didn't hesitate. 'Of course. But what about you, Luke?' She felt her breath coming fast and painfully now. 'What are *you* going to do?'

'I can look after myself, don't worry. I'll go out and see what's happening, and in the meantime Tom will take care of you. Tom?'

His henchman had returned to the room. 'Yes, Captain?'

'Take Ellie with Monique and Harry down to the cellars. I'll be back soon.'

He was about to leave, but suddenly Ellie touched his arm. 'Luke.'

'Yes?'

'Take care. That's all,' she whispered.

And as Luke watched Tom leading her away, he was reeling. *Don't think about the softness of her lips. Don't think about those sweet curves you know lie just beneath her ugly old gown...* 'Ellie!' he called. She turned round and he gave her a brief, dazzling smile. 'I will take care,' he said. 'And you remember to do the same. You hear me, French girl?'

For a moment she hesitated, though her smile when it came was shy yet radiant. *'Je vous entends, mon Capitaine,'* she whispered. 'I hear you.'

Chapter Seventeen

Monique was already in the hallway with her sleeping child in her arms and she looked terrified as she moved towards Ellie. *'Oh, mam'selle. J'ai peur...'*

'There's no need to be afraid,' Ellie soothed her. 'Luke will take care of you.'

'Here, miss!' said Tom cheerfully to Monique. 'Come this way. And don't worry, I'll carry the little 'un.'

Monique, not understanding, stepped back in alarm as he reached for Harry. 'It's all right,' Ellie said to her quickly. 'You can trust Tom.'

Tom gave Ellie his lantern to hold and nodded to them to follow him down the stone stairway that led from a door in the kitchen. There were cellars first, as Luke had explained; but then Tom handed Harry back to Monique and pushed aside a pile of wooden crates that concealed a low door. Opening it, he told Ellie to shine the lantern in there to reveal another, low-ceilinged cellar that was equipped, Ellie realised, with piles of blankets and tallow candles.

It was like being on the run again with her father.

Memories poured through her of similar hiding places.

Of a rat-infested barn where they'd hidden up in the loft, while the farmer and his sons searched around the yard below for reported intruders. Of a cellar they'd crawled into, beneath a house just outside Lille, while the soldiers tramped around above them, and she'd feared that her father's cough would bring discovery at any minute.

She forced herself into calmness as Monique looked around, shivering. '*Mam'selle*,' Monique was whispering. '*Mam'selle*, must we really stay down here?'

And Ellie assured her, 'You'll be safe here. And you must stay calm, for your child's sake.'

But Harry was already beginning to whimper in Monique's arms and Tom glanced at the child worriedly. 'I'll have to get back to the captain now, miss,' Tom was saying. 'And he asked me to give you—*this*.'

He handed her a pistol. *Dieu*, thought Ellie rather shakily. She slipped it into her pocket, before Monique should see it. How long would they have to hide? One, two hours? Perhaps all night? But if Harry was crying and the soldiers heard him, they wouldn't be down here for very long at all, because they'd most likely be hauled off to a prison cell.

Tom had gone and Monique was completely failing to soothe her child. '*Madame*. May I?' Gently Ellie took Harry in her arms and scoured her memory for one of the children's rhymes her mother used to sing to her.

> '*Ah! Dis-moi donc bergère,*
> *A qui sont ces moutons?*'

As she sang the old, familiar words, Harry began to smile. Ellie walked around, still humming softly, until she saw his eyelids begin to droop—and at last he was asleep again. Murmuring a silent prayer of gratitude, she whispered to Monique, 'Please, *madame*. Make a bed for your little boy in the corner—with those blankets, do you see?'

Monique did so quickly and Ellie lowered the sleeping child ever so carefully on to the makeshift bed. *Please don't wake. Please don't wake.* Harry let out a small sigh, then he settled back contentedly into a deep sleep.

Monique bent to kiss him, but when she stood up again, Ellie saw that she was brushing fresh tears from her eyes. 'My husband, Anthony—' her voice broke a little '—told me that Harry and I meant everything to him. And he always said—he said...'

'Oh, *madame*.' Ellie's heart overflowed with pity. 'Sit, please. Sit here with me.' She was already spreading a blanket over a stone ledge, then she took Monique's hand and they sat together, close to Harry.

Monique's tears were falling freely now. 'Anthony always said to me, "If anything should happen to me, my darling, you must get Harry to my brother, Luke, in England".' She raised her eyes to Ellie's. 'And the worst *did* happen. Anthony disappeared. I lost him.'

Ellie squeezed her hand tightly. 'If it distresses you to talk...'

'No. No! I want to talk about him! I want there to be *hope*—do you understand?'

Ellie nodded; Monique drew a deep breath and went on, 'We met three years ago, when Anthony was travelling in France, and we married in the summer. My Anthony was brave. *Too* brave. He was in such danger, always—and he knew it. "Go to Luke," he always told me—' She broke down again.

'You did exactly as he said,' Ellie soothed. 'And Anthony was right—Luke will keep you safe, I'm sure of it. But Monique—what happened to your husband? He was in the British army, wasn't he?'

Monique was gazing at Ellie with grief-filled eyes. 'Yes, he was in the British army. But he was betrayed. He was the most courageous man in the world—but even he could not save Les Braves.'

'Les Braves,' Ellie echoed. The Heroes. The letter in Lord Franklin's library. *I would suggest that we give our instructions to the group known as Les Braves...*

'Indeed, that's what they called themselves. They laughed about the risks they ran, they took life and death lightly, but they were truly heroes indeed, and they were sent to their deaths through treachery—' Her voice broke. 'And now I'm tired. So tired.'

Gently Ellie wrapped a blanket around her, and Monique leaned back against the wall with a little sigh, her eyelids already drifting shut. Ellie sat there with her mind whirling.

'Anthony was betrayed,' Luke had once said. 'Betrayed by high-ranking cowards.'

She reminded herself that Luke Danbury was in conflict with the law. He had stolen her father's precious compass to force her to get access to Lord Franklin's library. He was using her with a cold ruthlessness she felt she'd scarcely yet glimpsed.

And yet—she'd never met a man who'd made such an impact on her. A man who made a bone-deep longing for *something* surge through her veins with simply one look of his. Even down here, in the coldness of this underground hideout, heat flooded her anew at the memory of that afternoon in the garden when he'd trapped her in the snow-covered pavilion, trapped her with his hands cupping her cheeks and his mouth sweetly tasting hers…

For almost two years she'd been on the run. She'd been in fear for her life—but never, she realised, had she been as truly afraid as she was now, because she'd made herself terribly vulnerable, thanks to the wild emotions this man aroused in her.

And she could not afford to give way to such treacherous feelings, because Luke was absorbed in the fate of his brother and in some feud with Lord Franklin. He'd been engaged to an heiress—Mary had told her so—and quite likely wanted her back, so she, Ellie, must remember that she had no place in his future at all.

Monique and Harry slept on as the minutes went by. Ellie sat alert with the pistol in her pocket, although she got quickly to her feet when she thought she heard heavy footsteps upstairs and the sound of doors slamming, followed by gruff, questioning voices. She hurried to extinguish the solitary lantern and felt her heart hammering. *If the soldiers come down here and find us…*

Silence returned. She sat and tried to relax, but jumped to her feet the instant she heard the low door opening. Already she had her pistol drawn. Monique woke and was on her feet, too, gasping in French, *'Oh, God help us…'*

It was Tom. 'It's all right for you to come up now, miss.'

'They've gone?' asked Ellie quickly. She handed him back the pistol.

'They've gone,' answered Tom in a grim voice. 'But they've hurt the captain, the wretches.'

'Why?'

'He objected to their demands to search the house— but the officer in command told him to keep his mouth shut, and they all looked round anyway. Of course they didn't find a thing to charge him with and that made them mighty cross. So afterwards they dragged him outside for questioning.' He scowled darkly. 'Well, they *called* it questioning. But I heard it, and what they *really* did was taunt him for quitting the army. Taunt him about his brother.'

His brother again. Ellie felt her heart pounding. 'And he just had to stand there and take it?'

'He didn't *have* to, miss. He could have taken on the lot of them and we'd have helped him—I was with the captain in the war, in Spain, and it's hard to see a friend of yours being abused with lies, you know? But he told us—the Wattersons and me—before they came for him, to stay well out of it. He said, "Lads, they're not worth it." Of course, he's right. And let me tell you this, ma'am—there's lots of things been said about Captain Luke Danbury, but he's as good and brave a man as you'll find in the land.'

Ellie stood stricken. *Then why did he live like this, so shabbily, so disreputably? Why did he have such bad enemies?*

'Anyway,' Tom said gruffly, shining the lantern around the room, 'the French lady and her little boy—they've survived their ordeal, miss?'

'They're quite all right,' Ellie said. 'As you'll see.' She'd noted that Monique had already gone to Harry and lifted the sleeping child in her arms. 'But they need to get back to their bedroom, Tom. They need to be warm and comfortable.'

'Of course. And Captain Danbury's waiting to speak to you, miss, in the dining hall.'

Once they were out of the cellar, Mrs Bartlett herded

Monique and Harry away like a mother sheep with her lambs. And—*Now*, thought Ellie. *Now, I must get Luke to tell me everything.*

He was standing with his back to her, gazing into the fire. But he must have heard her footsteps, because he turned slowly round.

And she saw that one side of his face was marked by a livid bruise. She moistened her lips to speak, but could say nothing, because he was coming towards her, his eyes inscrutable. As though nothing at all had *happened.*

'I gather,' he said, 'that you kept Monique and her little boy safe and calm. I'm extremely grateful to you.'

She was shaking her head. Her heart was thundering against her ribs. 'Luke. I'm so *sorry* about all this. If only I'd warned you—'

He was close enough now to touch her. She gazed blindly up at him. Oh, his face. Lean, stubbled. Beautiful. Even with that fresh bruise, everything about him was beautiful, and she so wanted to trust him—and for him to trust *her*—that it hurt.

'Let me repeat, Ellie,' he said. 'I don't honestly think, even if you'd told me what Lord Franklin said, that I could have done anything to stop those soldiers turning up here and searching the place. Do you?'

'Perhaps not,' she breathed. 'But what did they want?'

His eyes still burned into her. 'I told you—there was a vague rumour about Frenchmen landing, but they had no proof. There are always stories about smugglers and foreigners along this part of the coast.'

He was making light of it for her sake, she knew. 'But to pick on *you*. Tom told me. Your face—'

'My fault. I started it.'

He gave a bleak smile, but Ellie didn't smile back. 'Luke,' she said, 'do you think it was Lord Franklin who ordered this?'

He was walking slowly over to the fire, but at that he swung round. 'What can I say about him, Ellie? When many people think that he's your protector and saved you from poverty and homelessness?'

'But surely,' she cried out, 'you remember that I ran from him, although you ordered me to go back? I never, ever felt I could truly trust him! And now I know it for sure—because he's no relative of mine! You suspected this from the start, didn't you, Luke? *Didn't* you?'

He didn't answer at first, but Ellie felt how the air in the room resonated with tension.

'It did occur to me,' he said. 'But how did you find out for certain?'

She shrugged. 'I suppose I found out in the traditional manner of scheming females everywhere. It was a simple matter of eavesdropping.'

'Eavesdropping?'

'I heard him talking to his mother, the formidable Lady Charlotte. By the way—did you realise her ladyship can *walk*?'

Luke's eyebrows lifted in surprise. 'No! The old schemer—after attention, I suppose. Tell me what you heard of her conversation with Lord Franklin.'

'It was short and to the point. He was instructing her that I must never, ever, be allowed to guess that he lied to me about my mother being some distant cousin.'

He'd come over to her again—close, *too* close, and her heart shook because suddenly she wanted more than anything to lean into his strength, his warmth. But she had to be strong, she *had* to be.

'You're right,' he said at last. 'I *did* suspect something of this from the start. And, Ellie, you need expert advice—guidance—on this. Lord Franklin is a powerful man.'

'So I gather,' she said, still trying to keep her voice light. 'With powerful friends and hidden motives. I already guessed as much, when I found that my room had been searched in London.'

'You found…'

'Yes. Someone had been through all my things. Nothing was taken, and everything was put back very carefully. But I knew.'

He nodded, frowning. Believing in her, she realised. 'Is there anyone else you can talk to?' he asked. 'Anyone else in London, whom you can go to for help? Some of the other French *émigrés*, perhaps?'

She gazed up at him, her eyes very bright. 'I know no one in London. Lord Franklin made completely sure of that. Anyway, who would listen to me? Who would believe me if I tried to speak out against Lord Franklin, of all people?'

'I would,' he said softly. '*I* would.'

Something in the way he said it—something in the way he was watching her—made her blood pound and her breath tighten in her throat.

The door opened and Tom was there. 'A word, Captain,' he said.

Ellie watched Luke leave the room, feeling something unfurling almost painfully inside her. Society scorned Luke Danbury, and certainly he made no attempt at all to present himself as a gentleman. But every word he spoke seemed filled, to her, with honour and integrity.

And that bruising on his face tore at her very heart-strings.

She would never forgive herself for letting her father's compass fall into Luke's hands. She still very much feared that her association with him could be disastrous. But all the same, just the brush of his fingers against her wrist sent shivers racing through her blood. And the way that he spoke her name—almost with tenderness—pulled at some corner of her heart that she hadn't even known existed.

As the light of the tallow candles flickered softly around the room, she went to sit at the big table and rested her face in her hands. As a child in Paris, she'd been a sheltered innocent, secure and happy in the love of her parents. By the time she might have started thinking as other girls did of pretty clothes and flirtations, she was absorbed in caring for her sick mother—and then, after her mother's funeral, she and her father were on the run together, travelling by night, hiding by day.

If, during those terrible months, Ellie gave any thought at all to her appearance, it was to make sure that she drew absolutely no attention to herself.

'I'm so sorry, Ellie. Really I am,' her father would say fretfully as he gazed at her travel-worn clothes. 'You should be enjoying yourself at parties, with friends. I can only hope that some day, when our running is at an end, you will find a man to love you as much as I loved your dear mother.'

She would stop him by hugging him and saying, over and over, 'Papa, I'm lucky to have you. I don't need anybody else.'

Or so she'd thought. But Luke! Luke only had to come into the room for her to feel that she wanted something from him in a way that she'd never wanted anything before. And the last thing she needed was for him to guess it.

Thinking she heard footsteps—*him, coming back*—she tried to gather her scattered thoughts and reached for a book that lay open on the table.

And her heart shook again with poignant memories, because it was a star atlas—just like the kind her father used to own. She gazed blindly at its pages, overwhelmed with emotion, while almost without her realising it, Luke came back in to draw up a stool and sat next to her.

You ought to send her back now, you fool, Luke told himself. The chilling voice of conscience inside his soul, inside his heart, was chiding him as bitterly as it had ever done in his life.

Ellie Duchamp was brave and vulnerable and alone. She was also quite possibly the most beautiful girl he had ever laid eyes on—especially since she wasn't even *aware* of her own beauty. She conducted herself with integrity and honesty through a life that must have been difficult beyond belief—and did she never even look in a mirror? Had no man ever told her that she had the most exquisite figure and a face that most men could only picture in their dreams?

He clamped down hard on the freshly surging desire that flooded his body and looked, as she did, at the star atlas. The book was open at the constellation of Orion. 'This book was my brother's,' he said quietly to her. 'Anthony knew and loved the night sky. Do you know anything about the stars, Ellie?'

'My father...' she began in a halting voice. 'My father loved the stars, too...'

Tears were glittering in her eyes, he noticed. He also

noticed that she was trying to wipe them away without him seeing.

'Ellie,' he said, 'I'm sorry about this. About involving you. About everything that's happened.'

'Don't,' she said, almost with fierceness. She'd pushed the star atlas aside jerkily and got to her feet, almost knocking her stool backwards. 'None of what's happened to me is your fault. It's mine. Do you hear me? I was a fool to trust Lord Franklin. A fool. I've made so many *mistakes...*'

Luke suppressed a low oath. She'd gone to stand with her back to him, gazing out of the window at the night sky above the sea; perhaps looking for the familiar winter stars that Anthony had loved so much.

He felt himself quite shaken by the urge to protect her. And more.

The best thing you can do, he told himself bitterly, *is to send her back to Bircham Hall and never, ever see her again.*

But he couldn't. It was as simple as that. He couldn't bear the thought of her leaving his life. Especially when she turned to him and whispered, 'Please, Luke. Tell me about your brother.'

And he did.

Chapter Eighteen

'Anthony,' Luke began, 'was two years younger than me. Our mother died giving birth to him and we saw very little of our father, who spent most of his time living the high life in London and trying to kill himself with drink. He died when I was ten.'

He ushered her back to a chair by the fire and sat close to her. 'It was my grandfather, Edward Danbury, who ran this house and the tenant farms—but times were difficult during the war, although he did his very best to hold the estate together.

'Anthony was always desperate to join the army. And when our grandfather died in 1810, Anthony went to join the Hussars in the Peninsula. As the heir, I stayed to look after the estate. But it was heavily burdened with debts.'

He shrugged, as if it were of no matter, but she saw how his blue eyes were haunted with memories. 'I did my best,' he went on, 'to hold everything together, arranging more loans to keep the farms going. At first Anthony wrote to me regularly, about the campaigns and the battles against the French. He wrote that the stars were different, there in Spain…'

He was staring into the fire, and Ellie saw how the light from the flames was flickering softly against his profile. *That bruise.* It hurt her almost unspeakably to think of him defying the soldiers, for the sake of his brother's wife and child.

Why had he become such an outcast? She clasped her fingers in her lap and found she was imprinting his features in her memory: the mane of dark hair, the proud brow and strong nose, the stubble-roughened jaw and expressive mouth. It must be past midnight and here she was, in this dangerous house, alone with this dangerous man—but she wouldn't have wanted to be anywhere else. Anywhere in the world.

And his eyes were bluer and more intense than ever as he turned to her and began talking again. 'After my brother had been in the army for a year or so, someone— Wellington himself, quite possibly—discovered that he spoke fluent French and Spanish. Anthony was recruited to the British secret service and was sent on a mission to the south-west of France, to make contact with the Royalist rebels who were fighting there to defeat Napoleon and get their exiled king back on the French throne.

'In the spring of last year—as you'll know—Napoleon's armies were defeated and Napoleon himself was banished to Elba. In the meantime, my brother had disappeared in France—either a prisoner or dead. A natural risk of the job, some might say. But I had reason to believe he was betrayed by the people he worked for. By the British secret service.'

She whispered, 'How do you know this, Luke?'

'Because I'd joined the army myself,' he said. 'As you know. I shouldn't have gone. I shouldn't have abandoned the estate, the farms. But I did, and by the October of

1813 I had crossed with Wellington and his army over the border into France. After that we were pretty much stuck there for the winter—Wellington wanted to wait till spring for the weather to improve, before striking up north towards Paris. But there were skirmishes with the enemy still, and one December night I was put in charge of a group of French prisoners. It turned out that one of them had known my brother.'

Ellie could see that Luke was gazing into the fire again now, as if this room, this house didn't exist. As if he was far, far away with the army in France.

'This French prisoner,' Luke went on, 'had been wrongly captured. They'd thought he was Napoleon's man. He wasn't. He was on *our* side, involved in encouraging rebellion against Napoleon in the south-west of France with a band of soldiers led by my brother. This prisoner—my brother's friend—was called Jacques.'

'Oh, Luke. Monsieur Jacques. I met him here, didn't I?'

Luke nodded. 'You met him, yes. And that winter night in Spain, Jacques told me how in the autumn my brother and several others—including Jacques—had carried out a dangerous mission for their London masters, delivering English guns and English ammunition to the resistance groups fighting Napoleon around La Rochelle. It was—supposedly—a prelude to English troops arriving. Anthony's orders were to make the deliveries, gather information, then go to the harbour at La Rochelle after midnight, to wait there for an English navy ship that would take him and his comrades, called Les Braves, back to London, to make their report. The ship never arrived. They'd been abandoned by their English masters.'

A betrayal. Just as Monique had said. 'Why?' Ellie whispered.

She saw Luke was flexing his right hand in its glove. 'My guess is,' he said evenly, 'that the government decided my brother and his friends were of no use any more. They'd served their purpose. They'd done what they were told to do—they'd supplied Napoleon's enemies, England's allies, with arms. As for the scheme to send over British troops next, to increase the pressure on Napoleon's army—' He shrugged. 'Everyone knows that the various ministers are always falling out—the heads of the Home Office and the Foreign Office, the Admiralty and the chiefs of the army. And perhaps someone decided the scheme was too expensive. Whatever the reason, it appears that the plans were cancelled. Buried. Which meant that my brother and his friends were doomed. Not only was their usefulness over, but they knew too much—which meant, as far as certain English politicians were concerned, that Les Braves were better off dead.'

Ellie made a low sound of horror.

'And so,' Luke went on, 'as I've said, the navy boat that was meant to pick them up from La Rochelle never arrived. My brother ordered his companions to split up and head inland, but some persisted in waiting by the harbour, still believing they would be rescued. Instead, they were captured by the enemy and shot.

'Jacques told me how he and my brother were separated in flight. Jacques knew that the English army had crossed the Pyrenees by then, into French territory, so he walked for days to reach the English camp where I was. He foolishly believed that if he told the English officers what had happened, how Anthony and his companions had been betrayed, then they might send men to look for my brother and other survivors. Jacques, in his naivety—' he gave a bitter laugh '—even hoped there might be some kind of retribution for the way Les Braves had been betrayed. Instead, Jacques was herded up with all the other French prisoners. As if he was one of England's enemies.'

Luke seemed to Ellie for a moment to be lost in thought. At last he spoke again. 'That night, I went to protest about Jacques's captivity to my commanding officer. But he announced that Jacques's fate was none of my business—I think he'd got wind of some War Office intrigue in the background, of some dirty business that needed to be kept secret. He told me that Jacques was to be kept where he was, and I guessed that one night soon Jacques would be found dead, to keep him from talking to anyone else. So I went back to him that night. I gave him money and I set him free—on condition that he try to find my brother.

'By then, I had resolved to resign my commission and to join Jacques in the hunt for Anthony. But within a week of Jacques escaping, an outbreak of typhus fever swept the camp and, along with hundreds of others, I was laid low. Many men died that winter—but not me. I had something to live for. I was going to survive, whatever it cost me, because I had one purpose in my life.'

'To find your brother,' Ellie said softly.

Luke had seen how the sympathy shadowed her face as he told his story. He nodded. 'To find my brother. To get *justice* for my brother. To uncover the men—the proud, powerful Englishmen in London—who had betrayed him and his comrades. By February I was just about able to travel, but was no longer considered fit to fight and was sent home. And I realised, when I got to this house, that Jacques had been trying to get in touch with me—to tell me that as yet, he'd found no proof that my brother was dead.

'Before long, Jacques arrived here—he'd acquired a fishing vessel and a loyal crew. I travelled to the French coast and back with Jacques, again and again. I sold up the remaining treasures of this house, to fund the search and pay for information, and together Jacques and I and his crew roamed all along the coast around La Rochelle and into the hinterland, searching for news of Anthony and Les Braves, hearing also how the British army had defeated Napoleon's generals at Toulouse and Napoleon had abdicated. Summer came—Jacques and I continued our hunt, but I was careless. I was captured by some French renegades who were still loyal to Napoleon. They thought I was merely a smuggler and let me go—after cutting two of my fingers off.'

Ellie let out a low gasp. 'Why?'

He gave her a bitter smile. 'I thought you might have known, since it's a traditional punishment the French like to inflict on their English enemies. Long ago, the battle of Agincourt was won largely thanks to the English archers, and in subsequent battles of that era, the French, if they took any English prisoners, cut off the first two fingers of their right hands, to make sure they would never use longbows again.'

'I'm sorry,' she breathed.

He shrugged. 'I've got used to it. After that, Jacques brought me home. He tried to tell me—in a *polite* way— that since I could no longer fire a pistol or wield a sword, I was as well staying here, in England. He was right, of course. The estate badly needed my attention—I'd been wrong to neglect it for so long. And besides, Jacques reminded me there were still things I could do.' He looked at her steadily. 'For instance, I could turn my attention to Lord Franklin Grayfield.'

She met his gaze without flinching. 'I know, now, that he works for the government.'

Luke nodded. 'Indeed. Lord Franklin is actually very highly placed, as an unofficial adviser to the Foreign Office. He's highly skilled in languages and diplomacy. He's entrusted with many vital and secret matters by government ministers—and during our last leave together, in the summer of 1813, Anthony told me that he suspected Lord Franklin knew everything about the planned venture to La Rochelle in September. I went to confront Lord Franklin in London, three months ago—but his lordship ordered his footmen to march me out of the house and told me that if I didn't stop investigating the betrayal, he would ruin me.'

He heaved in a breath. 'All in all, I had very little to lose—so of course, I *didn't* give up. That's why Lord Franklin hates me.'

'Do you think he sent the soldiers tonight?'

'It's possible. He could easily have sent them orders from London, to visit this house as a warning that I'm still being watched. To remind me that I should keep quiet about matters that don't concern me.' He shrugged. 'Perhaps I should take heed. Perhaps there is absolutely nothing I can do—'

Ellie broke in. 'But perhaps there *is*, Luke! I told you. I got into Lord Franklin's library today and I found letters in there. In particular, I found a letter to Lord Franklin about a British landing, from someone high up in government, telling him that the Les Braves expedition was to go ahead. There was probably more—so much more—and I could get it for you. You must let me help you!'

He'd gone very still. 'So it's there. But it's far too

dangerous. God above, I've already put you through too much. I can't—I *won't* ask you to do any more.'

'You don't have to ask me, because I'm offering. Please, Luke! And while you think about it, let me tell you the truth about my father.'

'Ellie,' he said quietly, 'have you thought properly about this? Doesn't it occur to you that I could be completely the wrong person for you to confide in?'

She lifted her face to his and he found her so poignantly brave, yet at the same time so vulnerable, that he felt his heart ache for her. 'Hasn't it occurred to *you*,' she answered, 'that at this moment I feel you're perhaps the only person in the world that I can trust?'

And that was it, Luke thought. Just those few, quiet words—and he was unarmed. He could no more turn her away than he could strike her or hurt her. She was more beautiful than he'd believed possible; heat was pooling in his loins, and a new, unbidden danger was lurking now. His desire to take her into his arms and never, ever let her go.

She trusted him. He balled his left hand into a fist, to remind himself to keep well away from her. 'Tell me,' he said, 'about your father.'

And she told him. He poured them both wine, then sat again and listened, marvelling that this delicate girl-woman should have endured so much. He listened, as she spoke in her low, musical voice; not looking at him but gazing into the fire, as if by staring at the flames she could resurrect everything she'd stored away in her heart.

'What most people don't realise,' she began softly, 'is that even after the Revolution, life in France was truly terrible for the ordinary people. They couldn't find work.

They starved. But Napoleon promised to get trade and commerce moving again. He offered people the precious gift of hope.'

She drew a deep breath. 'Napoleon employed my father to design roads. Roads were a vital part of the Emperor's plan, you see, to make France prosperous for *all* her people, and that was my father's desire, too. But gradually my father grew to realise that Napoleon no longer wanted those roads for the good of France, but for his armies. Napoleon wanted to conquer the world. And poverty grew in France again, because the war drained the country of men and money.

'When my mother died—' Ellie's voice broke, just a little '—my father tried to offer his resignation, but Napoleon refused to accept it. In fact, Napoleon was offended and angry, which meant that my father and I had to flee the country. I was seventeen and we were pursued, because I think Napoleon feared my father might try to sell his skills to a rival power.'

'Did your father ever consider that?'

'Never.' She shook her head firmly. 'He was no traitor. He decided we'd head for Le Havre first—he hoped to meet up with some relatives of my father's, but they no longer lived there. Then we realised our pursuers were on our trail again, and we had to head north...' Briefly she pressed her hand to her forehead, and again Luke felt a surge of pity when he saw the flash of vulnerability in her eyes, so quickly hidden.

'Many times,' she went on steadily, 'we were nearly caught by the Emperor's men. At last, we reached Brussels, and there we thought we were safe. But my father never really recovered from the hardships of our travelling. He caught a fever and became gravely ill.'

She was staring into the flames of the fire again. Luke spoke at last. 'Lord Franklin,' he said. 'Where does he come into it?'

She looked at him. 'He found me,' she said, 'last summer. He told me that he was in Brussels because, with the war being over, he was able at last to fulfil his dream of making a tour of all of Europe's museums and galleries. You know that he collects art?'

'I do,' answered Luke calmly. 'His passion for art is, I believe, genuine. But I also know that it provides an extremely useful cover for his other activity—working for the government.'

'Of course,' she breathed. 'Of course. And he offered to take me to London—I would have preferred to stay in Brussels, but my father knew he was dying and made me swear to accept Lord Franklin's offer of protection. I had to keep my promise. Do you understand?'

Luke nodded. *Once this passionate girl gave you her word*, he thought, *she would never willingly break it*. And once she gave you her heart—oh, her heart would indeed be worth possessing.

He realised she was still speaking. 'Lord Franklin,' she went on, 'took me to London. But in London, as I told you, I guessed—I was *certain*—that my room had been searched. Lord Franklin denied everything, of course—he told me I had an over-vivid imagination, and he banished me here. As I've also told you, I've since found out that he lied about being my mother's relative—why, I don't know.'

'From what you've told me,' Luke said, 'I think it quite probable that Lord Franklin took you into his care, in the full knowledge that your father worked for Napoleon— and in the strong hope that you might have vital information about the Emperor.'

'What information?'

'The names of Napoleon's supporters? Of his contacts?'

'But I know *nothing*.'

He saw that she was white with tiredness. 'I understand that. Listen, Ellie, we'll have to talk further about this. I'll need to give it some thought, but we'll do it at some other time, because you must be exhausted.'

He thought he saw her shoulders slump a little. 'But, Luke—'

'I believe,' he cut in, 'that Mrs Bartlett has prepared a room for you.' He was already picking up a candlestick. 'It's almost one in the morning, and it won't be possible, I'm sure you realise, to get you back into Bircham Hall at this hour. In the meantime, you'll perhaps be able to get a few hours' sleep here—'

He broke off abruptly. He'd been about to light the candle from the fire using his injured hand, but somehow he dropped the pewter candlestick and it clattered heavily on the hearthstone. Even as he bent to pick it up, Ellie saw him clamping down, hard, on his self-disgust. And suddenly, she found herself brimming over with emotion. *His crippled hand.* How he hated it. How he hated—himself.

He was trying to light the candle again. She went over to him and touched his arm. 'Luke.'

He swung round. 'What is it?' he said almost harshly.

She felt her heart breaking for this proud, wounded man, punishing himself so. 'I wish we hadn't met like this,' she said quietly. 'I wish everything had been different.' She reached up to touch his face, letting her fingers flutter oh so lightly over the bruise on his cheek, and Luke thought he saw the brightness of unshed tears in her eyes. Then she let her fingertips drift down to his lips.

'Ellie.' He almost bit out her name. 'This is no good. You're doing yourself no favours.'

'*You* are good for me,' she said softly. 'You're a good man, Luke. I feel safe with you.'

Then you shouldn't, he wanted to urge her. *In God's name, you shouldn't*.

But he was lost, utterly vanquished by what he saw in her eyes. He wove his fingers in her hair and pulled her face to his, gazing at her for precious, precious moments, and he thought he heard her whisper his name, just at the moment he touched his mouth to hers.

And he kissed her.

He clasped her close, breathing in her scent, her sweetness. She wrapped her slender arms around him, pressing herself against him. After that… After that there was no time for regret, only for the calamitous onslaught of passionate desire. As the longing thudded through his body, as he tasted her sweet mouth with his tongue and heard her let out a soft moan in her throat, he groaned and pulled her closer, feeling the slenderness of her waist as she kissed him back—and as he lifted his left hand to feel her breasts through the cloth of her grey gown, he was aware of her shuddering with need, drawing closer to him.

He knew he could have lifted her in his arms and carried her up to his bed, and made love to her in full. She was ready for him, her nipples were taut with desire; he could feel the soft curves of her lower body as she instinctively sought to press herself against his pulsing hardness, and whether she knew it or not, with every gesture of her innocent yet seductive body she was begging for him.

God help her, she was utterly desirable—and utterly vulnerable. Nineteen years old, an orphan and a friendless refugee. And he guessed that she'd guarded herself so fiercely in the past that she'd never even allowed a man to *touch* her before.

Until she met him, Luke Danbury. And now she was urging him with every breath in her body to make love to her. Now she was offering herself to him completely. She'd said that she trusted him.

That was why, with one of the greatest efforts of his life, Luke forced himself to drag his lips from hers, and pulled away.

Her lips were swollen, her green eyes were dark with need. Her lovely thick hair fell in voluptuous disarray around her face and shoulders. And his own fiercely aroused body was still thudding with longing for her. He gritted his teeth. 'I'm sorry,' he said. 'I shouldn't have done that. It was a mistake.'

And she stepped back as if he'd struck her. *You fool,* he told himself. *You utter, careless fool.*

Chapter Nineteen

Luke led her upstairs to a tiny bedroom where a fire burned in the grate. Ellie felt blinded with emotion. He hardly spoke to her again. Hardly even *looked* at her. What had happened? What had she done? Was it *her* fault?

'I think,' he said flatly as he stood by the door, 'that you'll find everything you need in here. I'll see that you're woken before dawn, and my men can get you home. I hope you get some sleep.'

Then he was gone.

She leaned her back against the door and listened to his footsteps fading. Something was hurting so badly deep inside her that it was as if a vital part of her had been torn away.

Luke was right. Whatever had happened between them must never happen again—she knew that. But ever since that kiss in the snow-covered garden, she'd lost her sense of what was right and what was wrong. She just longed, whenever he was near, for him to touch her—to kiss her and more.

Remembering what had just happened between them made her shake. She'd never known, never imagined, that a man's lips and tongue could create such a shockingly intimate caress. Had never dreamed that his hands on her sensitive breasts could send such heat and such yearning flooding through her to her very core.

But her body had known how to respond, there was no doubting it. She sat down on the bed and bowed her head, remembering how she'd clung to him. How she'd let her palms rove across his back, marvelling at the strength of his muscles while at the same time pulling him closer to her, inch by inch…

Dieu du ciel. So foolish of her. And yet she hadn't been able to help herself.

It was impossible that there could be anything further between them, and that was what he'd been trying to tell her. That was why he'd been trying to push her away, because he'd known very well that she was beyond reasoning. He was a man with a tormented past, scarred mentally as well as physically, and his whole being was embittered by what had happened to his brother. Besides—it came back to her with a jarring sense of hopelessness—he'd been in love already, he'd been rejected, and after that particular kind of betrayal, was he going to allow himself to become entangled with someone like *her*?

She, Ellie, was a homeless orphan. She belonged nowhere. Her father had worked for Napoleon.

And in a few hours, I have to get back to the Hall. I have to pretend that none of this has happened at all.

She sat on the bed and stared at the wall. Luke Danbury was a man who had chosen to live on the very fringes of normal society. He was trying to revive his estates by working the land himself, thereby alienating his landowning neighbours and attracting rumours that he collaborated with the free traders and with the French.

He was a bitter man with a vengeful heart; he was using her, as he no doubt used everyone he came into contact with. And yet—and yet...

She believed everything he'd told her about his brother and Les Braves. She completely understood his overwhelming determination to clear his brother's name. She believed in his courage, believed in his integrity. But the way he despised himself almost broke her heart.

She slept at last, only to dream of him as she turned restlessly on her pillow. She dreamed of his brother, Anthony, gazing out to sea through the long night at La Rochelle, waiting for the British navy vessel to take him home. But instead, Anthony was betrayed—and Luke had guessed all along that Lord Franklin was involved in that betrayal.

As for her—Luke Danbury had resolved to use her, and now he felt pity for her, because she was alone and friendless. That was all.

But when he touched her, her body was on fire for him. And that was what really, really frightened her. On fire for him.

She was wakened early by a knock at her door. 'It's six o'clock, ma'am.' It was Mrs Bartlett's hesitant voice. 'Time for you to be up, the captain says. If you please, ma'am.'

Ellie rose quickly and dressed—she'd slept in her chemise. When she got downstairs, the captain's men were gathered in the kitchen, talking together over coffee and bacon and eggs. She saw Luke there in their midst.

He turned to her and her heart shook as the memory of that kiss last night rippled through her, melting her insides again. Yet now he looked remote, almost forbidding. She would guess that he hadn't slept at all; she could see there were shadows under his eyes, and his jaw was dark with unshaved beard.

His face was expressionless as he came over to her. 'My men are ready to take you back to Bircham Hall. Joseph has been warned to look out for you and he'll let you in at the side entrance.' He drew a deep breath and lowered his voice. 'You've done all I could have asked and more. But you must *not* try to get into Lord Franklin's library again, under any circumstances.'

She gazed up at him. 'But you need to clear your brother's name!'

'I'll do it myself,' he said.

'So there's nothing more you want me to do?'

He shook his head. 'Not at all. It's too dangerous for you to be involved.'

'I've told you. I don't *mind*—'

'What I mean,' he said, cutting in, 'is that you will endanger me and my men if you are discovered. I should never have asked you—*forced* you—into doing what you did. And there will be no more of it.'

Ellie felt herself shaking inside, but she tilted her head proudly. 'I didn't think,' she said, 'that you were the kind of man to give up so easily.'

For a second Luke's blue eyes narrowed. Then he glanced over his shoulder towards his men. 'Josh,' he rapped out. 'Go and saddle up a pony for Miss Duchamp, will you?' He turned back to Ellie, and just for a moment she thought she saw a fierce, passionate regret burning in his eyes. 'Thank you,' he said. 'For what you did for Monique and Harry.'

She shrugged. '*Il n'y a pas de quoi.* It was no trouble.' But really she wanted to say, *Luke, I don't know what to do next. Because I cannot imagine not seeing you again, not being held in your arms again...*

She braced herself. Was already wrapping her cloak around herself, her head held high. Was already walking out into the courtyard, into the grey light of early dawn, where his man—Josh Watterson—was standing beside two saddled ponies.

Luke watched her ride off, sitting very straight in the saddle, in those clothes that were far too big for her, but which still couldn't hide the utter femininity of her figure. She was disappearing now, into the early morning mist.

And she didn't look back at him. Not once.

He took deep breaths of the fresh, cold air that blew in from the sea. He'd made hideous assumptions about the girl from the very start. He'd thought that she would be spoiled and silly, eager to come to London with the rich Lord Franklin in hopes of living in the lap of luxury and finding herself a rich English husband. He couldn't have been more wrong.

It sounded as though she'd lived through great danger and great hardship. Those months of flight must have been terrifying—he could imagine it only too well, travelling by night, living briefly in strange and alien places, always having to evade Napoleon's clever spies. She must have endured things that no well-bred girl should have to endure.

Then came her father's death—and Lord Franklin had taken her into his care, after falsely telling Ellie that he was a distant relative of her English mother's.

Why? Ellie had asked. Why would he do that?

And Luke had given Ellie what he was certain now was the answer—that Lord Franklin had hoped she might be in possession of information about Napoleon's agents, Napoleon's supporters—even perhaps the rumoured locations of the warehouses Napoleon was said to have stocked with quantities of arms in the event of his return from exile.

Though once Ellie had realised that someone had been searching her belongings and she'd tackled Lord Franklin with her suspicions, he'd banished her to the countryside. So she'd arrived, alone and lost, at Bircham Hall—and she'd played straight into Luke's hands, by letting him see her father's compass with its lethal inscription.

And hadn't he, Luke, treated her just as badly, just as cynically as Lord Franklin, by ordering her—compelling her—to get into Lord Franklin's library? And then—by *kissing* her?

He couldn't stop thinking about the way that she'd looked at him when he'd told her that by acting as she had, she was endangering him and his men. As if he'd stabbed her to the heart. Given her, in return for her loyalty and courage, another bitter taste of betrayal.

But, oh, her kiss had been sweet. If it hadn't been so early in the morning, he'd have been pouring some of Jacques's brandy down his throat in an effort to forget the scent of her dark curls, the taste of her silken lips, the feel of her soft breasts pressed against his chest. Last night, she'd been practically begging him to make love to her, and even now he felt the fierceness of *wanting* her spiking through his veins. The look in her eyes—the look that spoke of her belief in him, her trust—would stay with him for a long, long time.

She'd wanted him to make love to her; yes, him, with his damaged body and his bitter soul. And perhaps it

was the one honourable thing he'd done in his entire
dealings with her that he'd refused.

He realised suddenly that Monique had come out of
the house and was walking towards him, with her child
cradled in her arms. 'Monique,' he said. 'How are you
this morning? How is Harry?'

Luke's French was hesitant, but even so Monique
understood and smiled. 'We are well,' she said, softly
stroking her son's hair, 'thanks to you and that beautiful
French girl—the girl who was last night so kind to us.
So brave. Is she still here, Luke?'

He shook his head. 'Ah,' Monique sighed, 'I would
have liked to thank her properly. What is her name?'

'Ellie. Ellie Duchamp.'

Just then Luke's mare, Diablo, whickered in the
nearby stable and Harry reached out eagerly towards her.
With a laugh, Luke swung Harry into his own strong
grasp and held him up so he could stroke the mare's
glossy mane.

'Listen, Harry. We'll feed him together later on, shall
we?' Luke said. 'But now, I wouldn't be surprised if Mrs
Bartlett has something for *you*. Freshly baked bread, perhaps, and eggs she's just collected.' Carefully he handed
the little boy back to his mother.

'Thank you, Luke,' said Monique, 'for all your kind-
ness. And Ellie. You and she…?'

She let the question tail away.

'No,' he answered gently. 'No, there's nothing between us.'

'A pity,' she said and walked back into the house.

Luke stood there in the morning sunlight. Nothing.
There *had* to be nothing.

* * *

He got on with grooming Diablo until Josh returned to say that he'd got Ellie safely back into Bircham Hall without anyone except Joseph seeing her. Tom, meanwhile, had gone down to Bircham Staithe to gather what news he could about the soldiers last night, and after putting his mare back in her stable, Luke busied himself loading up a cart with some farming tools for one of his newest tenants, a young local man called Ned Rawling.

Ned was a former soldier who was trying to revive an area of arable land that had been abandoned during the war. A harrow and a hand plough, and some sacks of seed corn—Luke was piling them all on the cart, and would shortly be sending it off to Rawling, who had been told that the equipment was to be his for the next two months.

Rawling had looked disbelieving when Luke informed him of the loan. 'Captain, I can't even afford to pay you any rent!'

'I've told you before. You can pay me when your first harvest's in,' said Luke.

Now the cart was fully loaded and Pete Watterson was harnessing up a horse, ready to take it to Rawling's farm. But no sooner had Pete and the cart disappeared off down the track than Tom came riding into the yard.

'The soldiers have returned to barracks, Captain. And I heard they're being sent out on artillery exercises for the next few days, so they shouldn't be troubling us for a while.'

He hesitated and Luke narrowed his eyes. 'Nevertheless, you don't look very pleased. Is there something else you want to say to me, Tom?'

Tom put his hands on his hips. 'Yes. Yes, there is. And it's about the girl, Captain. The girl from Bircham Hall.'

Luke said quietly, 'Well?'

'You and me, Captain, we've known each other a long time.'

Luke's eyebrows lifted. 'We have. Anything else obvious that you care to state?'

'Yes. Yes, there *is*, and it should be obvious to you as well, Captain! If you ask me, that girl deserves a whole lot better than what you're doing to her, and that's a fact!'

'What exactly *am* I doing to her, Tom?' Luke's voice was dangerously polite. 'That she had to stay here for the night was unfortunate—but she slept by herself, in case you're wondering, and I've done my utmost to make sure she got back safe and unseen to the Hall this morning. What more could I do?'

Tom scratched his spiky hair. 'Even so—'

'I've told her,' Luke interrupted, 'that she is on no account to come near this place again. That she's on no account to do or say anything at all that would betray the fact that she and I have even met.'

His tone indicated that the discussion was over, but Tom stood exactly where he was, sighing and shaking his head.

'You know, Captain, sometimes I wish that you and I could just disappear. Start new lives somehow.'

Luke looked amused. 'What sort of new lives, Tom?'

'Now, *there's* the question.' Tom was still frowning, but then his face brightened suddenly. 'How about the pair of us going to Spain again? Do you remember all those little villages, far away from the cities and the battles? We could settle down in one of them, Captain! Grow oranges, perhaps, do some fishing. Drink wine with pretty Spanish *señoritas* at the local *taberna*...'

Luke laughed openly. 'I'd be bored witless within a week. And so would you.'

'No doubt you're right. And soon enough, you'd be sticking your nose in some business that wasn't your business at all. Just like you always do.'

'I'm righting wrong, Tom. Not sticking my nose in.'

'Well, Captain,' Tom said resignedly, 'whatever you want to call it, I'll be there at your side.'

'Glad to hear it,' said Luke calmly. 'Because I want you to come with me, now, over to the five-acre field by the ash plantation to help me dig some ditches.'

'You're not hoping to grow crops *there*?' Tom looked aghast. 'That field's been waterlogged for years!'

'Wheat grew there once. My grandfather told me.'

'Digging ditches,' Tom muttered. 'Your family's one of the oldest in the county. Your grandfather once had a dozen good farms and scores of men working the land for him—'

'That was a long time ago,' broke in Luke abruptly. 'And I'm not afraid of hard labour, are you? It's March, it's the planting season and there are jobs to be done. Get your horse ready and we'll head over there.'

Tom was already on his way to the stable, but Luke could hear him muttering. 'A rich heiress, Captain. That's what you should have found yourself. A rich heiress.'

Luke didn't actually mind physical labour, he reminded himself as he worked through the morning and into the afternoon with Tom—digging a ditch. He had never cared much for the way that wealth isolated you from the reality of how most people led their lives. He enjoyed the camaraderie of working in the fields with other men, and the sense of purpose he got from having obstacles to overcome and goals to achieve in trying to resurrect his estate.

The only advantage he could see in having money was that wealth might have given him more power. The power to get other men on his side, in the struggle to uncover the truth about his brother. Power to expose Lord Franklin. And perhaps to help and protect Ellie Duchamp.

Though it was Luke's fault now that the girl knew far too much for her own safety. With his spade, he heaved a fresh clod of earth out on to the bank and turned his face for a moment to the sun, listening to the shrill calls of the rooks in the nearby ash woods.

He hoped to God that Ellie would listen to what he'd said and stay away from the papers in that library. From now on it was up to him alone to get what he needed, because if Lord Franklin and his government colleagues ever knew what she'd done—what she'd *seen* in there— she could be arrested as a French spy. Even hanged as a French spy. *You fool, Luke. You selfish fool.*

It was almost two o'clock when Tom's voice alerted Luke to the sound of hoofbeats. 'Captain! Rider coming along the track!'

Luke turned sharply to see Josh Watterson galloping towards him, then pulling up his horse in a flurry of mud. 'There's news in the town, Captain. Napoleon's escaped!'

Tom had drawn up close. 'Ah,' he said scornfully, 'there's *always* wild stories about Napoleon.'

'Yes, but this time it's the truth! He's sailed away from that island of his, cool as you please, and got back to France. There's going to be war again.'

Tom Bartlett still looked doubtful. 'Steady there, Josh. Just because old Boney's escaped, it surely doesn't mean the whole French army will rise up for him, does it? And what about the new Frenchie King, who's just been crowned in Paris?'

'Running north as fast as he can towards Brussels, they say.' Josh had sprung from his horse and was gazing anxiously out to sea—as if expecting already to glimpse French ships on the horizon.

'Pah. He's spent his life running.' Tom turned to Luke. 'And, Captain, you and I know that by the time the British army had finished with them last year, Napoleon's soldiers were nothing but a starving rabble, all of them fed up to the back teeth of war and of their strutting little general!'

Luke took his time in answering. 'Napoleon has a strange effect on his men, Tom. I wouldn't be surprised if all his former soldiers flock to him again. In which case, King Louis will be begging the British and their allies to save his throne for him yet again.'

Josh was nodding. 'And there's something else, Captain. A rider from London told me Lord Franklin is on his way to Bircham Hall. He has guests travelling with him—important guests from the look of the carriages— and there's an armed guard, too.'

'Then I'd guess they'll be government men,' breathed Luke. 'Men of the highest rank, coming here to discuss in absolute privacy what to do about Napoleon. It sounds as if you might be right, Josh. It could be that the war is about to start all over again, one way or another.'

Tom's expression was sorrowful. 'So much for the wine and women in Spain.'

Luke nodded. 'It looks,' he said, 'as if you'll have to forget that particular dream for a while.'

Tom and Josh started talking earnestly to one another,

but Luke stood apart. If Anthony *was* still alive—a prisoner of the French—and if the war was about to break out anew, he was aware that Anthony's chances of survival were low. He had to act, and act soon.

And then—there was Ellie. How could he protect Ellie from the consequences of his own selfishness in dragging her into all this? *You must let me help you*, she'd said in her sweet, clear voice.

He couldn't let her. He'd already put her at grave risk by telling her too much, and he ought to get her to a place of safety, away from Lord Franklin's clutches. But he had to find Anthony. It was imperative that he find Anthony; he couldn't imagine a future without knowing that he'd done everything he could to save his brother.

Yet neither could he imagine a future without Ellie at his side. And that was impossible, he told himself. Impossible.

Chapter Twenty

When Ellie heard that Lord Franklin would be arriving at Bircham Hall that evening, she felt a cold sense of impending dread.

Not for herself—but for Luke.

She could not forget Lord Franklin's chilling threat. *To have Danbury at large, especially in the present circumstances, is intolerable. Something must be done.* She couldn't forget the soldiers who'd searched Luke's home and manhandled him. She thought of Monique and Harry—both mother and child so terribly vulnerable. So dependent on Luke.

Joseph had let her into the house that morning and got her safely up to her room. Mary had been a little quiet when she came to Ellie with her breakfast tray at eight, hurt no doubt to have been told last night by the maid Sarah that Ellie didn't need her. But later in the day Mary was distracted by the topic that now engaged the whole household. Indeed, the news that Lord Franklin was arriving here again threw all the staff into a state of near panic, especially as this time Mr Huffley had informed them that he wasn't coming alone, but with important guests.

They were due to arrive, Mary told Ellie excitedly, in the early evening—a rider had come from London to tell them so, soon after lunch. Footmen and bootboys, parlour maids and scullery maids; all had been set to clean and dust, to scrub floors and polish silver. Lady Charlotte spent the rest of the afternoon being wheeled around each of the reception rooms by her attendant footmen, giving the housekeeper her personal instructions about which flowers were to be brought in from the hothouse and generally glowing with self-importance.

'Bircham Hall,' she informed Ellie, 'has often hosted the grandest parties. And this time my son, I believe, will be bringing no lesser personages than the Home Secretary and the head of the Admiralty—they are all personal friends of his. "Bircham to me is a home from home, Lady Charlotte," the Foreign Secretary once said to me. Indeed, I wouldn't have been surprised if Franklin had told me that the prime minister himself was coming. He was here last year for two nights and he told me the hospitality at Bircham was incomparable—that was his precise word. Incomparable.' She looked around with satisfaction.

Miss Pringle followed Ellie around in nervous distraction. 'So wonderful,' she kept murmuring to Ellie, 'that his lordship is to be here again.'

Later that afternoon, Ellie retreated to her room, trying to read but unable to concentrate on a word. Since lunchtime, heavy clouds had swept in from the west, and outside the rain was pouring down—there would be no walks in the garden today.

Lord Franklin's visit *must* mean danger for Luke.

All day, she'd hardly stopped thinking about what had

happened at his house last night. She wanted to be alone with her memories of him and that kiss. She knew there could have been much more than a kiss. All the time, she'd wanted more with every fibre of her being.

She knew it was stupid of her, she knew it was wrong of her to give way to her feelings. But when her skin was still tingling from the memory of his touch, and her heart still shaking and her brain as scattered as the gusts of rain now battering against her window pane—then knowing what she *should* do was another matter entirely.

She'd truly hungered for him. Her body had been strung as tight as a violin string—not from dread or revulsion, but from the sheer longing that pounded in her veins as his beautiful mouth closed in on hers.

But he'd turned her down. *He'd turned her down.* Hadn't it been the only sensible thing to do? 'I'm sorry, Ellie,' he'd said, in a voice that chilled her to the bone because of the way he was distancing himself from her, drawing himself away. 'I shouldn't have done that. It was wrong of me. It was a mistake.'

Now she paced her room, hands clasped together in anguish. A bad mistake indeed, on her part—she'd been mad to let herself start feeling what she did for him, because he would not return her feelings. He'd known love in the past. Been let down by love, and now his brother was what mattered above all to him.

But last night it had seemed so easy to obliterate both past and future. Last night it would have been easy to forget everything, in that moment when his lips were on hers and his body hard against hers. His caresses had been soft as silk, but her knees had almost gone from under her as he drew her closer and his mouth moved against hers, warm and strong, and her breasts ached and a wave of pleasure rolled through her—pleasure so intense that she thought it might carry her away.

And, yes—she could no more have stopped herself from going to wherever his kisses were leading her than to stop breathing.

As well, then, she thought with bitter self-reproach, that *he* ended it—because she certainly couldn't have done.

It was almost six o'clock when Mary came in, full of excitement. 'Oh, miss. More news! Cook heard Mr Huffley talking to Mr Appleby. And Mr Appleby said that Napoleon's escaped!'

'But that's impossible, Mary…'

'No, miss! Mr Appleby says it will be in all the newspapers by tomorrow. And soon we'll be at war again, Mr Huffley says.'

Ellie clenched her hands, remembering what her father once said. 'At first, I thought Napoleon went to war simply to defend France from its enemies. But the fighting and the conquests went on and on, with thousands upon thousands dead. There *must* be an end to this war. There must be…'

She rose suddenly to her feet. *This* would be why Lord Franklin and his government friends were coming so suddenly to Bircham Hall. To talk in privacy about Napoleon. To talk about…war. Did Luke know? Would Luke be in danger? Would he try to do anything rash?

She realised that Mary was putting away some of Ellie's freshly laundered clothes and was saying, 'Now, miss, have you thought yet about what you're going to wear when Lord Franklin arrives? You'll surely want to look your best for his lordship's important guests. Perhaps you'll wear one of your fine London gowns?'

'No.' Ellie strove to keep her voice calm. 'I'll wear the grey gown.'

'Really, miss? You're sure?'

'Quite sure.'

Mary looked briefly crestfallen, but her face lit up with excitement again when Miss Pringle knocked on the door and hurried into the room. 'Elise? Oh, Elise, Lord Franklin has arrived with all his guests! And he wishes to introduce you to them. '

'Now? Before dinner?'

'Yes, indeed—you must come downstairs immediately!'

Lord Franklin saw Ellie the moment she walked into the drawing room and he came towards her with his face wreathed in smiles. 'Ah, Elise!' he called.

'My lord.' She curtsied and stayed where she was, but he quickly took her hand and led her to his companions.

'Elise,' he told them, 'is an orphaned relative of mine—a refugee from the turmoil in France. I was so very glad to be able to offer her a home here.'

'So generous of you, Lord Franklin,' she heard them all responding. 'So typically generous!' Though their eyes flickered over her with remarkably little interest and she was glad that in her drab gown, with her scraped-back hair and lowered eyes, there was little enough to hold their attention. *I can cope with this*, she told herself. *Soon they will forget I am here and I'll be able to slip away.* She barely registered any of their names or faces—until she saw him.

He was standing with his back to her. But when he

turned round, her blood ran cold. For it was the man with the pale eyes and the pale hair—the man she'd kept seeing in Brussels, whenever she ventured out of their attic apartment above Madame Gavroche's shop. The man she'd felt sure was following her.

He stepped forward and made a low bow as Lord Franklin introduced him to her. 'This is my secretary, Elise,' Lord Franklin was saying in a hearty voice. 'Gerald Malone.'

'*Mam'selle*,' said Gerald Malone softly. 'What a pleasure to meet you.'

This was the worst moment yet. The worst discovery yet.

Somehow, Ellie was able to hold herself steady. Somehow, she was able to acknowledge the man with the slightest of nods, as if she had not the slightest interest in him.

But this changed everything. This meant that not Napoleon's men, but Lord Franklin himself had been pursuing her and her father in Brussels.

By now Ellie was able to stay in the background, since Lady Charlotte was completely dominating Lord Franklin's guests with her strident account of the many comforts of Bircham Hall. 'You will find this place a true haven,' she declared. Ellie counted the moments until she was able to slip out unnoticed and make her way to the stairs. She had to get to the privacy of her room. To give herself time to think, before dinner was served.

But she halted on passing the library door, because to her surprise she could see it was open and the room was brightly lit. And someone was in there, standing by the bookshelves—Mr Huffley, the butler.

He looked up and saw her figure in the doorway. 'Miss

Duchamp,' he said. He looked even more harassed than usual. 'Are you searching for his lordship? I do believe he's in the drawing room.'

He was standing, she saw, by the shelves she'd examined yesterday. 'Thank you,' she said, 'but I've just come from there—I've already met Lord Franklin and his guests. You and your staff will be having a busy time, I fear, Mr Huffley.'

The butler sighed a little. 'Indeed. Such short notice. And what's more—' he waved his hand at the library shelves '—I've just been told by his lordship's business secretary that Lord Franklin needs to take certain files back to London when he returns—why, I've no idea. *"The files for 1813,"* Mr Malone said to me, curt as you please. *"The autumn of 1813."* Mr Malone said I was to transfer them to these boxes—' he indicated some packing cases on the floor '—and that he would check with me tomorrow morning that the right ones were packed. As if I can't be trusted with the task myself!'

He was muttering to himself by now, aware perhaps of his indiscretion in talking to her about Lord Franklin's secretary. But Ellie had heard enough. Her pulse was racing. Those files were to go to London? The very ones Luke wanted?

Mr Huffley looked at his watch and let out an exclamation. 'My goodness, is that really the time? Dinner will have to be served soon, and I haven't checked yet that the footmen have finished polishing the silver, or that the wine has been put out. I'll have to return to this later...'

Already he was hurrying towards the door, ushering Ellie out before him, turning the key in the lock. Outside in the corridor he mopped his brow. 'Miss Duchamp, may I ask you to take this key along to the housekeeper's room?'

'Of course,' Ellie said. 'Of course I will.' The butler hurried off towards the servants' staircase and Ellie stood alone, gazing at the big, cold key sitting in the palm of her hand. The vital evidence Luke needed was being taken from the library and sent back to London. Out of his reach, forever—unless she helped him.

Candles glimmered in the dining hall of Higham House, where Mrs Bartlett had just cleared away the remains of the evening meal. It was seven o'clock, and Luke and his men—Tom, the Wattersons and some of his chief tenants, men like Ned Rawling—had been studying maps of the Danbury lands and listening to Luke's plans for the fields which were to be ploughed and planted in the coming weeks.

But now Luke's men were talking about war. As an ex-soldier, Ned Rawling was anxious. 'If they're sending the British army to deal with Napoleon, Captain Luke, I might get called up again. I don't mind doing my duty. But there's the farm to think of now, and I've got my wife and little ones to care for.'

Luke tried to reassure him. 'I think it could be a while before it comes to war, Ned. And there should be soldiers enough already to defeat whatever troops Napoleon can summon up. Lord Wellington will have his Austrian and Prussian allies on his side as well, remember. So you must concentrate on your farm. On sowing your spring wheat and putting your ewes and lambs out to grass.'

The others murmured their approval. Ned nodded in relief.

'Thank you, Captain. The farm means the world to

me and my wife and two little ones. Some day I'll pay you back in full for everything, I promise.'

'I know you will,' said Luke quietly. 'But get the farm up and running before you worry about money. And remember that you're doing me a favour, too—for land that lies idle is of no use to man nor beast.'

Eagerly Luke's companions refilled their tankards from the pitchers of ale and began to talk again of lambing and crops and yields. But for a moment Luke's mind was far away.

Beyond the uncurtained windows, twilight was closing in, though against the darkening skies he could see the silhouettes of dozens of geese in flight, making for the nearby marshes to settle for the night. His men were immersed in plans for the future and memories of the past.

But Luke's mind was in turmoil. He couldn't stop thinking of the girl. Of the way she'd looked at him this morning, when he'd said to her that it was best if they didn't meet again.

For a moment, she'd looked stunned. Then she had shrugged and looked as if she didn't care—but Luke had seen that moment of raw fragility in her eyes and he knew what she'd be thinking. He knew she would see it as yet another rejection, another betrayal. But he had to keep telling himself that it was the only way. His only possible option.

There was a hurried knock on the door and Mrs Bartlett came in, looking agitated. 'Captain?'

Luke went over quickly to her.

'Captain,' she went on, 'Joseph's just sent over a messenger—a local lad—with this for you. He said to tell you that it's urgent.'

She handed Luke a folded, sealed sheet of paper, with his name written on it in a delicate feminine hand. And Luke realised, as soon as he took it, that the letter was wrapped tightly around—a key.

Chapter Twenty-One

Keep calm. Remember to hold your head high. Trying to fight down the knots of tension that twisted in her stomach, Ellie steadily descended the stairs to the reception hall, where Lady Charlotte had sent word that Ellie was to meet her before they went to join Lord Franklin and his guests in the dining room. The clock was chiming half past seven as Ellie reached the hall, and she saw straight away that her ladyship was already there, with her two silent footmen standing guard behind her bath chair.

There was an English expression that Ellie had once heard Mary use—*She had a face on her that could turn milk sour*—and how well those words described Lady Charlotte's look of utter fury when she saw Ellie. Her ladyship was dressed with great formality, in an old-fashioned purple satin gown encrusted with embroidery, and heavy jewellery on her neck and fingers.

And she looked at Ellie and said, '*What* do you think you have done to yourself?'

Ellie made a deep, deep curtsey. 'You are always telling me I should take more trouble with my appearance, your ladyship.'

'Yes? Yes?'

'So I did.'

'Of all the impertinent, insolent—' Lady Charlotte was searching for appropriate words to finish her tirade, but had to break off at the sound of the dinner gong being struck. Her lips pressed thinly together, she beckoned to her footmen to wheel her onwards into the dining room, with Ellie following in her wake.

And all eyes were on Ellie.

When they'd seen her earlier—when Lord Franklin had introduced her to them in the drawing room, with some vague words about her being a distant, orphaned relative—these men had let their eyes flicker over her with minimal interest—they'd been polite to her only for Lord Franklin's sake.

It was different now.

Less than half an hour ago, Ellie had set Mary to work. And now Ellie was wearing an exquisite, dusky-rose silk gown that clung to her slender figure and revealed her bare throat and the upper part of her breasts. She'd asked Mary to pile up her long dark hair in extravagant curls and Mary, her eyes gleaming with delight, had not only done so with some skill, but had also fixed a matching rose-red ribbon in her hair. 'Oh, miss,' Mary had exclaimed, stepping back in awe, 'you look beautiful!'

Ellie's attire was completely, utterly inappropriate for a young female who had not yet made her début in society. And Lord Franklin's guests—wealthy men, men of overwhelming power in the British government—were transfixed.

'*Messieurs*,' Ellie said, smiling. And curtseyed low to them.

* * *

All through the meal, even the well-trained footmen could hardly hide their astonishment at her transformation. What Lord Franklin thought was impossible to say, but he was a master at concealing his feelings. Ellie had never, ever seen that polite mask slip from his face—except when she'd told him, in London, that someone had searched her room.

Had that person been Gerald Malone? She'd not seen Malone in Lord Franklin's Mayfair house—but he was, without a doubt, the man who'd been following her in Brussels. He was sitting at the far end of the table now, and something cold trickled down her spine when she saw him suddenly lift his pale eyes to watch her.

He had tracked her down in Brussels for his master. *Lord Franklin probably hoped you had information about Napoleon*, Luke had suggested. *Names. Contacts.*

But Lord Franklin was a clever man, and now, as the first courses were brought in, Ellie's so-called protector hid his thoughts and emotions as well as ever, behaving towards her as if he were the caring relative he claimed to be. 'My long-lost French cousin' was how he described her again and again to his guests, as if she were an amusing trinket. 'I was so glad to be able to offer her a home here.'

'But what a shame,' they chorused, 'to hide such loveliness away in Kent!'

'It was her choice.' He turned to her. 'Wasn't it, Elise my dear?'

'Of course,' she answered softly.

He was amusing and polite, but Ellie saw how Lord Franklin's mouth said one thing and his eyes another.

Outwardly, he was appreciating the food and making light conversation. But his eyes were always moving, she'd noticed, always carefully scanning the company. He was listening, too, she realised, absorbing everything that was going on around him and aware of every murmur, every glance.

Especially since most of his guests' glances were directed towards Ellie, and that gown.

She smiled at them all demurely from beneath lowered lashes. She pretended to be lost sometimes for the appropriate English words, and the men competed to supply them for her. As the main courses were brought in, one of them said, 'It must be terrible for you, *mam'selle*, to hear that Napoleon Bonaparte is free again and is raising his army against France's rightful king. You were perhaps hoping that soon you might return to your homeland.'

Before Ellie could reply, Lord Franklin answered for her. 'There is no need to alarm Elise,' he said. 'No need to trouble her with politics. The rabble Napoleon calls his army will scatter soon enough. And Elise knows that, as my relative, she has a home with me for as long as she wants.'

'You should bring her to London, Franklin!' someone else was saying, glancing admiringly at Ellie. 'Truly, she'd take the *ton* by storm!'

Ellie saw Lady Charlotte give her a look of utter fury. But Ellie carried on play-acting. Flirting, even, until Lady Charlotte, almost puce with displeasure, announced when the desserts were about to be served that she and Ellie would retire to the parlour. 'We shall leave the gentlemen to their *important business*,' she said pointedly, 'of which there will no doubt be much. They can certainly do without silly distractions!'

The men competed to express their regret at her departure. 'Perhaps you will join us later, *mam'selle*?'

And another said, 'Lord Franklin has mentioned that you play the piano. It would be delightful if you could spare the time to entertain us!'

'I do hope so,' she said, smiling sweetly. 'It has been such a pleasure to meet you all.'

'Elise!' Lady Charlotte rapped out. 'Follow me, if you please!'

The minute they got outside, Lady Charlotte turned on her. 'You will go to your room for the rest of the evening, Elise. I will not have you insulting Lord Franklin and his distinguished guests a moment longer, with your state of—of *déshabillé*.'

'Very well, my lady.' Ellie curtseyed and walked steadily across the hall to the stairs.

Just what she wanted. To be dismissed. Just what she'd planned.

Then she heard the sound of dogs. Out in the grounds, baying in the distance. Her heart went cold. *Luke.* Had he received her message, and the key? Was he in the house yet?

If so, she had to to warn him. *Now.*

With the aid of the light of just one candle, Luke quickly explored the library. Joseph had let him in at the back of the house less than twenty minutes ago, then silently checked that all was clear as Luke unlocked the door to the library. After that Luke dismissed him. 'Go back to your work, Joseph,' he told him. 'I'll find my own way out.'

And he would—as soon as he'd got what he wanted.

From time to time, he heard the noise and laughter of Lord Franklin's guests in the distance; heard footmen, too, sometimes, hurrying to and fro. With luck, the meal would last for a long time yet.

Luke paused briefly in what he was doing and caught his breath—all those important people, with Ellie alone in their midst. He hoped she would have the sense to stay out of the way. To leave everything to him. This was dangerous business.

He worked on through the various letters and papers, thinking and making plans. If he found proof that Les Braves had been betrayed, perhaps he could force Lord Franklin's hand—get some kind of official declaration that Anthony and his comrades were loyal heroes and *not* traitors to the British cause. Though that would be little enough compensation, he thought grimly, for the grieving widows and children of those who'd died.

And Lord Franklin and his friends knew it. Knew that the revelation of those gallant men's betrayal and deaths would cause outrage if the truth were revealed. That, Luke guessed, was the reason why the files were about to be moved to London, for destruction. If war *was* to break out again, the government certainly wouldn't want it to be known that the reward for loyalty to one's country was disgrace and death. Besides…

His thoughts halted. His breathing stopped, because amongst the letters he'd been scanning was one written in broad black handwriting.

Your idea, Lord Franklin, is a sound one. You are right in saying this whole sorry episode needs to be obliterated—

He sprang to his feet as the door slowly opened. *Elise.* For a moment, he couldn't speak. She looked exquisite, with her dark curls piled to the crown of her head. And she was wearing a flimsy pink-silk dress that made her appear like a creature of his imagination. Of his dreams.

She was hurrying towards him. 'Oh, Luke. Have you found them?'

'Yes… But oh, God, Ellie, you shouldn't be here—'

'I decide what I should and shouldn't do.' She spoke calmly, but he thought he could hear a slight tremor in her voice. 'Luke, you told me I mustn't involve myself any more in the matter of your brother. But then, I was handed the library key—and I knew I just had to give you this one last chance to clear Anthony's name.'

He groaned inwardly. All he wanted was to take her in his arms and cover her face with kisses, then run with her from here—run *anywhere*, so she would be safe, so she would be his… 'Ellie,' he said again, his voice raw with tension, 'I know that I owe you the utmost gratitude. But I repeat that you shouldn't be here. And I must leave—'

'But you *can't*, Luke. That's why I've come! The dogs are out—I heard them!'

His heart sank, but he shrugged his shoulders. 'Then I will wait here.'

'But you might be *discovered* here. When they finish their meal, Lord Franklin and his friends—' he thought he saw her shiver '—might even come in to continue their business. There's nothing else for it. You will have to hide in my room.'

'Oh, Ellie. If we should be caught…'

Her expressive face was white, but utterly determined. 'We'll go up the back stairs, so you're not seen.' She nodded to the paper he held in his hand. 'You must bring whatever you've found and stay with me until you can escape. *Hurry.*'

He blew out the candle, ushered her from the library and locked the door.

In her room a fire had been lit and Luke saw that two wax candles cast their soft light over the exquisite furniture, over the rich carpets and thick curtains at the windows. Luke breathed in the delicate scent of lavender, conscious of his rough clothes, his obtrusive masculinity. Aware of the hideous danger he was putting her in.

She'd shut the door and locked it. Turned at last to face him.

'I'm sorry,' he said.

'What for? Why *should* you be sorry?'

Something tightened inside him, because even now, in this frankly impossible situation, he found himself looking through to the bedroom, imagining her on that bed and in his arms, yielding sweetly to him... *Fool.*

'I'm sorry for putting you,' he said, 'in this more-than-difficult situation.'

'You *didn't* put me in this situation,' she said steadily. Her hair was tumbling from its pins and she was trying to fasten it up again—completely unaware, he realised, of how her actions were making her breasts strain against the tight silk of her gown. Luke's throat was dry.

'I wanted,' she went on, 'to help you get into the library. I wanted justice to be done, for your brother—'

A dog howled almost beneath her window and she broke off; Luke remembered what she'd reluctantly told him about the time she and her father were chased by dogs. He wanted more than anything to take her in his arms and to make everything all right for her, but of course soon enough he felt the inevitable bitter self-mockery roiling through his veins. *Make everything all right?* Good God. He was the worst thing that could possibly have happened to her. And—

'I hear footsteps,' he whispered harshly. 'Someone's coming.'

At almost the same time they both heard a light knock at the door and a girl's hesitant voice. 'Miss, it's Mary. Are you in there?'

Already Ellie had flung a wrapper over her gown, as if ready for bed. 'It's my maid, Luke. Quickly. Go through to my bedroom.' She pointed, then went to open the door. 'Mary,' he heard her say. 'Is anything wrong?'

'I didn't realise you'd retired for the night, miss.' The maid sounded confused. 'I didn't even know the banquet was over, until Mr Huffley mentioned you'd gone.'

Ellie's voice was light. 'Oh, I was so tired after the sixth course, Mary, that I really couldn't face any more. So I decided to prepare myself for bed without troubling you.'

'It wouldn't have been any trouble at all, miss. Are you sure there's nothing you want? Your fire building up, perhaps? Your clothes putting away?'

'Nothing at all.' Luke heard Ellie feign a slight yawn. 'Although I wish it was in your power to silence those dogs outside—have you heard, Mary, how much longer they'll be making that dreadful noise?'

'Mr Huffley said that with all these important guests, the dogs are likely to be let loose all night. And he told us, too, that armed guards have been posted at all the gates—some of the youngest maids were ever so frightened. They say they won't sleep a wink tonight for fearing that the French might be landing in secret, miss!'

'I'm sure it's highly unlikely, Mary. But thank you for calling—I hope you sleep well and the others, too. Goodnight.'

'Goodnight, miss!'

The door closed, and Luke emerged from the shadows to see Ellie leaning with her back against the door, with a faint pulse visibly beating in her throat and fear in her eyes.

But she smiled at him. She smiled and shrugged. 'That was only my maid. But you'll have heard what she said, I'm afraid—that the Hall is well guarded.'

'No matter,' he said steadily. 'I'll find some way to get out. Ellie—you left the banquet early. Might people not have wondered why?'

She shook her head. 'But I didn't leave, you see.' For a moment Luke thought he saw the slightest hint of mischief in her eyes.

'You didn't...?'

'I was sent away before the end of the meal by Lady Charlotte. She told me I was a disgrace and a distraction.'

His eyes glittered with laughter, too. 'The gown, I suppose?'

'The gown. I wore it deliberately to annoy Lady Charlotte and to get myself banished.'

He smiled, but then his face shadowed. 'And that was all so you could get to see me, in the library?'

She was suddenly serious, too. 'I was anxious about you. And then, when I heard the dogs, I knew that I *had* to see you. You've found something, haven't you?' She pointed to the letter he held.

'Yes. But, Ellie...'

'Do you think,' she said, 'that I cannot keep a secret?

Whom am I going to talk to, about this? Lord Franklin?
Lady Charlotte? Who, Luke? Don't I *deserve* to know?'

  He sighed. 'Shall we sit down?' He indicated the sofa.
And there, as they sat side by side—*Not too close*, Luke
reminded himself heavily, *you mustn't get too close*—he
began to tell her. All of it.

Chapter Twenty-Two

'I think,' Luke began, 'that I've already explained to you how, in the early autumn of 1813, my brother, Anthony, and his colleagues, Les Braves, were sent on a secret mission to the south-west of France. Their task was to investigate the possibility of sending British troops there to help Napoleon's enemies.'

'They sailed to La Rochelle.' She nodded. 'You told me a British navy ship was supposed to collect them and never came. You said they were abandoned. Betrayed by their British masters.'

'Exactly.' He was still holding the folded letter tightly in his hands. 'Abandoned to their fate. Worse than that, the rumour was spread deliberately that they *had* to be left there—because they were traitors. And I believe that their fate was largely due to none other than Lord Franklin.'

She clasped her hands together. 'Oh, Luke. How do you know?'

He looked at her steadily. 'I've been aware for a long time that Lord Franklin was an unofficial adviser to the Home Office. His travels in search of art treasures and his mastery of foreign languages made him an ideal secret observer—and I believe he strongly advised that the

plan for the British to be involved in the west of France
should be abandoned. When questions were raised by the
family and friends of those who were lost, it was Lord
Franklin's idea to say that were guilty of treachery—thus
blackening forever the names of those brave men who
had given their lives for their country.'

Ellie was looking at the letter he held. 'And you've
found something that proves it?'

'Yes,' he said. 'Take it. Read it.'

She unfolded the paper in silence.

*Your idea, Lord Franklin, is a sound one. You
are right in saying that this whole sorry episode
needs to be obliterated. I agree with you that our
men—Les Braves—must not, after all, be rescued.
If Napoleon's soldiers capture them, then it is a
sad but necessary sacrifice. To also declare, as
you suggest, that they are turncoats and traitors
may unfortunately be necessary to ensure that their
names are never mentioned again. Thank you, Lord
Franklin, for your advice on this matter.*

Luke was watching her. 'You'll see,' he said, 'that it's
signed by the head of the Foreign Office.'

She was gazing at him steadfastly. 'Then this is your
proof, Luke. What are you going to do next?'

He'd risen to his feet. 'The first thing I must do,' he
said, 'is to make sure that you, Ellie, are not put in any
more danger.'

She rose, too, and stood defiantly in front of him.
'Luke, listen to me, *please*. I don't regret in the slightest
what I've done to help you. I would do the same again
and more. I've known all along that Lord Franklin was

not to be trusted and I know it even more now, because there was a man following me in Brussels, spying on me. And I saw him today.'

'You *saw* him?'

'Yes. He is Lord Franklin's secretary. Lord Franklin must have sent him last year to Brussels, to find my father and me—for information, perhaps, as you suggested.' She walked over to the fire, then turned to face him. 'And now—now that you have that letter—I want you to know that I don't expect anything from you at all. I wanted to help you achieve justice, do you understand?'

'What will you do now, Ellie?' he breathed.

Luke wanted her, and badly. He wanted to pull aside her wrapper and slip that silk dress from her exquisite form, and hold her and kiss her with the harsh desire that was becoming more and more relentless. And yet, it was, he realised, her dauntless *courage* that stunned him as much as anything. The way she coped with being alone. She had no family. No friends. And yet, even so, her sense of justice, of what above all was *right*, made her fight and fight and fight...

'What will I do now?' she echoed. He saw her shrug and try to smile—it tore at his heart. 'Some would say I have a wealth of opportunities ahead of me. For example, I attracted a great deal of attention amongst Lord Franklin's guests tonight. I could, I suppose, find myself a rich and eligible man to marry—'

He lifted his hand to stop her. 'Don't,' he said. Something was hurting in his chest. 'Please don't throw yourself away. Don't let yourself be deceived by any more false promises—'

She stared up at him, her face very pale now. 'Have *you* made me false promises, Luke?'

'I've tried not to,' he breathed. 'God knows, I've tried my hardest not to. But, Ellie, you must know, you must realise—'

He broke off. Outside in the corridor he could hear more footsteps. There were several people this time, and men's voices; over them all he could hear Lord Franklin's, growing louder. 'Someone has been inside my library,' he was saying angrily. 'An intruder. And he must still be here, *somewhere*, because all the outside doors are locked and the dogs are loose in the grounds. You must find him, do you understand?'

The footsteps came closer and stopped right outside Ellie's room. There was a sharp knock at her door—and Lord Franklin's harsh voice filled the silence that followed. 'Elise. Are you in there?'

'Hide,' she hissed to Luke. Luke hesitated, then headed for the adjoining bedroom. They wouldn't be kind to him if they took him. He knew that. But—*Ellie*, he was thinking. What would they do to Ellie?

He heard her open the door and say with incredible calmness, 'My lord. This is a surprise. Is anything wrong?'

Lord Franklin's voice was curt. 'I didn't realise you'd retired for the night.'

'I was very tired.' She sounded, thought Luke in amazement, as if she was merely mildly annoyed that Lord Franklin was troubling her at this hour. 'I was preparing for bed. I didn't expect to be disturbed.'

'And I apologise,' said Lord Franklin stiffly. 'But we believe intruders may have got into the house. You've not seen any sign of them, have you, or heard anything unusual?'

'Nothing at all.' Then she added, 'Beyond, of course, the noise of your guests.'

He sounded still uncertain. 'I'm sorry you've been disturbed. I wish you a peaceful night's rest.'

And he left.

She closed the door and locked it. Turned round to face Luke as he stepped out of the shadows. 'Thank you,' he said gravely. 'And now, it's best if I go.'

Her eyes flew wide open at that. 'Go? But even if you get out of the house without being seen, you *know* that the dogs are loose…'

'I'll manage,' he said quietly. He'd drawn a step closer. 'I have no right to put you through any more of this ordeal. Ellie, it's time for me to leave.'

She flung herself in front of him as he made for the door. 'No!' she cried. 'You cannot risk it! And I don't *want* you to leave!'

He stopped. 'Oh, Ellie.' His eyes burned into hers, dark with a need she suddenly recognised all too well, because it was the same need that burned in her, setting light to places she hardly knew existed. 'Oh, Ellie. Don't you realise just how dangerous it is—if I stay?'

It took just a moment for her to realise what he'd said. To feel his warning words scorching through her veins until she knew, with a sharp burst of utter clarity, that there was only one way this would end. Only one way she *wanted* it to end.

If she told him to go, he would leave instantly, she knew. He would shrug those broad shoulders of his, smile that sardonic smile and set off into the night, regardless of dogs, soldiers, guns, everything.

She said, in a voice that was so soft as to be barely audible, 'Stay with me, Luke. Please.'

She took the first step towards him and watched the blue of his amazing eyes burn brighter the closer she came. She lifted her hands—tentatively at first, then firmer—to press them against his chest, feeling something shake inside her as she recognised the heat of his body beneath his shirt. Felt the sheer strength of him.

For a moment, he stood very still. She heard his sharp intake of breath, was aware of him clenching his hands at his sides. *Please*, she found herself thinking. *Please don't cast me aside now. Not now.*

And then his arms came round her, pulling her against him. He kissed her.

And she was lost.

Almost reverently, Luke tasted the magic of her lips; they were so full and warm, and opened so sweetly to him, that he could do nothing but pull her ever closer, needing to feel the curve of her breasts against his chest, the softness of her abdomen against his loins.

He kissed her again and felt her hands twine around his neck, her mouth moving against his with the same urgency, the same demand he himself was feeling, and he thought, with a rasping surge of delight, that he heard her whisper his name in the French way. *Luc. Luc. Mon amour.*

He lifted his hands to her hair, exulting in the feel of it, the scent of it; revelling in that mass of raven curls that fell loosely now around her shoulders, the pins and the pink ribbon quite gone. He kissed the line of her cheekbones, the tip of her nose, the sweep of her lashes; then he took her hand in his, marvelling at how delicate it was, how perfect, as he led her towards the bed. All the time he was kissing her, then he was taking her again in his arms, reaching round to take off the wrapper and to start unbuttoning that beautiful rose-silk gown before sliding it down over her breasts.

He saw her gasp and cover her breasts with her hands.

'You are beautiful,' he whispered. He kissed her lips again, then leaned down to press his mouth against the crest of one breast, sliding his tongue across it gently. She gasped again, closing her eyes until he licked its tip anew and drew the nipple into his mouth.

She cried aloud, pulling him to her. *You should stop*, a harsh inner voice was telling him. But he didn't stop. He pulled that rose-silk gown all the way down her body and the other scraps of satin and lace she wore, and gathered her up in his arms and lay on her bed beside her, thinking that this was all he'd ever wanted since he first saw her on the road to Bircham Hall.

Her dark hair was spread out in rippling waves across the pillows. Her skin was milky-white, iridescent; her lips, like her nipples, were dusky pink. He arched himself over her to kiss her mouth, but with his good hand he traced circles around her breasts, toying with their peaks, hearing her soft moan of need. Then he let his hand trace down the gentle swell of her abdomen, to finally rest between her parted thighs.

'Luke...' she began. Her arms were reaching round his waist to under his shirt; she was running her hands across the taut muscles of his back and her voice was so full of passion, so full of want, that his hardness ached in response.

He eased closer to her, dealing at the same time with the placket of his breeches. Saw her eyes fluttering wide in shock as she felt the strength and heat of his maleness pressing against her abdomen. He eased his hips between her thighs and he pressed himself against the core of her.

She was hot and silken, and he wanted her so badly his desire was shaking him. He slid his hands beneath her hips and drove himself into her, seeing how her eyes darkened, her lips parted. He heard her catch her breath and murmur something; he was worried in case he was hurting her and he stopped, ready to retreat; but with a small sighing out of his name—*Luc*—she lifted her arms and flung them around his shoulders to pull him even closer, until her tender breasts were pressed against his chest.

She was supple and sweet and scented, and in that moment of madness she enfolded all of his being. He began to move harder, kissing her lips and her breasts; then he let his hand drift down to find that place, that tiny treasured place where his fingers set to work, and he felt her tighten herself around him and begin to sob out her pleasure. He started to move his hips again, driving his phallus deeper inside her; saw her squeeze her eyes shut and throw back her head, gasping his name again and other endearments—endearments he could scarcely make out, but he longed for them to mean what he hoped they meant.

She started to shudder wildly and he continued to pleasure her strongly, surely, until she lay limp and sated in his arms. And then he pulled out of her, at last, to find his own almost savage release.

Perfect. She was perfect.

Ellie lay tangled with him in the bed and slowly opened her eyes. The bedside candle had almost burned down, but there was light enough to see that Luke's eyes were closed, although his arms were still wrapped tightly around her. She marvelled at the strength of his hard shoulder beneath her cheek, the warmth of his skin and the steady rhythm of his breathing.

Then he opened his eyes. For a moment he gazed at her and she felt such a sense of belonging, of not wanting him to leave, that she could scarcely bear it.

He was drawing his hand—his gloved hand—up her side to her face, touching the curve of her cheek and the line of her throat as if to memorise them.

She closed her eyes. She had known from the start that this man was dangerous. She guessed he was also honourable and brave and true, which made things worse, not better. If she'd been able to tell herself he was a rogue and was just using her, then she could have dismissed everything she felt in his arms and told herself, *He's nothing to you, nor you to him.*

But she couldn't.

There would never be anyone else like Luke. She'd been a fool to think she could order herself not to feel how she felt. That this man could, and now would always, she guessed, mean everything to her.

He'd loved someone else, and after being rejected he'd turned his back on respectable society. Now he was obsessed—understandably—with the task he'd set himself of proving his brother's innocence. He'd made love to her passionately just now, but only because she'd begged him to. Heaven help her, she'd ordered him to her room and put him in a position where he couldn't refuse. Colour rushed to her cheeks and pain flooded her heart.

Suddenly she realised he was drawing her closer again.

'Ellie?' he was saying softly. 'Tears, Ellie? I didn't hurt you, did I?'

'No,' she whispered. 'No.'

Still holding her in his arms, he was leaning back and looking at her in the shadows, and she didn't know how to prevent him seeing everything that was in her face—all her hopes and fears and longing.

So she reached out for his damaged hand and started to remove the black glove. She heard his sharp intake of breath—but she didn't stop.

Tenderly, like a caress, she peeled away the leather and pressed her mouth to his palm; then she kissed the two stumps that marked his cruel injury. Caressing them with her lips; unable to stop herself loving him. Because she *did* love him, she realised, with a sudden sense of her own enormous vulnerability.

'Ellie...' he breathed. He cupped her face, and he kissed her. He kissed her eyes and cheeks and lips, and he began making love to her again—slow and strong and devastating—until she stopped caring about her future or his past. Until all that mattered was how she felt, *now*, in this precious moment in time. She ran her hand deliciously over his powerful chest and arms, feeling how his smooth skin was stretched taut over warm, rock-hard muscle, until once more he was deep inside her and she felt the fire burning, felt his lips on her taut breasts, his fingers at the heart of her need.

And soon she was sobbing out his name again, and breaking into a thousand pieces all around him.

Chapter Twenty-Three

She woke hours later to realise it was still dark, but he was moving purposefully around the room and she realised he was already dressed in shirt and boots and breeches.

'Luke,' she said, trying to keep her voice calm. 'What time is it?'

He turned to her, his hair tousled, his jaw rough with stubble. 'It's almost five,' he said softly. 'And I have to go.'

He probably hoped to be gone before she woke. And even as the thought ran coldly through her veins she sat up, quickly pulling on her silk wrapper. 'But will you be safe? Getting out of the house and the grounds, I mean.'

He was easing on his long coat, every movement of his conveying the lithe power of his body. 'The dogs have been locked up,' he said. 'The guards and the soldiers are at the main gates still, but I can get over the wall.'

She was aware that something hard and tight was knotting like a ball in her stomach. *Luke*, she wanted to ask. *Luke, will I see you again?* She stifled her sudden cold fear and said calmly. 'How do you know about the dogs and the guards?'

'Because I've been downstairs.' He came a little closer, so she could see the gravity of his expression. 'And I've put that letter back.'

She must have made a low exclamation of shock. 'But your brother. You need the letter to prove the truth.'

'I know the truth,' he said quietly. 'And some day I'll find a way to tell the world exactly what happened to my brother and Les Braves. But, Ellie, I can't produce the letter without you being implicated.'

'That's not necessarily true. And anyway, I don't care...'

'I do. And, Ellie, there's something else you must know. Tom sent over a message to Joseph early this morning. Jacques arrived last night at Higham House, and he says that Anthony has been found alive in France.'

She let out a low exclamation.

'I have to go to my brother,' he went on. 'I have to find him. You understand?'

'Of course,' she whispered. 'Of course...'

He was pressing a brief kiss to her forehead. 'The servants will be up and about shortly—Ellie, I must leave. But I'll be in touch very soon. I swear it to you.'

He was already standing, fastening up his coat.

'Luke?'

He turned to her. 'Yes?'

There were a thousand things she wanted to say. A thousand things she wanted to tell him. *I love you. I will always love you.* 'Luke,' she said quietly, 'take care.'

'I will,' he answered. 'For *you*, I will.' Then he left, closing the door almost silently after himself.

She gazed out of her window after he'd gone. The garden was still in pitch blackness and she saw no lanterns or flaring torches, heard no sounds of dogs or men in pursuit of a lone, shadowy figure.

She went slowly back to her bed and lay there, aching with missing him. She remembered his mouth on hers, his body in hers, and the sweet, searing pleasure that had sent her senses soaring. She'd never guessed. Never dreamed it could be like that. She'd moved now into a forbidden, unknown world, and her life could never be the same.

The morning passed for her in a daze of thinking about Luke—of *missing* Luke. *I have to go to my brother*, he'd said. *I have to find him.* She didn't see Lady Charlotte until the early afternoon, when her ladyship joined Ellie and Miss Pringle in the dining room for a late lunch. Ellie was dressed in her plain grey gown today, but she could tell that Lady Charlotte was recollecting every detail of the shocking pink dress last night.

Poor Miss Pringle's eyes darted nervously between one and the other, as Lady Charlotte consumed soup and dry toast and explained in a tight voice that her son and his guests had been closeted in Lord Franklin's private suite all morning, continuing their important business. 'You are to stay out of their way, Elise. They must on no account be disturbed by your wayward behaviour, as they were last night.'

Ellie struggled to concentrate. *What would Luke be doing now? How was he going to reach his brother? Would he sail to France with Jacques? Wouldn't it be dangerous?*

There was a knock at the door of the dining room and Mr Huffley came in. Lady Charlotte looked displeased. 'Well, Huffley?'

'My lady. Lord Franklin and his guests are taking a temporary break in their business—and Lord Franklin wishes to see Miss Duchamp in his library.'

'In his library? Now?'

'Now, my lady. If it is not inconvenient.'

Ellie felt her mind whirling. What could he want with her? Lady Charlotte was ready with an answer. 'No doubt,' she said, 'my son wants to reprimand you for the way you dressed and behaved last night. For the way you attempted to shame him in front of his distinguished guests. No doubt—'

'Excuse me, your ladyship.' Ellie rose abruptly from her chair and followed Mr Huffley out of the room. Could Lord Franklin know that Luke had seen those papers of his? Could he somehow know that Luke had spent the night in her room? One thing was for certain—she would soon find out.

She knocked on the door of the library and entered, to see that Lord Franklin was on his feet and looked as if he had been pacing to and fro. She curtseyed. 'My lord.'

'Elise.' His voice was cold. He beckoned her to sit, then sat also, behind his desk to face her. 'Well,' he said. 'Last night, we found no trace of the supposed intruder. No trace at all.'

She gazed back at him steadily. 'No doubt your security arrangements are excellent, my lord.'

'I certainly hope so,' he replied softly.

He'd been tapping a finger on his desk, but suddenly he reached out for a thick diary that lay nearby, pulled it towards him and began to flick through it. Ellie glanced towards the open box sitting on the floor by his desk. In it was the file in which she'd found the papers about

Luke's brother and his friends. In it was the letter ordering the abandonment of Les Braves on the coast of France; which Luke had put back for *her* sake, giving up all hope of justice for his brother.

She wanted to say to Lord Franklin, *I know what you've done. I know you recommended that brave men be abandoned to the enemy and labelled as traitors for your government's convenience...*

Suddenly she realised Lord Franklin was talking again. 'London,' he was repeating. 'I said, Elise, that I'm taking you back to London with me. Did you hear me? I'll be returning there early tomorrow. So I wish you to pack your things—'

'No.' She half-rose from her chair. 'My lord, I have no wish whatsoever to go to London. I assure you that I'm perfectly content to stay here—'

'So I've heard,' he broke in. His voice hardened. 'In fact, I've heard that you like to consort with low-life wastrels, down by the harbourside in Bircham Staithe.'

Ellie gripped the sides of her chair, feeling quite faint. Lord Franklin got to his feet, still talking, and his words washed over her like waves of ice-cold water, chilling her blood and making her limbs nerveless. He told her that his secretary, Gerald Malone, had found out that a group of Revenue men had seen her one night, on the streets of Bircham Staithe.

That night when she'd tried to run from here. The night those rough men had caught her and Luke had rescued her. She'd been seen—and identified. She fought hard against panic. Had they seen her with Luke?

Lord Franklin sat down again and rested his hands on his desk. 'Do you happen,' he said softly, 'to have met a man called Luke Danbury?'

Fresh shock rippled through her. 'How could I?' she breathed.

His lip curled. 'Well,' he said, 'I was rather hoping you might tell *me*. There are rumours, you see. And the best way to end them is to get you away from here. You have the rest of the day to prepare yourself for travelling with me to London. And please be under no illusion that you will get the chance to flaunt yourself, as you did last night. I think the best tactic will be to find you a suitable husband, as soon as possible—a French aristocrat, perhaps, who might be willing to take you back to your own country once Napoleon is dealt with. You need, *mam'selle*, a husband with a will as strong as your own.'

Ellie was on her feet. 'You have no *right*. You have no right whatsoever to take control of my life like this, because you lied to me. You're no relative of mine. And your mother is a fraud, too—she can *walk*, and you must know it—'

'Silence!'

For a few moments all Ellie could hear was the sound of the clock ticking on the mantelshelf. At last Lord Franklin leaned forward. 'Oh, Elise, be careful. Be very careful. If you should feel the unfortunate urge to object to my actions, then I heartily suggest that you think again. Your father. Remember?'

She sat down again, feeling quite cold with the knowledge of what he could reveal—that her father once worked for Britain's arch-enemy, Napoleon. With a new war perhaps imminent, Ellie knew that, as Luke had once warned her, she could find herself interned in an English gaol. But *marriage*? She wouldn't. She couldn't.

He gave a tight smile that was completely without warmth. 'You can take Miss Pringle with you to London—

she will serve as your companion until a marriage is arranged. And I shall tell Huffley to find out whether your maid here is prepared to travel with you—'

He broke off at the sound of a knock at the door and went impatiently to open it. 'Ah. Huffley. Yes, I did want you. There's a box of papers on the floor, by my desk…'

He moved out into the corridor and Ellie was on her feet, straining to hear his voice. 'Yes,' he was saying, 'everything that's in the box needs to be burned in the garden. *All* of it. Send a couple of men in for it, as soon as you can…'

By the time Lord Franklin came back in, she was sitting down again, smoothing her skirts. Her heart was thundering, but somehow she managed to listen calmly to what Lord Franklin was saying to her.

'Well,' he began, 'I think we have everything in order. London, tomorrow. A change of scene for you indeed.'

Ellie tilted her chin to meet his gaze. 'Does that mean I'm free to go, my lord?'

'You are—for now.' Ellie stood very slowly. 'Oh, and one last thing,' Lord Franklin added smoothly. 'If I hear anything of your name being linked with that man Danbury again, then I'll ruin him. His reputation, his estate, his tenants—everything. You can be very sure of that.'

Ellie walked steadily from the room, closing the door behind her.

Up in her bedroom, she found Mary dusting and tidying. 'Mary,' she said, 'will you please find Joseph the footman and send him to me?'

'He's polishing the silver for Mr Huffley, miss. He might not be able to get away—'

'Tell him it's urgent. *Now*, Mary.'

The maid hurried off. A few moments later, Ellie heard a quiet knock at her door. She flew to open it and ushered Joseph inside.

'Joseph,' she began, 'you must get a message to the captain. You must tell him I have to go to London tomorrow and—'

'Ma'am,' Joseph broke in, 'he's preparing to set sail for France, on Monsieur Jacques's ship.'

She stepped back. 'Today?'

'This evening, ma'am—as soon as dusk falls.'

His brother, of course. He was going to rescue his brother. And whether he wanted her to or not, she would do anything to help him.

Anything.

Chapter Twenty-Four

Luke was pacing the beach, his boots crunching on the shingle. He was trying to curb his impatience as the minutes went by; knowing full well that Jacques's sailors would only dare to bring his ship in close once darkness began to sweep over the sea.

Jacques had been waiting for him at Higham House early that morning when Luke got back from Bircham Hall. From Ellie's bed. A pang that was almost pain shot through him, as he remembered how beautiful she'd looked last night as he slid that silk gown from her body. He still had the lavender scent of her skin in his nostrils; he could still hear her low cries as she clasped him to her. He had taken her innocence. He'd had no right to do so.

Jacques had confirmed in person this morning that Anthony had indeed been found. He'd been a prisoner of the French, but had escaped and made his way to the coast to find a ship for England. Weak from his imprisonment, Anthony had caught a fever and become very ill, Jacques said; but a community of nuns just outside the port of Le Havre—who wanted none of Napoleon and dreaded the prospect of war again—were looking after him well in their convent.

'I heard all this from a trustworthy source. Indeed, I was assured your brother grows better daily,' Jacques told Luke. 'I wasn't able to reach him myself—my ship was under surveillance and we had to sail away. But there is no doubt it's Anthony. He is waiting for you, *mon ami*.'

Now, as the night gathered, Luke could see Josh and Pete Watterson pointing to their rowing boat, which lay beached at the sea's edge. Jacques was with them. 'Captain Luke!' called Josh. 'Time to go! We can see the ship out there!'

Tom came over to bid Luke farewell. 'When we meet next, Captain,' he said confidently, 'you'll have your brother with you, I'm sure of that. But…' and he hesitated '…that won't be quite the end of it. You know what they say, Captain? About Anthony being a traitor?'

'I'll deal with that.' Luke's voice was calm, but his eyes were grim. 'Believe me, I'll deal with that.' He was looking out to sea, where in the twilight a white sail glimmered and the light of a lantern flashed once, twice.

Jacques was calling to him from the rowing boat. 'Luke? Are you ready?'

'That's it,' Luke said to Tom. 'Time for me to go.'

But he hardly got more than a few yards, because Tom had gripped his arm and was saying hoarsely, 'There's someone coming down the cliff path, Captain. *Look*.'

Luke swung round. Customs men? Soldiers?

And then Luke was staring incredulously—because the person hurrying towards them was Ellie.

God's blood, no. At the sight of her—all wrapped up in her old grey cloak, carrying her valise—Luke felt a great anguish in his heart. Had it been easy to leave her arms this morning? To leave her warm bed? No. Had it been easy, to say, *I have to go to my brother. I have to find him*—and then to turn his back on her? No. A thousand times, no.

For Luke knew he might not be able to return. Luke knew that Anthony was a marked man, and so was he. Even if he brought Anthony back, he would still have a hard fight on his hands to clear his brother's name—a fight which the government would be eager to win as swiftly as possible, especially if war with Napoleon was looming once more.

He knew it was quite possible that arrangements might be made for both Anthony and him to be silenced. He knew that he should have kept away from the girl from the beginning. But as he watched her hurrying towards him along the beach, with his men and Jacques staring at her, he realised that she had come to mean far, far too much to him.

Being with her filled a great void in his heart and his life. It cancelled out the emptiness left by the way he felt he'd let down his estate and his family. Had even started to heal the bitterness he felt at the way Anthony and his brave comrades had been treated.

But Luke knew that he was a fool and worse for wanting her more than he'd ever allowed himself to want anything.

She was within a few feet of him now, and her footsteps were faltering. Jacques, with his familiar sense of loyalty, was keeping Luke's men out of earshot. Ellie's face was lifted to Luke's—it was troubled and uncertain, but still so lovely. What was she doing here? What was she thinking of?

'Luke,' she said, still clutching her valise, 'I had to find you—'

And then, drowning her words, the shrill cry from one of the Watterson brothers. 'There's a Revenue cutter sailing round the headland, Captain! We need to get going. Especially as the wind's getting up—those storm clouds show there's a nasty squall coming in from the south, and if we don't go now, we're not going to make it.'

Already Luke felt the first lash of the wind on his face and the sting of raindrops. 'Push the boat out, *now*.' Then he spun round on the girl. 'I've told you. I have to leave for France. What were you thinking of, coming here?'

Her face was white, her eyes haunted. 'Something happened at Bircham Hall and—'

'Are you in danger?'

'No. No, I'm not. But—'

'Then you must go back there,' he said more harshly than he meant. *'Now.'*

'I can't,' she whispered. 'Take me with you.'

He stared at her blankly, then rubbed his hand across his eyes before drawing in a rasping breath. 'You are not helping me,' he said. 'You are not helping me.'

The storm caught them within minutes of setting off from the shore. The wind and the rain lashed at the rowing boat as if it were a child's toy and the waves tossed it from side to side. Jacques took the tiller while the Watterson brothers hauled at the oars and the girl sat hunched in the bow, her face almost hidden by the hood of her cloak.

Luke swore under his breath. *This was impossible.* He could see Jacques's ship, riding at anchor; could see the crew leaning over the side, anxiously watching the struggles of the storm-tossed boat. And the Revenue cutter! God almighty, if he looked round, he could see it as well, still a good distance away, but...

'They're gaining on us, Captain!' Josh Watterson was shouting, his arm muscles bulging as he pulled the oars.

'Row harder,' Luke shouted above the wind. 'You can do it. We're almost there!' He could see Jacques's second-in-command on the deck of the ship, giving orders for the hauling up of the anchor. And suddenly Luke realised that by some miracle, the wind was swinging round in their favour; Jacques wrenched the tiller hard to take advantage, the boat hurtled over the waves and within moments it was lurching alongside the ship. Eager arms were reaching out to haul Luke on board. But Luke was pushing Ellie forward, and Jacques, black-browed, was at his side to help him.

'This one first!' Jacques shouted up to his men. But in almost the same breath he turned back to Luke and muttered, 'To bring the girl. *Sacré bleu*, Luke. Are you mad?'

Maybe he was, thought Luke tiredly as he sat an hour later in Jacques's tiny cabin. But this was truly the first chance he'd had to contemplate the full extent of his madness, because from the moment he, Ellie and the Wattersons were on board Jacques's ship, it was as if all hell had broken loose.

Scarcely had they all been hauled up from the rowing boat when the storm had unleashed all its savage power and the boat had been swept away, no doubt to emerge on some Kentish beach in the days to come as smashed driftwood. The Wattersons immediately joined with Jacques's crew to struggle with the sails and the ropes as the ship headed out into the Channel; Luke watched and shouted out the progress of the Revenue cutter to them, while two of Jacques's men took Ellie below deck.

Their expressions said more clearly than any words what they thought of bringing a girl on board. And now that the storm had subsided a little and Jacques and Luke were able to take a brief moment below deck to review their plans, Jacques didn't spare his words.

'To bring the girl with you. To put us—and her—at such risk!' Jacques rubbed his forehead tiredly. 'I saw her pleading with you on the beach. But have you gone mad?'

Luke stared at him. 'Good God. You think that I *wanted* to bring her?'

Jacques let out a sigh and poured two brandies. 'Very well. I'll accept, for now, that you had no choice, and perhaps some time soon you'll explain. But we still have rough seas to cross, and I must go up again and take the wheel.' He swiftly swallowed a large portion of his brandy. 'All I can say is—thank God your friends the Wattersons were forced to board my ship also, because without their help I think my ship might have foundered. Do you still want me to land you near Le Havre?'

'If it's true what you say—that Anthony is being sheltered in a convent there—then, yes.'

Jacques nodded. 'There might be soldiers around—you realise? But even in desperate times, the military tend to respect convents. Listen, *mon ami*. I'll put you ashore by night and I'll wait out at anchor for you as long as I possibly can. But there's talk of armed risings, both in support of Napoleon and against him. And if you're captured, I might not be able to get ashore to help you.'

Luke nodded. 'I realise that, and nor would I expect you to. You've done enough and more.'

Jacques reached out his hand to briefly clasp Luke's left one. 'You saved my life,' he said, 'when I was a prisoner and I'll never forget it. We'll get you to Le Havre, and I'll give you all the help I can. But as for the girl—'

He broke off as someone banged on the door of his cabin. 'Monsieur Jacques! There's a fresh squall blowing up from the south-east. You're needed.'

Jacques grabbed his black, salt-stained coat and left. A moment later Jacques was back, roaring, 'Luke. You're needed, too. You can haul on a rope one-handed, can't you? Up on deck with you, *mon ami*—now!'

For the next hour the small ship was tossed like a cork on the boiling, foam-flecked waters of the Channel. Ellie lay curled on the bunk in the tiny cabin that Jacques's men had taken her to, a cabin that was little more than a cupboard.

She knew that she'd had no choice other than to come to Luke. No choice, yet he was so angry with her. *You are not helping me.*

She lay fighting her nausea and fighting her weakness—she may even have slept a little—until she opened her eyes to realise—was the sea a little calmer? Was the ship rolling a fraction less violently? And then, above the creaking of the ship and the distant shouting of the sailors, she heard someone knocking on her cabin door.

She sat up. The door opened and Luke's tall figure filled the space there. Despair twisted into her ribs like a knife. He was angry with her. He despised her. She rose to her feet, unsteady still. 'Luke. I know that what I've done must seem foolish and rash. But I had to come to you—'

He crossed the tiny room in two strides, his eyes taking in her pallor. 'Sit down again, Ellie. Have you been sick?'

She sat carefully, pushing her loose hair back from her face. 'I'm a bad sailor, I'm afraid.' She tried to smile. 'I'm always sick at sea.'

'Oh, Ellie.' Luke spread out his hands. 'Now you're having to endure *this*. And back at Bircham, they'll be searching for you. What will everyone think? What will Lord Franklin think?'

'He'll be thinking,' she answered quietly, 'that I've spoiled his plans yet again.'

Luke had spied a wooden stool in a corner; he dragged it out and sat opposite her. 'Explain.'

'He told me this afternoon that he was taking me to London.'

'To London? Why?'

'He told me he was going to find a husband for me. A *French* husband.' Something caught in her voice. 'Someone who would take me back to France and keep me under control. I objected. I told him I knew he was no relative of mine and that his mother could walk—I said that the two of them were frauds. He was furious.'

Luke half-smiled, but at the same time he was shaking his head. 'Oh, Ellie,' he said again. 'So you came to find me. To come to France with me. But France is dangerous. What am I going to do with you?'

'You don't have to do *anything* with me,' she said, looking so pale and so proud that Luke felt his heart wrench. 'You can leave me in France. It's my country—remember?'

'And a country that will soon be at war, quite possibly.' There was frustration and anger in his words. 'England

and the allied powers cannot possibly allow Napoleon to regain his throne. There could be soldiers everywhere, and you know that my first duty is to get Anthony out of there.'

'You need not think that I will be a burden!' She had fire in her eyes now and spots of colour in those desperately pale cheeks. 'Luke, I am not your responsibility, and I never intended to be—I came to you because I had to bring you the letter!'

She was reaching for her cloak, delving into its deep pocket. Luke stood stock still, not understanding. 'The letter? But I put it back. I told you it had to be left where it was. I told you that I would challenge Lord Franklin over it when I got back to London. Once I've made sure that Anthony is safe—'

'Lord Franklin was going to destroy it, Luke!' Her voice burned with passion. 'He was going to have *all* those papers burnt within the hour—I heard him giving the orders. I could not let him do it—do you understand? I was with Lord Franklin, in his library. He had to go outside to speak to his butler, and I found the letter. I took it.' She thrust it at him.

Once more Luke held the letter in his hand. He stared at it in disbelief.

'You're angry with me,' she was saying in a low voice. 'Because now you have to decide what to do with me.' She gave a little shrug.

'Angry? Oh, God, no. How could I possibly be angry with you for long?'

He spoke almost with despair, but Ellie, hearing the sheer tenderness in his voice, felt his words trace patterns of swirling heat all down her arms, her spine, her abdomen. Suddenly he shifted to sit next to her on the tiny bunk and she was aware of him with every fibre of her being. Aware of his hooded blue eyes, of his beautiful mouth, too close to hers…

'You could tell me I'm a burden, at the very least.' She tried to laugh. 'As if you didn't have enough to deal with. I didn't mean to cause such trouble to you, Luke.'

'A burden?' he echoed. Disbelief etched every syllable. 'Oh, Ellie…'

He said her name as if it were a caress. His strong hands cupped her face, then slid round to bury themselves in her hair. She felt a dark pulse start up in her bloodstream—low and deep and insistent.

'Luke.' She tried to back away. 'You mustn't feel that you need to be kind to me.' There was a huge ache in her throat, almost blocking it. 'I'm used to coping. Used to being on my own. I've always *preferred* to be on my own.'

'Why?'

'Perhaps…' She hesitated. 'Perhaps because it was less dangerous that way.'

His hands were softly stroking her shoulders. 'I felt the same,' he said quietly. 'For such a long time. Until I met you, Ellie.'

And Ellie couldn't seem able to do what she knew she should. Couldn't make herself push him away.

Especially when he drew her close—and kissed her.

In that tiny cabin, the kiss exploded all around them. Luke's hands held her fast as his lips tasted and caressed hers; but then—with perhaps the greatest effort of his life—he held her away from him, his hands resting with the lightest of touches on her shoulders. He realised that his breath was catching in his throat as he absorbed her adorable face and inhaled the faint scent of lavender that lingered on her silken skin and tumbled hair.

But now—he groaned inwardly—now wasn't the time to make love—there wasn't even time to *talk* properly. This wasn't the place, on board this flimsy little ship, on the way to rescue Anthony. She was still weak after the effects of the storm, though she tried to hide it, and there was danger all around. And yet he wanted her again. He wanted *all* of her.

God forgive him, he'd used her badly in his tormented effort to find his brother and to clear his name. In fact, since he first set eyes on her on the road to Bircham, he'd done his damnedest to see her merely as yet another weapon in his battle to save Anthony.

But all the time, she kept catching him unawares. Catching him on the raw. Piercing the wall of granite he'd put around his heart that he thought was there forever—until Ellie Duchamp came into his life. By some miracle, this girl was yet again illuminating the darkness that had wrapped itself around his heart. Was making him think that, yes, finding Anthony was still his life's mission. But after that—what about after that? If Ellie wasn't part of his life, then there was no point to anything at all.

He must have looked graver than he'd thought. Forbidding, even, because now he saw Ellie shrink away from him just a little. He took her hand quickly. 'We need to talk,' he said. 'Properly. But meanwhile, I have to help Jacques to get the ship safely to anchor off the French coast—and then I have to find Anthony.'

'Of course.' Her voice was intense. 'But I meant what I said, Luke. Once we've found your brother, you needn't worry about me. I can make my own way back to Paris, and there I'll look for somewhere to stay. Get a job, perhaps, as a governess, or a lady's companion—'

He cut in almost roughly. 'Don't ever talk such nonsense again. Do you hear me?' He felt a wave of emotion that was almost raw hurt for her—and near-loathing for himself. *He* had done this to her? She felt that he cared for her so little that she was already thinking of *leaving*?

He pulled her closer. Pressed his forehead against hers. 'Whatever happens, Mademoiselle Duchamp,' he whispered, 'you're staying. With me. Is that quite clear?'

She shook her head. 'Luke. Oh, Luke, you don't have to…'

'Nobody,' he said, '*nobody* makes me do anything at all that I don't want to do.'

'But I know there was—there *is*—somebody else. Someone who hurt you badly. I understand that.'

'Oh, God,' he breathed. 'Do you mean Caroline? Caroline Fawley? That was a mistake—I knew it from the start.'

'But you were to be married to her. And when she broke off the engagement, you were so hurt that you left to join the army.'

He almost shouted with laughter. 'Is that what they say?'

Her eyes were wide. She looked stunned. 'Isn't it true?'

'No,' he breathed. '*No.*' He gathered her into his arms. 'Listen to me. I didn't love her. I *never* loved her. And she didn't love me.'

'Then why…?'

'She found me attractive,' he said simply. 'Dangerous, if you like. A challenge, especially since her father objected to me strongly. As for me, I'm afraid I saw the marriage as a way of saving the estate, but fortunately for both of us, I couldn't go through with it. I told her that she could have the privilege of breaking off our engagement. I told her I would take the complete blame—society could say what it liked about me.'

His expression darkened a little. 'And believe me, society *did*. Caroline made quite sure of that. Society condemned me as a worthless rogue, which was why I went off to join the army in Spain. As for Caroline, I forgot about her long ago, and believe me, I was well rid of her. It's you I'm thinking of now, Ellie. Always. Always. Do you believe me?'

Just then they heard a shout from outside. 'Luke. Are you there? We need you, up here!'

'I must go,' he said to her. 'But I asked you a question. Do you believe me?'

She nodded slowly, her eyes wide and serious. 'Luke, you must find your brother. And then—*then* we'll talk.'

Luke resolved he would make it his mission to convince her that being his was her only option. 'I'll find Anthony,' he assured her gravely.

'Do you know exactly where he is? You'll have to land by night, won't you?'

'I'll have to land by night, yes. And I know he's being cared for in a convent near Le Havre, but I'm not quite sure how far it is from the town...'

'I have maps,' she broke in eagerly. 'Maps of my father's, in my valise. You see—we lived for a while in Le Havre.'

He stared at her, astounded, and then he began to laugh. 'Oh, Ellie. Ellie, you are wonderful.'

'Luke! We need you!' From up above, on deck, someone was shouting his name again. She was hastily open-

ing her valise. 'Are you going ashore at Le Havre alone?'
She handed him the map.

'Speaking French as badly as I do?' He shook his
head. '*Not* a good idea. I'm planning to take one of
Jacques's men.'

'Take me,' she said.

'You? No! I wouldn't dream of endangering you...'

She tilted her chin stubbornly. 'Take *me*. I've told
you—I know Le Havre and its neighbourhood. And if
you do meet with any of Napoleon's soldiers, then a man
and a woman are far less likely to be stopped than two
men travelling together—especially since Jacques's men
all look full of *piraterie*.'

He smiled. 'You mean—like pirates? Piratical?'

'Piratical, yes! Exactly!' She stood there, determined
and utterly lovely. 'Take me, Luke.'

'I *cannot* expose you to fresh danger...'

'I'm not letting you go from here,' she breathed, 'until
you promise you'll take me.' On tiptoe she reached up to
kiss him so sweetly that his pulse pounded and his loins
were on fire.

And Luke agreed.

After that, he worked on deck with Jacques and
his sailors almost all night. At four in the morning he
snatched two hours' rest; then before dawn the Wattersons rowed him to a tiny cove less than half a mile from
Le Havre. With Ellie.

Chapter Twenty-Five

Afterwards, whenever she remembered that journey with Luke, she realised that even though she'd known they were in great danger, she'd felt herself to be brimming with hope and even happiness—because Luke was at her side and he needed her.

The Watterson brothers were desperately reluctant to leave Luke on French soil, but he was resolute. Ellie had shown him her map of the coast beforehand, pointing out to him all the details she remembered, of the port of Le Havre and its hinterland.

'I once visited the village of Montvilliers, where the convent is,' she told him. 'It's only three miles from the coast, but of course we'll be best avoiding the main roads. Will we be walking?'

Luke nodded. 'I think so. Hiring horses would draw attention on us.'

'In that case, on foot, we can go *this* way—' she pointed at the map '—and this way, along the river and through the woods. You see?'

Jacques had already warned them repeatedly that they would have to be careful. 'Remember, we don't know how many local men will be gathering to support Napoleon. War is coming again without a doubt, and it will be dangerous in the next few weeks for any Englishman in France.' He looked at them both sharply. 'You'll travel as husband and wife?'

'As husband and wife,' said Luke.

They set off along a narrow track that led them away from the sea and, as they walked through the lush green fields and unfurling oak woods of Normandy, Luke constantly marvelled at Ellie's enterprise, at her optimism. How would he have managed without her? He wasn't sure.

Jacques had been right to warn them to be wary, because even though they were well away from the town and the main roads, there were people around: labourers in the fields, housewives feeding their chickens out in the yards of their cottages. An ancient French farmer coming towards them with his horse and cart was clearly curious about these strangers on the road, and it was Ellie who responded lightly to his questioning, telling the man they were travelling to Rouen to visit her family there.

'You'll have to watch out,' the farmer said, nodding at Luke, 'or your strong husband might be snatched up for Napoleon's army.'

Luke understood that and held up his maimed right hand. *'Hélas, monsieur,'* he said.

'Perhaps not,' the man muttered. 'Perhaps not.'

The road was becoming busier as the sun rose higher, and if anyone spoke to them, Ellie was the one who answered back cheerfully. Luke laughed and told her that he must look, to the French, like a silent hen-pecked husband. And he smiled inwardly with satisfaction when he saw her colour slightly at the word, *husband.*

Ellie had left her precious valise in Jacques's care, on the ship, but he guessed that she would have her pistol concealed inside her cloak, somewhere. And he had a knife ready, under his coat. Even with his left hand, he could still use it to defend them from enemies. To defend *her*.

During this brief but all-important mission, Luke didn't allow himself to think too much, or to make any assumptions about their future. But he couldn't stop himself being aware of her, so acutely that it was as if she were a part of him. She walked steadily beside him, in her old shapeless cloak—but he was seeing her as she'd been that night in her room at Bircham Hall. In that sinuous silk dress. *Out* of that dress.

She was beautiful. She was courageous. She had risked *everything* to come with him on this journey, and yet she demanded nothing in return. 'You needn't worry about me,' she'd said in that tiny cabin on the ship. 'I can make my own way back to Paris and look for somewhere to stay. Get a job, perhaps.'

Ellie. Everything about her caught so fiercely at his heart that it wrenched him and left him almost breathless with wanting her to be his and only his.

She was ahead of him now. She'd stopped on the brow of a hill where a valley opened out before them and she was studying her father's map. When she turned to him, her eyes were serious, yet somehow burning with hope. 'The village is down there,' she told him. 'By the river.'

He nodded, his gaze never leaving hers. 'Ellie,' he said. 'I want you to know that I will never be able to repay you for all that you have done. But when we get back to England—when Anthony is safe...'

She nodded. 'When Anthony is safe, we'll talk then. Come, Luke.' She reached for his hand. 'We're almost there.'

They descended the track into the valley and soon they were crossing the stone bridge over the stream. As they walked down the cobbled street of the village, there were people all around them, farmers and housewives, and Luke felt the tension prickle at the back of his neck. But Ellie led the way calmly, as if she wasn't even aware of the stares aimed in their direction, until at last she walked up to an old woman sitting by the well and said, *'Madame. Où est le couvent, s'il vous plaît?'*

She was asking for the convent. Luke hoped to God they'd got the right village and that all this wasn't in vain. That Anthony was still alive. He wasn't a man who believed in prayer, but he prayed now.

The old woman pointed and said some rapid words, which Ellie of course understood. Ellie led the way down the road to the low stone building in the shadow of the church and she knocked at the door. A nun came to open it and Luke heard Ellie explaining something about a sick Englishman. He heard her speak his brother's name.

The nun answered, talking volubly, and then they followed her black-robed figure through an archway to an airy inner garden that was filled with apple trees in the first flush of blossom.

Ellie turned to Luke. 'The nun says that he is through there. In a private bedchamber.' She pointed to where the nun was waiting by an inner door. 'You must go to him, Luke.'

He touched her hand, once; her eyes were clear and

bright, and the expression in them gave him hope. *She makes my life worth living,* he realised suddenly.

The nun, her black robes swishing, led him through to a large whitewashed room with an iron-framed bed in one corner. The sheets were white, the pillows were white and the sunlight shone down into the room from a high window. And there, with his head and shoulders resting against the crisp pillows, lay his brother.

Luke thought at first that he was asleep. But Anthony opened his eyes at the sound of visitors. And slowly, he began to smile.

'Luke,' he said. 'My big brother.' His smile broadened. 'You certainly took your time.'

Ellie sat outside in the shade of an apple tree, breathing in the sweet scent of the flowers, aware of a group of sparrows twittering loudly on the tiled roof of the convent. Anthony was here. The nun had said he was recovering well. To know that Luke and his brother were reunited was worth everything.

And yet at the same time her heart was aching.

The last few hours had been perfect—just the two of them, united and purposeful. She had felt of use to Luke, vitally necessary, even, to his quest. She'd been able to let her love for him quietly flow through her as they travelled the road today and talked together—her laughing over his poor French, him needing her and yet being there for her, so that she was aware always of his quiet strength.

She was in love with him, which meant that she'd made herself vulnerable in a way she'd sworn to herself she never would. *When Anthony is safe,* Luke had said to her, *we'll talk then.*

But she could not forget what Lord Franklin had said.

She'd not yet told Luke of Lord Franklin's final, chilling warning. *If I hear anything of your name being linked with that man Danbury again, then I'll ruin him. His reputation, his estate, his tenants—everything. You can be very sure of that.*

When Luke came out into the sunshine, her heart turned over. He was so familiar to her now, so dear to her, and, yes—her blood raced—so desirable. He didn't need fashionable clothes, he didn't need to preen himself as other men did. She loved him as he was, with his shabby long coat and dusty boots, and his disregard for his tousled mane of hair and his stubbled jaw. His complete lack of vanity was one of the many reasons why every bit of her was pierced with wanting him.

I'll ruin him...

She rose to her feet, a bright smile fixed to her face. 'Oh, Luke. Is your brother going to be all right?'

He put his hands on her shoulders and gazed down at her. 'Thank God, he is.' His voice was husky with emotion.

She put her arms round his waist and pressed her cheek against his chest. 'I'm so very glad,' she breathed. Then she looked up at him. 'What next? Can he travel home?'

'Indeed. I've told him Monique and Harry are waiting in England for him and I've told him I'm going to clear his name. He's coming home with us—but now, Ellie, I want to talk about you and me.'

The only sound in that sunny garden was the splashing of the fountain and the chatter of the sparrows on the roof. He drew her back to the stone bench and he told her that she'd come to mean everything to him.

'I have very little to offer you,' he said, 'chiefly a broken-down and decrepit estate. But you will have me. You will have my heart. I love you, Ellie.'

Her whole being overflowed as he spoke those words. This man had made her realise the desires and dreams that burned deep within her and had more than fulfilled those dreams.

I love you, Ellie. She heard those words over and over in her mind. She began to feel hope—and that was what terrified her most of all.

Luke was lifting her face with his hand under her chin, so her eyes would meet his. 'Tears?' He frowned. 'Ellie, all the time I've spent with you, yet so rarely have I seen tears.'

She drew a deep breath and she told him. She told him what Lord Franklin had said that last day in the library.

The set of his jaw was grim, just for a moment, then he said softly, lethally, 'We'll see about that. But I'm not moving from here until you've said yes to me.'

'But, Luke—'

He stopped her the only way he knew—he kissed her.

Luke had never before felt entitled to happiness. For a long time now, his life had been ruled by the belief that he should have somehow been able to save his brother and that he'd let down the tenants on his estate. Since Caroline, he'd never contemplated marriage.

But now he kissed Ellie until he forgot about the problems that still faced him; until he forgot about Lord Franklin's treachery and all the bitterness of his own past. He kissed her until there was no one else but her in his world—nothing else except her taste, her scent, the way her body fitted so perfectly in his arms. He held her face between his palms and kissed her again and again. She kissed him back, and only when both of them were breathless did he pull away. 'Say yes, Ellie. Say that you'll marry me.'

'Yes,' she breathed. 'Oh, yes. But what about—?'

'Lord Franklin?' He smiled—a glad, defiant smile of hope and of confidence in whatever lay ahead. 'We'll see about that as soon as we get back to England. When the time is right, I have a few things to say to his lordship.'

Chapter Twenty-Six

London

Just for a moment, Ellie's heart tightened with fear as the hired carriage progressed slowly along the ever-busier streets of the crowded city. Self-consciously she smoothed out her satin pelisse and the silk skirts of her evening gown. *Can I do this? What if I let him down?*

But Luke was beside her. Luke took her hand and held it, his grasp warm and strong. 'This,' he said to her softly, 'will truly be an evening to remember.'

She glanced up at him. 'But, Luke,' she said innocently, '*every* night with you is a night to remember.' He leaned to kiss her, his lips so tender yet so strong. Reluctantly she pulled away a little. 'But do you think it's wise to attend this ball?'

'I think,' he said, his eyes suddenly grave, 'that it's essential.'

Ellie nodded and gazed out of the window at the other carriages, the crowds on the pavements. Then she turned back to him, and asked the question that women everywhere asked, 'Do I look all right?'

He lifted her hand to his lips and kissed it. 'You look *exquisite*.'

She sighed with happiness and nestled against him as the carriage headed on towards Clarges Street—and Lord Franklin's house.

It was two weeks now since they'd returned to England with Anthony, on board Jacques's ship. They'd taken Anthony to Higham House, of course, to be reunited with his wife and his little son.

Ellie stayed there, too, with Luke. 'I want us to be married, Ellie,' he'd told her again that night as they walked along the beach and gazed out to sea, watching Jacques's ship disappear over the horizon. 'As soon as possible.'

'But Lord Franklin. He threatened to ruin you—'

'Lord Franklin is in London. He won't even know for a while that you're here with me. He'll have other matters on his mind. And when he does find out—' Luke's face was suddenly grim '—believe me, I have ways to deal with his threats.'

'You mean the letter? But he has such powerful friends, Luke!'

'I have something else. You'll see.' He was smiling again. 'Soon, we'll pay him a visit in London, you and I. But in the meantime, I have you all to myself. And I'm going to make the most of it.'

Arm in arm, as darkness fell, they walked back to the house and he led her up to his bedroom. He gathered her in his arms and guided her to the bed in the corner. And his mouth possessed hers once again—tasting, teasing, caressing.

Like the night in her room at Bircham Hall. Only now, she knew what lay in store. Now her body knew what pleasure awaited her, and the craving for him made the kiss more intense and made the low pulse down *there* beat that much harder. Somehow he'd parted her bodice so his hands could cup her breasts, and then his mouth was sucking the tip of each one in turn.

She clung to him, feeling as if her body were not her own, but his. As if she'd known, since the first moment she'd seen him on the road to Bircham, that there could never be anyone but Luke. She was racked by the depth of her own longing.

'Ellie...' he breathed as he let his gaze devour her face and body. His blue eyes burned with heat and his voice was raw. He began to kiss her again, only more deeply this time, with his tongue exploring the inner silk of her mouth, and she felt his hand stroking the softness of her inner thighs, slipping his finger against her most intimate place.

She was nearly beyond control. Nearly. The desire for him was like molten silver in her blood, turning her into heat and fire, burning for him. Her legs had fallen apart and he was easing himself between them, easing himself into her. She felt the blunt, velvety head of him pressing against her until, giving a little cry, she opened to him and he was sliding into her, filling her, hard and sure and sweet.

Almost desperately, her hands were under his shirt, caressing the corded muscles of his shoulders and back, gripping his lean hips; while he covered her throat and her breasts with kisses, drawing a nipple in deep. An all-engulfing heat was pulling tighter and tighter at her core and she lifted herself to meet him, crying out his name as her world burst into cascades of light.

And she slept all night in his arms.

* * *

They spent ten days and nights at Higham House. For Ellie it was a time of pure happiness—she dismissed, for now, her fears about the future and she pushed from her mind the sadnesses of her past. Luke was busy spending time on the estate and talking—*being*—with his brother.

Anthony was still recovering from his illness, but often Ellie would see the brothers walking slowly down to the beach, or along the familiar cliff path. Monique and Ellie were content to leave the two of them together, knowing they were sharing memories of their youth and possibly sharing their experiences of war and hardship that they might never recount to the women they loved.

Monique was eager to learn English, and Ellie sat out in the courtyard with her when the sun shone, talking with her while Harry played with a toy horse that Anthony had made for him. Ellie loved watching father and son together. *Some day*, she thought. *Some day Luke and I might be so blessed.*

That was an idyllic time, but she knew it had to come to an end. And when Luke told her they must go to London, she was ready. 'Where will we stay?' she asked.

'I have a house,' he told her.

She turned to him in surprise. They'd been out riding together—Luke wanted to see how the wheat fields on Ned Rawling's farm were faring—but now they'd returned and Luke was holding Ellie's horse as she dismounted. 'A house?' she repeated.

'Nothing grand,' he said quickly. 'It's in a street off Cheapside. It was rented out to a London merchant, but he moved out a while ago. I have a reliable couple who look after it for me—and now it will be a useful base while I continue with my plans.'

'It sounds,' she said, 'as if you mean business.'

'I do.' His expression was grave. 'It's time for me to confront Lord Franklin. Ellie—will you come with me?'

She felt something cold trickle down her spine, but she reached for him and pressed her cheek against his chest, and felt his heart steadily beating as he wrapped his arms around her. And the coldness—the fear—had gone.

'You don't have to ask,' she said softly. 'You know that, don't you? I'll go with you anywhere. *Anywhere.*'

Ellie had found Lord Franklin's Mayfair mansion to be cold and unwelcoming and chillingly large, with servants who were as remote as the statues that stood all around, in every niche and corner. But Luke's house in Wood Street was smaller and cosier. It was run by a middle-aged couple who reminded her of Tom Bartlett and his wife, and they couldn't have been more welcoming to her.

They called her *Mrs Danbury*, or *Ma'am*, and indeed, Luke had already slipped a silver band on her wedding finger. 'Soon,' he promised her, kissing her forehead. 'Soon I'm going to make you my wife, Ellie.'

'Only when you've dealt with Lord Franklin,' she reminded him. 'Our wedding can wait till then.'

'Then I trust,' he said gravely, 'that we haven't long to wait.'

That was when he told her that Lord Franklin was, the next night, holding a party for all his important friends. 'He's recently brought over some art works he acquired in Paris,' he explained, 'while Napoleon was in exile. He's got them all out on display and he's eager to show them to his guests. You and I are going, too.'

She was aghast. 'Luke. He won't let you in! And as for me... You've not forgotten, have you, how he told me that he'd ruin you, if he found that I was seeing you again?'

He drew her close and kissed the tip of her nose. 'I thought you trusted me, Ellie.'

'I do. Oh, I do. But...'

'Tomorrow night,' he told her. 'The party is tomorrow night. And I want you to look stunning, do you understand? Tomorrow morning, you're going to see a modiste. The gown will have to be ready-made, but no matter—you'll still be the most beautiful woman there.'

Now it was eight o'clock on the night of the party, and the hired carriage was turning down Piccadilly to take them to Clarges Street and Lord Franklin's house.

Ellie had wondered how she would feel to see again the house where she had been so alone and so afraid for her future. But with Luke at her side, everything was transformed. As the carriage pulled up, she leaned across to him and whispered, 'You look wonderful, too.'

And he did. He was dressed in a simple but well-tailored black tailcoat and light-coloured breeches that suited his physique perfectly. His shirt and neckcloth had been checked over by Ellie, who had placed a plain silver pin that he told her had been left to him by his grandfather in the snowy folds of the cravat.

'Luke, you're almost a dandy,' she teased him. He'd taught her the word, when she'd exclaimed over the fancily dressed gentlemen she'd noticed on the streets of London.

'I sincerely hope not,' he said, screwing up his face in distaste.

'Nevertheless.' She reached up to caress his cheek. 'You're so handsome that all the ladies will be after you.'

He was easing on his black leather glove over his right hand, but he stopped and said, 'Too bad. Because I don't want any of them except you.'

And now, they were climbing out of the carriage and Luke was leading her up the wide steps to Lord Franklin's imposing front door. On either side flambeaux burned, and liveried footmen stood to attention, waiting to greet the guests.

'Sir.' A footman bowed his head to Luke. 'May I see your invitation, sir?'

'No need,' Luke replied crisply. 'I assure you, his lordship is expecting me.' More guests were arriving all the time; the steps were crowded and Luke took advantage of the crush to brush the footman aside and usher Ellie in. He handed her pelisse to another footman in the hallway, and the staff and guests who were already gathered in there, beneath the great candelabra, turned and stared.

Because Ellie looked exquisite. She wore a flowing, low-necked gown of green silk, with no adornment except green ribbons in her piled-up hair and a silver chain around her neck. The modiste had picked the gown out for her and made several minimal alterations, but otherwise it fitted her slender figure perfectly. The other women, most of them considerably older than Ellie, were dressed in stiff, formal gowns of satin and lace. They wore fabulous jewels and feathered headdresses—but all the men's eyes were on Ellie.

Luke led her in amongst them all. 'Perfect,' he said to her gently under his breath. 'You look absolutely perfect.'

'Danbury.' The word came out like an explosion of

sound. Lord Franklin was there, in front of them, and his face was as black as thunder. 'Danbury,' Lord Franklin repeated. 'How did you get in here? Who let you in? And... Elise?'

He gestured abruptly to the nearest footman. 'Show this man the door. Immediately. Elise, you will stay. I need to speak with you—'

'No.' Luke stepped forward. 'I need to speak with *you*, Lord Franklin.' A crowd had gathered round, silent, awestruck. 'You will be interested to hear, my lord,' Luke went on—his voice was calm and clear—'that my brother, Anthony, has recently returned from France.'

Lord Franklin took a step backwards.

'You,' Luke went on, 'and some of your colleagues—who are here tonight, I believe—will be glad to hear of his safe return, I'm quite sure. Especially in view of the extraordinary service he and his friends performed for our country—a service that I'm certain you will agree has not, up till now, been fully recognised by those in power—'

'Stop,' said Lord Franklin. His face was tight with anger as he turned to his gathered guests. 'If you will excuse me, ladies and gentlemen, I need a moment in private with this—person.' He swung back to face Luke. 'You'll come to my study, Danbury?'

'I will,' said Luke. 'But first...' He turned to Ellie. 'Will you wait here for me? Will you be all right?'

'Of course.' And she wanted to add, *You know that I'll wait forever, for you.*

For almost a quarter of an hour, Luke was closeted with Lord Franklin in his study. The other guests pretended everything was as normal; there were musicians, there was dancing, people played cards, couples flirted; but Ellie could tell they were looking round all the time, avid for gossip. Avid to know what was happening.

Some of the women came over to talk to her. 'You are Lord Franklin's relative, are you not?' they asked curiously. 'But he told us you had returned to France!'

She pretended not to understand their English. She sat there as the music and the chatter filled the air, and she thought of nothing but Luke.

And when he came back into the main room, at Lord Franklin's side, she was on her feet, fighting the urge to run to him and put her arms around him.

He appeared calm and composed, but Lord Franklin looked tense with suppressed rage. The whole room fell silent—even the musicians stopped playing.

Lord Franklin stepped forward. 'Ladies and gentlemen. You came here tonight to see my latest paintings from France. You have been very patient. Will you follow me upstairs to my gallery, so I may show them to you?'

They clustered around him and followed him up the sweeping staircase. All except for Ellie. Luke came over to her, took her hand and pressed it to his lips.

Her heart leapt when she saw the fierce joy in his eyes. 'It's over,' he said. 'It's done. Let's go, my love.'

Outside Luke hired a hackney cab to take them back to his house, and on the way he explained everything to her.

'I had the letter, of course,' he said. 'The letter from his library, which told us of his part in the betrayal of Anthony and Les Braves. "I want medals to be issued to all those men, Lord Franklin," I told him. "Those who died and those who lived. They were treated abominably by the British government."

'Lord Franklin was furious, and tried to deny it. "I warned the girl," he told me. "I can still have you and your estates ruined, Danbury." And it's true that perhaps he could—he and his friends are very powerful. But I told him that there was something else.'

'What, Luke?' She was nestling against him as the hackney rattled along Pall Mall. She was daring to feel hope. Hope for Luke, and hope for their future together.

'A few months ago,' Luke went on, 'I heard some rumours about Lord Franklin—rumours connected to his passion for art. I asked Jacques to make enquiries for me in France. And he found out what I suspected. During the last years of the war, Lord Franklin sent English gold—illegally—to Paris to purchase from undercover dealers some works of art that he desperately coveted. What he did would scandalise London if it were known. Imagine—liaising with the enemy in wartime! What would his government colleagues think?

'Tonight,' he went on, 'Lord Franklin was horrified to realise that I knew this. I said I would keep quiet about it—if he arranged for the heroism of Les Braves to be publicly acknowledged. But I also reminded him that if he ever, at any time in the future, decided to try to get some sort of revenge on Anthony or me—or *you*, Ellie—then I would reveal his treachery in full. It's done, my darling. It's over.' He gathered her in his strong arms. 'I love you. I need you. And the future is all ours.'

He kissed her, long and deep, until the cab driver called out, 'Wood Street! You're home, sir!'

But of course, thought Ellie. *Home was anywhere that Luke was.*

Epilogue

Kent

It was the perfect place for a wedding. The church overlooking the sea was tiny, but there was enough room for all the people who mattered—Anthony and Monique and Harry, Jacques and his sailors, the Bartletts and the Watterson brothers. Luke's farming tenants had crowded in, too—they were brown from working in the summer sun, because it was early July, and the crops were ripening steadily in the fields, while the sheep grew fat on the summer grass.

Last night a display of fireworks had illuminated the sky, further along the coast—the Kent regiments were returning, after their momentous victory at Waterloo in June, and the celebrations went on till midnight. The war was over. Napoleon had been sent into exile on St Helena. 'And this time it will be for good,' Luke told Ellie. 'There'll be no escape for him from there.'

But Luke was worried for the returning soldiers, Ellie knew—he feared there might not be enough work for them all. 'Especially those who've been wounded,' he said to her.

She knew he was thinking of his own damaged hand. 'You can employ some of them to work on the Danbury lands, Luke, can't you?' she ventured. 'Not many, I know—but it will be a start. You still have fields that haven't been cultivated for years. There are farms that have lain empty for too long.'

'After our wedding,' he'd promised. 'I'll make plans for all that. After our wedding.'

Ellie had chosen Jacques to give her away. 'A wise choice, *mam'selle*!' He'd beamed. 'A fellow countryman—what could be better?'

And now, as Jacques led her along the aisle in the sunlit stone church, she could see Luke standing with Anthony, his groomsman, at his side, both of them wearing dark tailcoats. She saw Monique in the front pew beaming at her, and Harry jumping about at her side. 'Aunt Ellie! Aunt Ellie!'

Ellie was wearing the green silk dress she'd worn to Lord Franklin's party, with a cream lace veil draped over her head and shoulders. She carried a simple bouquet of wild white roses that Monique had gathered for her that morning and, as she drew near to her husband-to-be, Luke turned to watch her, his eyes alight with admiration and wonder.

Luke was there for her. Luke had *always* been there for her, she realised. In a way, her life had only begun when he stepped out of the shadows and accosted her on the road to Bircham—so long ago now, it seemed.

Loneliness. Fear. Despair. All those emotions were behind her now. 'You look wonderful,' Luke said softly. 'Are you ready?'

'I'm ready,' she breathed.

* * *

After the ceremony she walked across the grass with Luke to his parents' and his grandfather's graves, where fresh wreaths had been laid. Luke touched his grandfather's headstone lingeringly. And then a chaise and pony—the chaise garlanded with summer flowers—rolled up at the lych gate to take them back to Higham House, where there was to be a party for all the guests. Mrs Bartlett, Ellie knew, had already hurried off there to check that the food would be ready and plentiful.

Ellie was going home, as the wife of the man she would love for the rest of her life.

The eager guests surrounded them as Luke helped her up into the chaise. They threw scented rose petals and called out their congratulations and their good wishes for the pair. Luke settled her into the chaise next to him—Tom was driving—and in front of them all he swept her veil aside and leaned to kiss her; how they clapped and cheered!

'Mine forever,' he whispered.

'Forever.' She kissed him back, knowing the service had been a formality, because their vows had already been exchanged outside the sunlit convent in Paris and their hopes and dreams had been shared together ever since.

Tom had the reins in his hands and was about to set off. But just then there was a sudden clamour and Ellie saw that little Harry, held in Monique's arms, was reaching out to Luke. 'Ride. Want a ride,' he was calling.

'No,' Monique was scolding, 'no,' but already, with a husky chuckle, Luke was holding out his arms to his nephew.

'Come on up, then,' he said, settling Harry on his lap. 'The more the merrier.'

Harry sat contentedly in Luke's lap. And Ellie's heart was overflowing as the chaise set off, with all the wedding guests following them in a happy throng along the cliff path.

Soon—as soon as they were alone together again—she would tell him that he was going to become a father.

A perfect day. A perfect future.

* * * * *